THE SEAS BETWEEN US

RUTH HAY

For all my readers, past, present and future.

Auld Lang Syne
By Robert Burns

Stanza IV We twa hae paidl'd in the burn,
Frae morning sun till dine;
But seas between us braid have roar'd
Sin auld lang syne!

For auld lang syne, my dear,
For auld lang syne,
We'll take a cup o' kindness yet
For auld lang syne!

A Book of Scottish Verse
Ed. R.L. Mackie
Oxford University Press, c. 1934

About This Book

***The Seas Between Us** is the sixth book in the **Prime Time** series, which began with Anna Mason's story in* Auld Acquaintance.

Anna Mason has transformed her life by learning to welcome challenges.

With the help of her Samba friends, she has enlarged her existence and found another home in Scotland. Now that the mystery of Helen Dunlop's past is finally laid to rest, Anna can look ahead.

In this concluding book of the series, Anna must try to overcome her doubts about the younger man, a talented artist, who claims her as his soulmate.

Both she and Lawren set out on journeys to discover more about their parents' generation and the reasons for the life-altering decisions that broke families asunder. In tackling these quests, they must each integrate the lessons of the past which will allow them to create a better future.

You will meet old friends again and follow their relationships including the exciting story of how Anna's young protégé, Fiona, finds her true path in life.

A future romance blossoms in this novel!

Chapter One

❦

"Well, thank goodness you're here at last!"

Susan could not disguise the relief in her voice when she opened her front door to find Anna Mason standing there.

"I know! I know! It's been way too long, my dear friend, but it's not all my fault. You and Jake have been in Florida for months now. How is he doing?"

Susan ushered Anna into the kitchen, their usual gathering place, and switched on the kettle before answering. Anna could see the tension in Susan's back view and began to dread what she would hear next. Susan was always the stalwart one of the Samba group and if she could not cope with events in her life, what hope was there for the rest of them?

"It's not as bad as we first thought." Susan turned back to Anna and her expression was serious but not as worried as Anna had feared. "There was certainly a relapse in June while you and Alina were in Scotland, but with his sister's extra care, and Florida warmth, Jake has recuperated better than expected. He did have to resort to his wheelchair for a time but he can manage with a stick for part of the day now."

Her voice dropped a notch in volume and she leaned closer to Anna and whispered urgently.

"You'll notice a change in his appearance, Anna. I know you won't show any shock but I wanted to warn you ahead of time."

Anna found this warning to be quite alarming but she took a deep breath and prepared herself to act as normally as possible should Jake appear suddenly.

Susan spoke at the usual volume as she turned attention from her concerns to those of her friend.

"Now, Anna! I want to hear everything. So much has been happening in your life and I need to catch up."

"Do you mean to tell me that Maria and Bev haven't been in touch with you all summer?"

"No, I can't say I have been out of the loop completely. There were texts and e mails while I was in Florida but nothing to compare with hearing the information from the person most concerned."

"Well, I am happy to supply whatever updates I can, Susan, but tell me what you know already."

Anna settled back in her chair and sipped the coffee Susan had poured. Turning the conversation back to her friend would give her a moment or two to gather her thoughts and try to find an entry point to the problems she had hoped to solve with Susan's help.

"Now, let me see. I first found out about Lawren Drake when you asked me to show you his portrait paintings in my old law offices in town. Of course I suspected there was more to it than just artistic curiosity on your part but I sensibly refrained from comment."

"Just as well you did. I had no intentions other than to find an artist for a portrait of Helen Dunlop at that point."

"So you say!" Susan smiled, with the knowing expression on her face that indicated her superior instincts when it came to her Samba friends' concerns. "I did get a surprise when things moved ahead so fast, though. Before I knew it you and Alina were off to Scotland and Lawren Drake was to follow you in a few days."

"Yes, I admit it all happened very fast but I was still motivated by an urgency I felt to acknowledge Helen's presence in her Oban house with a suitable portrait. Nothing else was on my mind then."

"Aha! So you admit there was more to the relationship than a business arrangement very soon after he arrived in Oban?"

"Now, Susan, I am sure Bev explained my hesitations to you. A personal attachment was not on my horizon then, but I was drawn into the whole portrait thing step by step. I discovered I would be front and centre of the work and that opened up a connection with Lawren that was both personal and emotional. It may have seemed fast to everyone else, but to me it was a slowly evolving situation and one that I never imagined could happen to me again."

Anna placed her right hand over her left as she spoke and Susan noticed at once.

"Right! Let's cut to the chase! I want to see the famous ring."

Anna held out her left hand and Susan gently turned the silver ring on Anna's middle finger until she could see the inscription. "I can't pronounce it or even read it from here but I have been told what it means; soulmate. Am I right?"

Anna swallowed and nodded. She still found it difficult to calmly recall the firelit room in the Oban house where Lawren placed the ring on her finger to match the partner ring on his. The scene was burned into her memory but it was a private moment so powerful that she could not trust herself to talk about it without tears welling up in her eyes.

Susan patted Anna's hand in a motherly fashion. She could not help a sense of satisfaction in the outcome of the romance since she had been instrumental in their connection at the beginning stages.

"Are you happy, Anna? What are your plans for the future?"

A shadow passed swiftly over Anna's features. The change was not lost on Susan.

"What's wrong? Has something happened since I've been in the states?"

"Nothing specific has happened. It's just that life has intervened. Neither of us is a teenager with unrealistic and overconfident hopes for the future. We are dealing with two separate lives and responsibilities and it isn't easy to blend those together."

"Of course, it isn't easy! But there's a more important issue."

Susan held Anna's gaze and asked the crucial question.

"Do you love him, Anna? They say love will always find a way."

"Oh, don't worry about that part. He is the most incredible, talented, sensitive man in the world and I am so lucky to have found him. I won't pretend it was a simple matter to make love to a man after so many years on my own but he was tender and patient with me beyond anything I could have expected and I am reborn in many ways."

Susan was surprised to hear this intimate account from Anna. Things had certainly changed in her friend's life to make her so open about her feelings. She could not help wondering what the problem was when the essential part of their relationship seemed to be going so well.

"That is wonderful news, Anna. I could not be happier for you." She paused while these words reassured her friend.

"So, what is the problem that brought you here today?"

"You know me too well, Susan." A deep sigh escaped from Anna's lips but she was committed now. Much had been held inside while she waited for Susan to return from Florida. Now was the chance to unburden herself.

"Truthfully, I am finding it hard to adjust to this new lifestyle with Lawren. First of all he is younger than me and there's no denying it. I know it's foolish but I worry about what people will say. And it's not just me. Lawren refuses to accept any money from me. He is fiercely independent and won't even move into the condo with us. And that's another thing! Living with Alina is non-negotiable. My commitment to her predates any with Lawren and I must consider her needs, despite anything she may say about it.

I can't move in with Lawren. He works in a tiny studio and needs his own space to concentrate on his profession. It seems as if everything has changed since we left Scotland."

Susan sat back and let Anna unreel her worries without interruption. She was used to hearing clients in the legal office spill their problems all over her reception desk while they waited for their lawyers to be

free. She had developed the skill of analysis and knew that clients could solve their own problems, in many cases, if they heard them repeated back to them in a less emotional frame.

"I am sorry for burdening you with this, Susan. You have enough to worry about without me heaping my problems on your shoulders. I apologize. I'll go now before I embarrass myself any further."

"No you will not. Sit down again, Anna. I will make us some lunch and I want you to go out to the garden in a minute and call the dogs in. You need some canine comfort and I have some answers for you. On you go now. You'll find Jake out there. Wheel him back in with you for lunch."

Anna stood, wiped her eyes and pulled herself together mentally. It was good to follow simple, direct instructions and would give her a break from the disconnected thoughts that circled endlessly in her brain these days. Susan had always been wise. If she claimed to have answers, Anna was more than ready to listen.

Lunch was a lighthearted occasion. The dogs were happy to see Anna again and sat with their huge heads leaning on her knees while she ate a sandwich and sipped fruit juice.

Her first sight of Jake proved how right Susan was to

warn her. He had shrunk inside his clothes and the shakes were more obvious now than previously. Despite this, it was Jake who carried the conversation in the kitchen, regaling Anna with anecdotes about the dogs' antics in the warm Florida seas where they happily retrieved thrown sticks in a tag team style, to the applause of an admiring crowd.

As soon as the food had been cleared, Jake excused himself to go for his afternoon rest, wheeled his chair around, called the dogs to follow, and the two friends were alone again.

"Thank you, Susan."

"For what, my dear?"

"For giving me this space to gather my wits about me. Seeing Jake has put my silly worries into perspective. I will find a way to work out my problems but I must say it is a tribute to you both that your marriage has survived, and thrived, in spite of calamities that would have shattered many a relationship.

How do you do it?"

Susan turned her head and looked out of the kitchen window for a moment. It was rare for anyone to acknowledge the effort she had put into her marriage. Her devotion to Jake was something accepted now and her role as caregiver was taken for granted even by close friends and family.

"Well, Anna, as you know, when a relationship starts out it is impossible to predict the future. Life happens, as they say, and life brings both the good and the bad times. I think the strength of the love a couple discovers at the start of their relationship is the key. In ancient times a sword was tried in the fire over and over to strengthen its metal and its flexibility. The few swords that survived the process were things of great beauty and rarity, but superior materials had to be there from the beginning."

"I see what you mean, Susan. That was quite poetical but are you saying that my relationship with Lawren is not of a lasting quality?" Her voice shook a little as she spoke.

"Not at all! I haven't even met the fellow yet!" Susan decided not to mention the brief and unfortunate occasion in the coffee shop when she and Alina had confronted Anna and Lawren.

"Also," she continued, "I have a much better opinion of your ability to make good choices than you seem to have Anna. You have spoken very lovingly of your Lawren today and that is the best beginning I could hope for. However, I do have some advice for you."

"Please go ahead. I am grateful for any help." Anna gave Susan her full attention. Whatever wisdom she cared to share was badly needed at the moment.

"First of all, I must tell you that the Anna I see today looks fitter and more glowing than I think I have ever seen. You may not be aware of it but you are standing straighter as if you can see life differently now. These small signs tell me you are on the right path but this is not going to be like any other relationship you have ever had. The times are different and the situation, assuredly, is different.

The age thing is a non-starter. Get over it Anna. Truly, today no one cares about that. As to his independence; well, take that away and he would be someone you might not even like. He has built a life for himself and your job is not to tear it down but to blend yours and his together as much as is reasonable. From what I have heard, Lawren Drake is a true artist and his art is essential to his sense of self. Leave the studio alone. All men need a cave to retire to. It keeps them sane!

Basically, what I am saying is that the image of two doves cooing together nightly by the fireside may not be in your future. The question you need to answer is; how much togetherness is necessary and beneficial for both of you? Your relationship is still very young. Try a couple of date nights a week. Send Alina to visit me or to catch up with A Plus matters and play house together. See how that works out. In time you will know what you need as a couple.

My best advice is to drop the worry. Enjoy this stage of your love story, Anna. It is a gift."

Anna was laughing, crying and shaking with relief at the same time. Her confidence shot sky high. All she had needed was this confirmation. It had been difficult to discuss the situation with Alina because of her initial negative feelings about Lawren but now she felt as if a pathway had been cleared in front of her and she could safely move ahead. The path might not be traditional in style. It would be their own unique style.

She could not wait to throw herself into Lawren's arms and clear the air between them. Of course, they would sort things out. Why had she ever doubted that they would?

Susan got a hug so powerful that her feet left the floor for a second.

"Go on! Get out of here! I expect to meet this amazing man soon, don't forget!"

"Susan! You are a wonder! Thank you a million times! I'm going! I'm going! Say bye to Jake for me."

She watched at the window as Anna practically skipped down the front steps and into her car.

Susan wondered if they would ever formalize their relationship and marry. Her advice was not pointing in that direction but if Anna could gather her courage around her, as she had done so often in recent years, then anything was possible. The truth about the years they might have together was a stark reminder. When love strikes in the sixties, and later, decisions have to be made with appropriate speed.

Chapter Two

The passage of time was occupying the mind of Alina also. Three months had passed since she and Anna had returned from Scotland to their home in London and these were three months of adjustment.

She was delighted to watch Anna's happiness blossom as she grew accustomed to the fact that she was a couple again. Many cozy chats late into the night revealed how she had overcome her reluctance to share a bed with Lawren. Alina was pleased to be Anna's confidante but she was not able to make a connection with Lawren despite making herself scarce at the other end of the condo and actively keeping herself busy so as not to see or hear anything private when Lawren was spending the night.

She knew this was a stumbling block for Anna, but, really, how could she expect a comfortable threesome to be formed from the close relationship she and Alina had shared for so long?

When she was being honest with herself, Alina knew she had not been as supportive of Lawren as she could have been.

It was the old green-eyed monster, of course. Initially she had been trying to protect Anna from the heartache of a failed romance. And who could blame her? This younger man appearing out of the blue and worming his way into Anna's life so quickly had all the earmarks of a scheme to steal her money, if not her heart. Alina was on the defensive from the beginning and could not be faulted for that sincere concern, she felt.

And yet, her mental images of the day the portrait had been unveiled in the large bedroom in the Oban house could not be denied. The painting was a masterpiece, acclaimed by all who assembled there to see it. Anyone could recognize the feeling for Anna that was clearly there in the painting. Yes, it was a romanticized version of Anna, but that was significant in itself if this was how the artist perceived her.

Things were different after that, culminating in the night when Anna received the ring.

The two friends had talked about it often afterward. Indeed, it had been the main topic of conversation all the way home to Canada in the plane to the point where Alina had been hoping for a change of subject.

The matching rings were a romantic gesture, of course, but not a formal promise of marriage. Alina realized she derived some comfort from this fact although she would never say so to her friend.

Did she really hope this new relationship would peter out and fade away? How could she even entertain such a thought? Anna's happiness was paramount and surely Anna had made every effort to reassure her that the situation between them would not ever change. But life had changed, nonetheless, and that was the problem.

Lawren was not comfortable in the condo when Alina was present. He had told Anna it was a feminine environment and he felt like an intruder, which Alina interpreted to mean she should not be there.

Anna refuted this, saying it was preposterous and he meant only that it was so different from his spartan existence in the studio, that the contrast between their financial levels was unavoidable.

It was good that he could acknowledge this contrast. The man had nothing other than his talent. The condo and the business were jointly owned by the two friends. Alina was just as protective of their shared business earnings as she was of Anna's emotional security. The first move he made to insert himself into A Plus was the moment when she would finally take a stand. But could she afford to antagonize Anna by criticizing Lawren? The threat of her diminishing eyesight was ever present in her mind. Aligning herself against Lawren could backfire badly and leave Alina out in the cold. When it came to choosing between a friend and a lover, most women would choose the latter.

No, best to avoid a confrontation. Life had changed for all of them. It could not be denied. She would continue to be watchful, of course, but it would be advisable to cast around for ways to get Lawren on her side. The last thing she wanted was for him to turn Anna against her.

Alina picked up a trowel and donned her gardening gloves. She would divide some of those spectacular hostas and move them to another location. Digging around in the soil would relieve some of her frustration, if only temporarily.

Floor space in the studio was almost non-existent. A number of new canvases were stacked against the wall in preparation for a shared gallery show at the beginning of October. He had committed to seven works and now realized that was unrealistic. Four were completed but he deliberated about substituting sketches or partly-finished pieces for the remainder.

He could always use the initial drawings he had made of Anna. Leafing through the samples, he picked out one of her face turned up to the sun. It was done without her knowledge and showed an appealing innocence. He looked it over with his professional eye and saw that its rapidly-drawn lines conveyed a freshness of approach capturing the sun and wind of the Iona beach scene.

Involuntarily, a finger traced the pencil lines of Anna's profile and his objectivity fled. So much emotion now imbued the sketch. He could instantly recall the feel of her soft skin when he cupped her face in his hands and told her how beautiful she was to him. It had taken a number of tellings before she believed him and relaxed into his embrace but now he could not wait to see her again.

With a grimace he turned back to the task in hand. How soon could he finish the paintings and have them moved to the gallery's storeroom? This would create a free space in his mind as well as in the studio. There was much to think about.

Money was one of the most crucial problems between them. Anna insisted on paying for a hotel where they could spend the night free of restrictions. He had sternly refused unless he could pay the bill himself. His back muscles tensed at the thought. Not even a sweet, generous woman like Anna would be permitted to pay his way. He was only too aware of the discrepancy between their incomes and not one of her friends or associates would ever be able to accuse him of sponging off an older woman with property in two countries and a thriving internet business. The gallery show was his attempt to get on a more solid footing financially. There were many wealthy art lovers in London. If he could catch the eye of only one patron who would sponsor his work, the entire situation with Anna would turn around and he could hold his head up high.

He had been offered portrait work in Scotland and was saving that for a back-up plan should the gallery show fail to produce results.

Placing the sketch carefully aside, he wiped his hands on a wet cloth and grabbed his leather jacket from a peg near the door. There was another matter of concern to him in addition to his relationship with Anna. His father had recently fallen and broken his hip. The phone call from the hospital had reminded Lawren how old his father had become and how important it was for him to return the care his parent had given him. There was no one else who could answer the old man's pleas. Only seeing with his own eyes would reassure him his father was still fit to live on his own.

Lawren clattered down the wooden steps and ran outside to where his bike waited in the garden shed.

In moments he was speeding out Richmond Street and heading north uphill to Arva. He knew a country road where the cool air would blow the cobwebs from his brain.

"Anna, are you busy? I've just had another call from my father."

"Oh, Lawren! How is he? Is he out of hospital yet?"

"I'm afraid not. He's due to be released in a day or so. I'm heading up there now to have a serious talk to him about the future."

"Can I do anything? You won't want me there when you have personal matters to discuss but give him my regards please."

"That's good of you, Anna. I am sorry we won't see each other tonight."

"We'll have other nights, Lawren. I'll be thinking of you, my darling."

The warm feeling that Anna's voice always created in him, soothed his worry until he reached St. Joseph's Hospital. The bicycle rack was handy and as he locked his cable around the metal posts he was glad, not for the first time, that his cycle made the journey much shorter than it would be if he had to search for a parking spot inside the large parking building.

Each time he reached his father's room, it struck him again how much his father had aged in the last year or two. Perhaps it was the surroundings that brought the fragility of the older man into clear focus, but it was obvious that decisions now had to be made for his father's safety.

"Hi Dad!" Lawren bent down and kissed the old man's pale cheek. "How are you today? Did you manage a few hours sleep?"

"No one could sleep in this damn place," grumbled the tired voice. "It's like rush hour at Union Station in here any hour of the day or night."

Lawren had heard this refrain before. "If you are too tired, I'll come back later."

"No, no, my boy! Ignore me. I need to talk to you. I've been thinking."

Lawren felt reassured by this statement. The last thing he wanted was an argument with his father over where he would live next.

"Help me sit up a bit. Push these pillows behind me, but carefully. My hip is still tender and the physio fellow had me moving about too much this morning. Young idiot!"

Once he was comfortable, Lawren pulled over a chair and settled down close to the bed. His father's voice, that once had the capacity to be heard from a great distance, was now a feeble whisper at times. He did not want to miss anything significant in this conversation.

"I don't want you to worry about my accommodations, Lawrie. It's all planned. When I leave here I will go straight to the nursing wing of the Chartwell Residence for Retired Persons. Don't look so surprised. It's been arranged for years now. I had no intention of burdening you with my querulous old age.

No, don't protest! Much as I love you, there's no chance we could manage to live together in my small apartment even if we wanted to. This is the best solution."

Lawren was only partly surprised at this revelation. His father had always had a mind of his own and planning ahead was one of his best characteristics. It was this tendency which had steered Lawren through years of study and supported his desire to be an artist by providing him with the best education available. His father's handling of money was always exemplary. He had invested carefully after much research of the financial markets. Not even his only son was aware of this plan for luxury retirement living, but he was more than pleased to hear about it.

Before Lawren could respond to the news, his father raised a hand and signaled for silence.

"Let me finish. I need to get this off my chest now. There's no guarantee of how much time I have left and I want you to do something for me."

Lawren's eyebrows lifted and his golden eyes darkened. What was coming next?

"You know the family history, my boy. There are things I regret and one of them is that you have been cheated of your heritage by my actions as a young, foolish man. No, don't deny it! It's too late for prevarication. The facts are the facts. I can't make the trip to England that I meant to take. I have left it far too late but I want you to go for me. If you can find the old place, I want you to take a photograph and bring it back to me. If you can find out whether or not my older brother lives, I would like to know about that too. The money and all the information I have is in the envelope by my bed. I brought it with me in case ...."

Here his father's voice faded out completely and the tired old eyes closed. Before he succumbed to sleep, his shaky fingers pointed to the drawer on the bedside table. Lawren gently took his father's hand and placed it back by his side, covering the old man's chest with a sheet and blanket. After he had closed the window blinds, he tiptoed over to the drawer again and removed a thick envelope, placing it unopened in his inside jacket pocket.

"Thanks, Dad," he whispered. "Rest well. I'll do what I can. Thanks for everything you've done for me."

The cycle trip to the university campus took only a few minutes but Lawren could not have described any part of it. While his physical body observed traffic and pedestrians, his mind was fully occupied with the implications of the information his father had delivered. The weight of the envelope in his jacket reminded him with every movement that more complications were about to descend on his already-complicated life.

He rode swiftly over the bridge and sought out a quiet corner on the fringes of the campus where no one would disturb him. Going back to his studio would have led to more distractions and he had to concentrate on whatever the envelope would reveal.

He settled on a bench in a leafy courtyard between buildings near the art department portables and leaned his bike against the back support. His hands were slightly shaky as he prised open the heavy brown package and began to read.

My Dear Son,

You will find in here details of the location of Hartfield Hall in Wiltshire, England. I apologise for misdirecting you before this. I mentioned Kent because at that time I was reluctant to let you investigate our family history in case you stirred up a hornet's nest that I was unwilling to explain, or to deal with.

Now, it is clear to me that I have done you a disservice in concealing your origins. You know only the basic story of how I chose life with your mother over my own inheritance. I made this choice without thought of any future child of my marriage. Something I regret deeply.

I know little or nothing about what has happened to my English family over these many years. At first it was anger that kept me silent but later it was a sense of shame. Not that I was ever ashamed of taking your mother with me to Canada to start a new life, you must understand, rather that I had allowed bitterness to cut me off completely from those who were my foundation and my ancestry.

The Drake family is an ancient one with many branches, some of which may derive originally from Sir Francis himself. If you can travel to London you will see the remarkable Drake Jewel in the Victoria and Albert Museum.

My childhood home was surrounded by a large estate run by my father with an autocratic hand. From this estate derived the family's wealth.

Make yourself known to whomever is in charge there. My younger brother, who inherited everything when I fled, is named Henry; presumably Sir Henry George Albert Drake the third. He will recognize you by your family resemblance, although your eyes are your mother's alone.

This is the year you turn sixty, Lawrie. I have waited too long. Don't delay.

Return to me as soon as you can and mend this rift in my family. It is the only thing that will give me peace of mind.

All of my love and my memories go with you.

Your father,

Edmund Francis William Drake

When Lawren reached the end of his father's letter he released a deep breath and realized he had been holding his breath in amazement as he read. His first thought was to wonder why now, why at this point? In seconds the answer came. His father was afraid of dying and feared the end of a family line.

The urgency of the requests impacted on Lawren. There was no time to waste. He must go to England, and go soon.

Immediately he was faced with two conflicting priorities; the gallery show and Anna. Each was interconnected. His impulse was to see Anna right away but as he looked around him it was clear that the evening was far advanced. The last stragglers from the evening extension courses were striding past him on their way to parking lots and buses. Perhaps it was best to sleep on the information he had been given and see Anna in the morning when he had time to process it all.

His next thought was that there would be little sleep that night. He must work on the unfinished canvases for the art show and arrange for them to be delivered to the gallery.

With this decision, he returned the letter to his pocket and zipped up his leather jacket against the chill air. He jumped onto his bicycle and raced downhill to Richmond Street. As his legs pumped fresh blood into his brain again, Lawren Francis William Drake had much to think about.

Chapter Three

"Lawren, what happened at the hospital last night? "

A groan was the reply to Anna's question and she immediately realized she must have woken him up from a sound sleep.

"Oh, I am sorry, my darling! I'll call back later in the day."

Before she could put the phone down she heard a throat being cleared and the words, "No, wait, Anna!

I was working all night but I need to see you today. Unexpected things have happened. Give me an hour to get myself together and I'll meet you."

"Do you want me to pick you up at the studio? I think you should come here and have a meal and then we can talk privately."

"I have some phone calls to make first and I would rather cycle to Rosecliffe. I need to clear my head."

"That's fine. Just be careful on the roads. I'll have food ready whenever you get here. Are you all right, Lawren?"

Anna could not stop herself from making the last enquiry. She knew he did not like too much female fussing but sometimes a quick answer prevented hours of worry.

"I'm fine. I'll see you soon."

She would have to be content with that response for now.

She went into the kitchen and began to put a simple meal together; fresh bakery bread, eggs, grated cheese and sliced vegetables for a quick omelet, coffee and tea at the ready. Sometimes Lawren preferred one and sometimes the other. She unearthed, in the freezer, a bag of the cinnamon donut centres he liked and put them out to defrost.

It was a fine September day and perhaps they could eat outside. She always found bad news to be more acceptable in the outdoors. She quickly chided herself for presuming the news was bad. Yet, his tone of voice clearly betrayed concern and anxiety. She hoped his father was improving. She well knew how upsetting it was to watch a parent deteriorate. She had not yet had a chance to meet his father although he knew about her.

Fortunately, Alina was at the warehouse this morning preparing for the busy Christmas season online. She liked to supervise operations although the new manager was more than competent. Alina often said no one could appreciate how important it was to photograph knitwear effectively, better than the creator of that knitwear.

Anna was well aware that Lawren was not always comfortable when Alina was present. She and Alina had talked about this endlessly and Alina had made every effort to excuse herself when Lawren came over to spend the night, but he was a sensitive man and alert to atmosphere in a way Anna had never encountered before. She thought it was part of what made him such an outstanding artist. She blushed when that thought led to his comparable ability as a lover as well.

She knew it was the honeymoon period for them, marriage or not. She had already determined never to bring up the subject of marriage. She was quite content with their present arrangement, other than the fact that getting time to be together was becoming more difficult rather than easier. They say absence makes the heart grow fonder, she reminded herself, but the corollary; out of sight out of mind, was a warning.

She was ever conscious of her age. How many years might they have together before illness or weakness would affect either one of them? Secretly she expected the deterioration to be more likely for her. Lawren was remarkably fit for his age as evidenced by his ability to cycle several miles after very little sleep. She could not say it, but she did worry about him whenever she drove in London. The streets were increasingly busy with vans and trucks and, nowadays, the whole length of Wonderland Road had streams of traffic at all hours. She was much more aware of cyclists on the road now and hoped other drivers were equally cautious.

How would she cope if he was ever involved in an accident? It would be as if she had been granted a vision of heaven and then had it snatched away from her.

Don't be such a silly woman! Her practical Scottish mother used to say there was no point in borrowing trouble. Anna gave herself a mental shake and remembered Susan's advice also. They were two mature adults. Whatever problems presented themselves, surely they could solve them, one way or another.

She had reason to remind herself of this decision an hour and a half later when Lawren showed up at her door. He was windblown and somewhat more breathless than usual so she refrained from questions until she had ushered him inside and heated the pan for the omelet while he relaxed on the sunny patio.

Glancing through the plate glass windows she could see how restless he was. He fingered his shoulder-length hair and pushed strands behind his ears, then jumped up and walked the garden as if his thoughts had taken over his body. He was about equal in height to Anna but his physique was fit and honed to perfection. She could have stood there admiring him for hours but curiosity made her hurry with the food.

What now?

She waited impatiently until all the plates were emptied and he finally sat back with steaming coffee in the large mug he preferred. It was known already as 'Lawren's mug' and kept for him.

"Damn, Anna! That was good. I didn't realize how hungry I was."

She reached over and rubbed his shoulder. "I am glad you feel better. You are beginning to look more relaxed. Now, please tell me your news. What could have kept you up all night?"

"It was the gallery show and the paintings I needed to finish. I decided to include the one you saw in the studio the first time you came there. Remember?"

"I certainly do! I still think it is one of your best but what was the rush to finish? Don't you have several weeks before the show?"

"You are right, of course. It wasn't the prime reason." He sat up straighter in the lounge chair and Anna knew the main topic of the conversation had arrived.

"I saw my father last night, as I had mentioned. He told me a number of things that shocked me. He has made arrangements to go from the hospital to a residential home for seniors."

"But, that is good news, surely? You were concerned about where he could go to recuperate."

Anna was even prepared to offer Lawren's father a place with her, temporarily, if necessary, but now she was glad that complication in her life would not be required.

"Absolutely! That was just the beginning, however. He made a request that floored me completely. He wants me to seek out the Drake estate in England and bring back information about the family."

"What? I thought you were permanently cut off from the family many years ago."

"I thought so too. Now he says he regrets this and wants to introduce me to the family heritage .... and, he wants me to do it *soon!*"

Anna sat back and tried to absorb this news. Now she understood the urgency of completing the paintings. It was obvious that Lawren took his father's request seriously and had every intention of meeting the obligation that had been thrust on him.

She deduced at once that he would be leaving for England and their lives would be separate again. Coming fast on the heels of this conclusion was the thought that he was doing the right thing.

If someone in her own family had ever had this impulse to re-establish connections across the Atlantic, her own life might have been very different and Helen Dunlop might not have been a relative she never met face to face.

"You must go, Lawren. I will check out travel arrangements for you, if you like. Do you know where you are heading? We can look for accommodation and transport links online. I can do all that for you and you can finish your gallery work. When do you think you will be able to leave?"

There was a silence that stretched out for a minute. Anna saw Lawren's face dissolve into tearful relief despite the hardening of his jaw in a vain attempt to control the emotion.

"I could not have expected you to be so understanding, Anna. My dear Anna! Since my mother died I have never known the comfort and sweetness a woman can bring to a man's life. Come here!"

She held him in her arms until he had gained control then briskly kissed him and pulled him into the small office where the computer and internet awaited.

After an hour researching the county of Wiltshire and exclaiming about its ancient history and amazing old towns, houses and gardens, Anna could see that Lawren was wilting with fatigue and they were no closer to the actual location of Hartfield Hall.

"Look, my dear, you had best go to bed and sleep for a couple of hours. I'll continue with the search and find a travel plan to suit you."

Lawren nodded in reply and needed no further persuasion. After tucking him into her bed, Anna kissed his forehead and tiptoed back to the computer.

She had an idea of where the estate might be located but maps were notorious for changing scale so that places looked much closer than they were in reality. The best she could come up with was a village in the Nadder Valley in the west of Wiltshire where there had been a railway station for well over a century and a half, making the trip from London by rail an easy connection for Lawren. From there he would be on his own, exploring the local area and asking the kinds of questions that should provide the information his father was no longer clear about. Tisbury would have country hotels or pubs where Lawren could stay while he ventured into the countryside. It was impossible to guess how long it would take for him to find what he was looking for and there was always the chance that it was a fool's errand and age had dimmed his father's memory.

Anna wished she could go on this adventure with Lawren. It was tempting to leave Canada behind and escape to a place where neither of them was known and their current problems might be forgotten.

She soon rejected this impulse. It was a very personal odyssey he was embarking on; one that would require an adjustment and re-evaluation of his family history. It was best that he take this journey on his own and return to her once he had gradually incorporated his new understandings into his personality.

She accepted this necessity, but, at the same time, she found herself thinking about something she had promised to do for herself in deciphering her own family secrets. A trip to

Glasgow where her mother and father met and married might help her find out the whys and wherefores in her parents' decision to leave their Scottish life behind in such a final way.

There were unanswered questions on both sides. Lawren's father wished he had not waited so long. Anna did not want to face the same regret one day in the future.

While she was still coming to this conclusion, she heard Alina's key in the door and rushed to meet her with a whispered warning that Lawren was asleep nearby. Alina said she was aware that he was inside as she had spotted his bicycle in the driveway.

"What's up?" she asked. "Have you two resorted to daytime assignations to avoid interruptions?"

Anna could not summon up a smile at this feeble joke and Alina soon saw the serious look on her friend's face. "Sorry! I didn't mean to offend you by that tactless remark. Tell me what's been happening."

They headed for Alina's suite at the other side of the condo where their conversation would not be likely to disturb Lawren. Anna wanted him to sleep until he woke naturally, knowing this would help him to deal with these rapid changes in his life.

It took a full ten minutes to give Alina an outline of the events of the last twenty-four hours. To Anna's surprise she grasped the implications at once and encouraged Anna's idea to do her own family research in Glasgow.

"Don't worry about me," Alina added. "This gives me the opportunity to do something I have been thinking about. I want to invite Philip to stay here with me for a trial period. After all, I have seen him on his home ground in Manchester and I think it's time he saw how I live here in London, Ontario."

"I think that's a wonderful idea, Alina! Philip will take good care of you, and the condo and business will be in safe hands while I am away. You should have told me you had this in mind."

"No need to fret about it now, Anna. Everything has fallen into place perfectly for all of us. Philip is badly in need of a break since the Olympics ended and I have another good idea for you."

"You are full of surprises today, my friend!" exclaimed Anna. "What is it?"

"Well, when you have done your research in Glasgow, why don't you and Lawren meet up in Oban for a week or so. Is the house free in September?"

Anna was delighted with this suggestion and hurried to the office to check the website where all the bookings for the McCaig farmhouse were kept up to date. She scanned the month of September and found her brother Simon had booked the second week for himself, Michelle, Donna, their older daughter, and one of the grandkids. There were no further bookings until October.

She rushed back to inform Alina and grew more and more convinced this was an excellent idea.

"If I time it right, "she exclaimed, "I can see Simon and Michelle, *and* my niece and her daughter before they leave. I have not been out to Alberta for years and I miss them. They can meet Lawren, too!"

"You see! A good plan works for everyone," Alina agreed with a touch of smugness. "It looks like we all have plenty to do in the next few days but before you run off, Anna, there is something important for you to consider first."

"What do you mean?"

"Well, if you are ever going to have success in finding out about your Scottish family, you need to write down everything you know about them from your parents or from other sources."

"Oh, I see what you mean. I can hardly arrive in Glasgow with nothing and no place to start the search.

I will do this as soon as Lawren has decided when to leave for England. Thanks, Alina. Smart thinking, as usual!"

Lawren slept until the skies had darkened. He proclaimed he felt much better but Anna insisted he join she and Alina for a meal. While he was enjoying a second helping of pasta and chicken, Anna carefully lifted his bicycle into the back of her car and returned to the condo to prepare a folder for him of the results of her online investigations. She had included all the relevant price options as she did not want to volunteer to fund the expedition and insult his independence. His first trip to Scotland was a business expense for Helen's painting. She doubted she could persuade him to accept an air fare again.

Lawren hardly complained about the car ride home to his studio and Anna was relieved that he did not need to tackle the cycle journey in the dark.

"It's good to have even this short time alone," he admitted, once they were on their way. "We haven't managed a night together for far too long. It's my fault, Anna. I don't want you to think I am not keen to make love to you again. I love you so much; more than I can say. Every day adds to the feeling I have that you are the best thing in my life. I want to give you everything and I am counting on the art show to make that wish a reality."

Anna knew he was watching her profile as he spoke to gauge her reaction. She desperately longed to stop the car and cover him with kisses but dared not lose her concentration on the road ahead. A brief flash of insight made her grin as she imagined what she would say to a police officer after they had caused an accident in the middle of a busy road.

"Lawren Drake, I am having serious difficulty keeping my eyes on the road here. You know how I feel about you. You have already given me more than any man has ever done. I feel such joy just knowing you are in my life and that has nothing to do with proximity. No matter where you are, that closeness we share is real and immediate." She swallowed and was glad the dim interior of the car hid her blushes. She was not used to fulsome expressions of her emotions any more. It was another thing she needed to adjust to in this new shared life she had acquired so unexpectedly.

A low throaty voice emerged eventually from the seat beside her. "Anna Mason, I know the location is not the most glamorous, but you will share my bed in the studio tonight before I let you drive home. Put your foot down woman, and get us there fast."

If anyone had been watching, they would have seen an unremarkable automobile suddenly moving into top speed and heard the sound of laughter floating behind it like strains of loud music from a car stereo.

"Silly young fools!" the observer might have concluded, and for a few wild minutes Anna and Lawren might well have agreed with this assessment.

Chapter Four

Fiona Jameson, recently-qualified Scottish Wildlife officer, clamped her uniform cap firmly over her brown hair, now gathered securely in a tidy bun low on her neck. She was not used to the headgear, having previously preferred to keep her head and hair free of encumbrances even in wild weather, but now that she was an official, as it were, she was required to dress the part when on official business.

Her assigned territory was mainly north of her home base of Oban, and stretched from Skye on the west coast to Glencoe in the interior. It comprised everything from rugged mountain terrain to coastal plains; tourist towns to estates and castles and all manner of landscapes in between.

Fiona was as excited at the prospect as she had ever been about anything in her whole life. Indeed, it felt as if her life had been merely a preparation for this job. Her independence, driving skills, love of wildlife photography and delight in closely observing Argyll's open spaces, were the key to her successful graduation.

She would be reporting to the local office of Scottish Natural Heritage in Fort William and could not wait to earn a good reputation for solid decision making and concise reports.

Her courses in sustainable economic growth, and management of Scotland's conservation and protection areas, had opened her eyes to the importance of securing the natural heritage of the country. As a former taxi-service driver she thought she had seen many beautiful areas of her homeland but she now had an understanding of its special land and seascapes and a new, fierce pride in maintaining them for future generations.

For the next several months she would be under the close supervision of senior managers. She knew she was only one of some seven hundred staff doing a huge variety of jobs but she was determined to succeed in the one job she wanted to claim for life. She knew her Granny in heaven would be proudly smiling down on her.

She checked her equipment, counting off the GPS, the powerful binoculars, the mobile phone with earpiece and a backup large-scale book of maps. She carried a laptop for reports which could be sent directly to the head office when in a WIFI zone, and her own special, Digital Single Lens Reflex camera, a gift from Anna and Alina on her graduation. Should the occasion arise to take some spectacular photographs, she would be ready. The very thought sent a shiver of anticipation through her.

Today's tasks required two stops at vastly different areas. She had been told to 'keep an eye on' the Glencoe Wood Estate. Apparently some Canadian had purchased a section of mainly wooded hillside land and divided it up into lots sized from just one square foot to a maximum of 10, 000 square feet.

These lots were sold to exiled Scots in Canada who wanted to possess property in a conservation area and thereby obtain the paperwork to enable them to use the courtesy title of Laird, Lord or Lady.

Fiona was shocked when she heard about this. She could not believe it was legal but was assured that the owner of the company, Scottish Lands, had some legal entitlement and the expressed intention to save this section of land adjacent to Loch Linnhe from developers.

The main concern of Natural Heritage was to protect and preserve, not only the ancient oak and birch woods on the site, but also to save the mammals, bats and birds that made their homes there.

Fiona had been made aware that a rare Nathusius' Pipistrelle bat had been sighted in the area, in 2011.

She had no clue what, if anything, a person from Canada would do with a couple of square feet of land in a wood in Scotland but she understood the necessity to watch carefully for any damaging activity.

The only Canadians she knew well were Anna Mason and Jeanette McLennan, George's wife. Both seemed eminently sensible to her and not the types to take risks in a vulnerable forested area but, then, her previous experience of many kinds of people warned her not to make assumptions.

She pulled the Land Rover off the A828 well south of the village of Duror and decided to climb the hillside and survey the Glencoe Wood site through her binoculars.

The length of the loch was the predominant land feature and it took some adjustment to find the site in question. She began by focusing on the top of the hillside opposite and found at once the silhouette of a noble red deer. Although the autumn hunting season was in full swing she prayed that the deer would flee before a hidden marksman could find him. She watched with bated breath until he turned his antlered head and vanished swiftly down the other side of the hill.

Before she could re-focus, she heard the sound of an axe and quickly scanned downwards until she found the source. Partly hidden by a densely-wooded section was a small caravan, what the Americans called a trailer. Outside this, a man was chopping down a sapling.

Fiona's heartbeat increased substantially as she realized what the man intended to do. He had set up a portable barbecue, and he obviously planned to cook some food on it once he had burned enough wood to create the required heat.

She ran down the hill at top speed and threw herself into the Land Rover grating the gears as she slammed into forward. In a few seconds she was on a lochside trail near the caravan and jumped out of her vehicle, remembering, at the last minute, to bring her camera to record the infraction.

It required several calming breaths before she could bring herself to talk in the quiet manner she had been instructed to use.

"Excuse me sir, can I ask what you are doing?"

"Can't you see, miss? I am cooking my lunch." His aggrieved tone of voice incensed Fiona further and she once more used deep breathing to settle her temper. Was this man an idiot?

"I must ask you to douse the fire at once, sir, and remove your vehicle from this area before any further damage is done."

"Excuse *me*! This is my property and I own the rights to it."

"Can you prove that, sir? This is a conservation area and therefore protected."

"Look here, I have come all the way from Nova Scotia to claim this land. I mean to stay here for a day or two and take pictures to show the folks at home. I have a certificate of sale and a title deed and a reference map in the trailer if you insist on seeing it. "

"I *do* insist, I'm afraid! You may have some title to this plot of land but you do not have permission to drive a trailer across other land to reach it. You have broken several laws already and the potential for further damage is obvious."

"But, but I have *paid* for this!" He drew himself up to his full height of 5 and a half feet and puffed out his chest, saying, "Do you know you are addressing Lord Mackenzie?"

Fiona could hardly restrain her laughter. Her cheeks flamed with the effort. So the information about these fake titles was only too true. She had heard that some small Hebridean islands off the west coast were sold to rich foreigners who owned the titles that the original owners of the island had held, but this wee man on a tiny plot of land declaring a lordship was too ridiculous to be believed.

Her instinct was to laugh out loud and dismiss his claims but there was also a faint sense of pity that he had paid good money in Canada to participate in this scheme, and no doubt cared deeply about his Scottish family heritage. He had the clan name for certain sure. She knew many Scots over the centuries had fled from their native land to Nova Scotia, Newfoundland and beyond. Wasn't Anna's family originally from Glasgow?

"Now, let's be sensible, sir. I can see you are not intending to cause any harm. You are just a bit unaware of the laws here in Scotland. Let's douse the fire and we'll say no more about it for now.

I'll be back tomorrow to confirm that you have moved on to a supervised campsite nearby. I am sure you will not damage any more trees. Take as many pictures as you wish." As she spoke, she moved over to the barbecue and poured her own drinking water supply over the flames until the heat was gone. 'Lord' Mackenzie was deflated by the official manner and appearance of the young girl and he decided to cut his losses and eat cold snacks for lunch. He reasoned that if he argued the toss with her, he would be wasting time on 'his' expensive plot of land and who knew if he might end up in a Scottish jail?

Murmuring under his breath about crooks who stole a guy's hard-earned money and misrepresented their claims, he climbed back inside the caravan to find something to eat and to fetch his video camera.

Meanwhile, Fiona had taken a few photographs of her own and settled into the driver's seat of her Land Rover to write up an official report. There was no harm in lingering on for a few minutes so the man would realize she meant every word she said.

"Well! I think that was a successful intervention," she proclaimed, with a satisfied smile as she saved her report to be sent on its way to Fort William later in the day.

Her next location was one she had requested specially.

Ever since she and Anna Mason had found and hand-raised a tiny Scottish wildcat kit, she had been fascinated with the rare species. Few Scots had ever seen one of the breed as they were masters at keeping out of sight. The tiny abandoned kitten in the barn at Anna's farmhouse would have died without the care and attention the two women had lavished on it.

Fiona was particularly proud that they had tried, deliberately, to keep their scent away from the animal so that it would not be truly domesticated. Despite this intention, they had named it Sylvester and watched with delight when the tiny creature began to grow on a diet of enriched milk.

Long before he had shown his true wild and aggressive nature, Sylvester had been claimed by the local vet and taken to an animal shelter. Fiona and Anna paid visits to the sanctuary from time to time and found, to their delight, that the adult wildcat had not forgotten them even though he was now mated to a semi feral cat and had a litter of his own.

Fiona never regretted the intervention. Her relationship with Anna Mason had really developed during the period when the kitten was living deep in the recesses of one of Anna's kitchen cabinets. That relationship, and the coaching Anna had volunteered, had been essential to Fiona's present career and now she was in a position to repay her debt to Sylvester.

Scottish Natural Heritage had determined that wildcats had been shot by gamekeepers thinking they were killing off feral cats who preyed on the eggs and young chicks of grouse and other wild birds.

A program to help gamekeepers to distinguish between

the two types of cat had been initiated and early results were positive. Once the keepers had seen a series of pictures showing the comparative sizes of the wildcats to their much smaller domestic relatives, the incidents of wildcat deaths were reduced.

Fiona was anxious to help cut these unnecessary deaths to the lowest possible number and had asked if she could visit any estates in her area where gamekeepers had not yet been contacted.

She had been given a location on a large estate where there were two gamekeepers. The busy autumn season meant these two men were often out on the hills with hunting parties or escorting fishermen to prime sites on the fast-flowing rivers that poured out of the mountainous areas.

Previous attempts to contact the keepers had been unsuccessful and Fiona was determined to correct that situation.

Following procedure, she entered the estate by the long driveway that led eventually to the Scottish baronial castle. As she parked on the gravel forecourt, she noted it was a fine example of the style with the main tower building stretching five stories high into the sky, surmounted by the imposing triangular gables the local people called 'crow-stepped'. Turrets could be seen projecting from both corners with the decorated, stone supports that kept the turrets from falling. She estimated their original purpose was to provide the castle owners with a longer view of whoever might be advancing to attack.

Several lower buildings had been added to the structure over the centuries and these housed stables and store rooms, but Fiona felt the strength of the building lay firmly in the defensive tower itself.

She reached up to tidy her hair and pull her jacket firmly into place. The castle was on land belonging to the Duke of Argyll and she was not sure who of the clan Campbell might be in residence there. She had better be prepared to meet anyone. Straightening her shoulders, she marched up to the old oak doors on the ground level of the tower with a firm step that contrasted with the nervous quivering she felt inside. There was a metal pull attached to a bell at the side of the door which she managed to reach by dint of standing on her tiptoes. A deep clanging sound reverberated somewhere inside the tower and she waited to see if there would be any response. Silence. She was just about to try again for the third time when the door creaked and slowly opened.

Fiona thought it was like a scene from a horror movie. *Who would be behind the door? Perhaps a wizened old family retainer, a dark-clad butler with a haunted face, or a tiny ghost child from a long-past era?*

She was scaring herself into what her Granny used to call 'a blue funk' so she stepped back to calm herself. She was not usually given to flights of fancy and this was not like intrepid Fiona Jameson at all.

A tousled young man in stained work clothes and with filthy hands stood in the narrow opening of the door and berated Fiona before she could say a word of explanation.

"What are you doing here? No one uses this door nowadays. You should have come to the stables or the estate office. I am in the middle of mucking out and I am on my own today. I can't stand here listening to you, whatever you may need. Follow me and hurry along!"

With this aggrieved complaint, the man hustled her through the narrow door opening and into a dark hallway with stairs ascending to another level. He pushed the front door back into place by leaning his body against it.

Fiona immediately saw how difficult it must have been to open the old door and felt annoyed that she had not been told which entrance to the estate she should have used.

The hallway was even darker now the outdoor light had been excluded and Fiona blinked to adjust her vision and almost missed the hurried figure disappearing through another door hidden at the back of the staircase. Fortunately, this door was left ajar for her so she followed the sound of rapid bootsteps and eventually came to an outside exit to a large cobbled yard around which stables were arranged on two sides.

The figure she was following had already disappeared again. Calculating that she had not exactly made a good first impression, she decided not to yell out her name and business, but began to walk from horse box to horse box along the L shape, peering inside and feeling increasingly grateful that large and curious horses were not peering back at her. She finally tracked down the stableman shovelling manure onto a wheelbarrow and from the tension in his back view she confirmed that he was not happy to be disturbed.

Clearing her throat, Fiona asked politely, "I won't interrupt your work if you can just direct me to the location of either of the estate gamekeepers?"

This attempt produced no result at all so she tried again. "I am on official business, you know. I represent the concerns of Natural Heritage."

He straightened up at this pronouncement and wiped sweat from his brow leaving a large brown smear there. "Well, *I* represent a very busy, hard-pressed man trying to keep this place running and I don't appreciate being lectured to by a slip of a lass."

Fiona's blood was up. She had tried to be polite and professional but this fellow was really getting under her skin. She remembered her training just in time but it was with a considerable effort that she was able to produce a calm tone.

"I don't believe I have been lecturing. I am here to provide a service and I don't appreciate your verbal attack. Perhaps I will return on another day."

She turned on her heel with her head held high, and walked smartly away looking for an exit gate.

What a rude man! Who does he think he is? We are all busy people with a job to do. I hope I don't run into him the next time I come here.

This refrain running in her head was abruptly interrupted by a loud shout of "Wait!"

Couldn't be for me, she determined, and kept walking toward a double-railed gate.

"Please, wait!"

At the second call, she turned slightly and found the stableman running after her.

What have I done wrong now? This can't be good.

"I apologize! You caught me at a bad moment. Neither stable boy turned up for work this morning and a group of riders are arriving in a couple of hours. That is not an excuse for being so rude to you. Please tell me your purpose. The keepers are both occupied but I can contact them by mobile phone if there's an emergency."

Fiona looked up into grey eyes in a tanned face topped by floppy dark hair and liberally smeared with what might well be manure. There certainly was more than a whiff of the smell around him. His boots were positively clarty, as Granny would say, and his shirt sleeves, rolled up to his elbows, had not escaped contamination. He untied a cotton scarf from his neck and wiped at his hands and face as he stood waiting impatiently for her information.

"It's about the wildcat survey," she began quickly. "I wanted to show the keepers some pictures to identify the species so that unnecessary culling of these very rare mammals can be prevented."

"Do you mean you have called me away from my work to tell me about *cats*?"

There was no mistaking the irate tone of voice and the red tide that flooded his face. Fiona stepped back and went directly into a bold frontal attack before she could stop her reaction.

"Look here! The Scottish wildcat species is the last remaining example of the type in the whole of the British Isles. Gamekeepers have been slaughtering the few that are left because they think they are just wandering feral cats. On the contrary, they are a magnificent wild animal and this information may help to preserve them into the next century."

She stopped abruptly in her tirade and realized she had been speaking to this stableman as if he had personally threatened the kitten that Sylvester had once been. She had totally lost the required professional objective manner that had been drilled into her and, undoubtedly, destroyed any vestige of sympathy and cooperation this man might have provided.

"Excuse me!" she continued. "I must be talking to the wrong person. When could I meet with the estate owner to discuss this matter?" She tried to maintain some kind of dignity in her speech although it was not easy under the circumstances.

A wry chuckle escaped his lips at this question. "You'll have a distance to go to find him, I'm afraid.

He's likely in a palace in Qatar at this moment and doesn't set foot in this place very often which is why we are seriously understaffed."

"Oh, I see! Well, I will leave you to it. I apologize for wasting your valuable time."

"Wait a minute!" He almost reached out to catch her sleeve then withdrew his hand when he saw its condition. "I can't fault someone who feels so passionate about Scottish wildlife. Give me any materials you have and I will promise to show them to Fergus and Roddy when they return. Come back in a few days, Miss ……..?"

"Ah, it's Fiona, Fiona Jameson. Thank you, Mr.…….?"

"Just call me Gordon. As I was saying, come back to collect the materials and you can assure yourself the task has been done properly." He reached into a slit pocket in his tweed waistcoat and drew out a card which he offered between two comparatively-clean fingers.

"Call me on one of these numbers and I'll make sure to be

here. I don't want to be labelled as someone who stood in the way of Scotland's natural heritage."

Fiona was unsure whether or not he was laughing at her but she chose to believe his words were sincere. She dared not criticize any further or her probationary period might be in jeopardy should he place an unsatisfactory comment on her record.

"Thank you. I'll be off then," she said, and she sprinted to the gate leading to the gravel parking area and the safety of her Land Rover, with nary a backward glance.

On the drive back to Oban she berated herself for losing her temper and being so high-handed with someone who was not responsible for the situation.

She rehearsed, and rejected, a dozen versions of the official report on the visit that she would soon need to submit. If she phrased it carefully she might not be in danger of a formal rebuke.

She quite forgot, for some days, to examine the grubby card she had been given.

Chapter Five

"*Have you heard from Anna lately?*"

This enquiry was accompanied by a strident voice in the background that sounded to Bev as if young Annette was impatient for her supper.

"Yes," she replied over the escalating screams. "*She tells me she is heading to Scotland soon.*"

"Oh, just wait a minute will you, Bev. I'll settle this wee one down and be right back.

Now don't disappear on me!"

"*I won't, don't worry!*"

Bev settled down on the nearest kitchen chair and listened through the phone as Jeanette soothed her daughter and no doubt provided something she could suck on for the time being.

Bev was reminded of long-ago days when her own two boys were small, and getting herself into a shower was a task requiring the organization of a field general. She smiled. It was a sweet time in her life despite the fact that her soldier husband was often overseas and she was, in consequence, a single mother.

The boys were well grown now and off about their own affairs. She had different priorities these days. There was her new and much-loved husband, Alan, who had given her his love and trust along with a new country, a farm and a restaurant supplying farmhouse teas to tourists who visited the animals Alan cared for. Kirsty, Alan's elderly mother had happily relinquished care of her son, and his farm, to retire to her own people on Skye when Alan married. Bev reminded herself that she had acquired a whole large, Scottish family as well as a completely different lifestyle from that of her life in Canada.

She was never lonely now. Sometimes it seemed there were not enough hours in the day to accomplish all that needed to be done. And yet, she relished every minute of it.

"Right you are; I'm back! Wee Anna's teething and she isn't happy when I am distracted by someone or something."

Bev smiled to hear the baby name that had given the grown-up Anna such pleasure when she first met George and Jeanette's second child at her christening in the summer.

"Give the wee darling girl a cuddle from me. She's still the loveliest child I think I have ever seen."

Jeanette laughed. *"Don't you encourage her!*

George says she'll have a swollen head from all this praise if we don't put a halt to it soon."

"Good luck with that!" warned Bev with a laugh.

"Now what were we talking about before we were so rudely interrupted?"

"You were asking about Anna."

"Right you are! So what's been happening with the romance?"

"Well, she said it was tricky to get time together because Lawren is busy with art work for a show."

There was a pause on the line. *"There's also a bit of a situation with Alina."*

"What would Alina have to do with it? Those two are the best of friends.

Surely you're not suggesting there's some jealousy going on?"

Jeanette's tone was concerned rather than annoyed but the message was clear. No one should dare come between the two lovers who had declared themselves soulmates right here in Oban.

"That's the last thing Alina would want, yet you can see how awkward it would be to have honeymooners right on your doorstep, as it were.

They have separate suites in the condo, of course, but I gather it's Lawren who feels like a bit of an intruder in the all-female environment."

"Ah, that is a problem! I imagine a starving artist isn't exactly rolling in enough money to buy separate accommodation."

"Exactly! He is a proud man though. Anna says it's difficult."

"You said she was coming over here soon? Don't say they've split up already!"

"No, no! Nothing like that! It's good news. Lawren's father has asked him to go to what was originally the family estate in England and try to mend the long-term dispute between them. Anna will join him in the Oban farmhouse when he returns via Glasgow."

"Wait a minute! Isn't the house let out to Anna's brother and his family this month?"

"You are quite right about that, Jeanette. Anna is hoping to coordinate her arrival so she can see Simon again and no doubt introduce the family to Lawren."

"Sounds like a good idea. I hope it all works out. How are things with you, Bev? You said the summer tourist season was good."

"It certainly was! Eric and his dog shadow, Duncan, were the hit of the summer but I'm worn out with baking scones and making huge pots of tea. Visitors can certainly drink and eat plenty when they've been following sheep and sheepdogs on the hills."

"Poor you! You'll get a bit of rest after the September weekend, no doubt, and then you'll be bored stiff!"

"I doubt it! Alan has plans to visit Skye. He wants to buy some long-legged sheep. He says the signs are there already. He predicts the snow will be deep this winter."

"Oh, heaven forbid! I want to get out and about with this wee one in her pram this year."

"Speaking of Annette; she's really quieted down this last few minutes."

"And so she should! I've been walking about the room with her in my arms while we've been talking and now she's fallen fast asleep."

"Right, that's my cue to go! Try to get some rest while you can, Jeanette. It'll soon be time to fetch Liam from nursery school."

"Too true! We'll talk soon, my dear!"

"Oh, just one more thing, Jeanette, I think I will ask Anna if the Samba group can add one more name to the roster."

"Goodness me! That's a departure from custom! Who do you have in mind?"

Jeanette sounded very curious at this proposed change to a long-standing Canadian cohort.

"Why, you, of course! You are a perfect fit and I am positive Anna will agree."

"But! But! What will happen to the name?"

"We'll just add J at the end. Sambaj sounds quite exotic, don't you think?"

"Bev, I am so touched. I would be proud to be a member. It's a real privilege to be part of the Canadian Connection."

"We'll have a special ceremony when Anna arrives. Bye for now."

Bev put her phone back on the kitchen counter. She looked out of the rear windows and smiled to see the view of green fields and heather-clad hills ascending to the sky. She never tired of this ever-changing scene.

Today there were scattered dots of white sheep roaming along the high ridges. Alan would be up there with Prince forging ahead of him to spy out the land. She knew Alan was safe with the dog nearby. He would protect his master with his very life if necessary.

Bev turned back to her baking duties. All the ingredients were arranged in order on the countertop and the oven was warm. Another batch of cheese and raisin scones would soon be ready for the next group of visitors. That's if Alan and Eric didn't find them first.

She grinned at the thought and picked up Kirsty's old wooden spoon. It was better than any modern metal spoon for mixing dough.

Old and new together. Past and present blended like the ingredients in the big yellow baking bowl.

Life is an interesting recipe, she thought. The surprising element is always ready to be added to the mix. She poured a little applesauce into the bowl as she considered the changes that had happened to the Samba group's members over the last couple of years.

"And now we have found another Canadian, far from home, who fits right in. Sambaj definitely has a nice ring to it."

Bev applied her strong right arm to the mixing and continued to think about life's surprising twists and turns.

Chapter Six

W hat I Know:
> *My parents, Angus and Marion McLeod were married in Glasgow in 1946.*

"No! Wait a minute! That's not right. I need to start further back than this."

Anna had only just begun to type the list of what she knew about her mother and father when she realized chronology and precision were going to be of vital importance. She shuffled the papers on which she had jotted down rough notes over the last two weeks. Today was the first time she had tried to organize her information on the computer. It was not starting well.

She leaned back and sighed deeply. Her mind was distracted by the farewell scene at the Aboutown bus terminal this morning when she had waved Lawren off on his trip to Toronto, and subsequent flight to England.

Both of them were disappointed that they were to be separated so soon after they had really become a couple. They had stood forlornly together in a corner of the terminal building waiting for the bus and jealously watching the other travellers. Several couples were obviously excited to be setting off on a Fall vacation. They whispered together and held hands while they checked their travel itineraries.

Anna almost ran to the booking counter and asked for a seat on the bus transport so she could join Lawren, but they had discussed this possibility endlessly and it became clear to Anna how important it was for him to take the trip independently. It would be an emotional journey into a past that strangely paralleled Anna's. Neither of them had grown up with extended family members around them. In both cases, the stories of early escapades and the names of previous generations were missing from their childhood memories.

Anna's theory about this was that those memories were perhaps too painful to be recalled when, for whatever reasons, decisions had been made to sever relationships by emigrating.

In Lawren's case, his father and mother had left England for Canada. In Anna's case, her parents had left Scotland for Canada, but the results in each situation were very similar. Two branches of families were apart and virtually unknown to each other and, as far as either Lawren or Anna knew, also forgotten.

Anna had been amazed to discover a Great-Aunt Helen who had taken the trouble to seek her out and to leave Anna, in her will, a property in Scotland. A great sadness in Anna's life was that she had never met the aunt whose legacy had changed her life so completely. She fervently wished that Lawren might be spared this sad disappointment. If he could trace any Drake family members she knew he would be the better for it and his questions might be answered.

It was in an attempt to answer her own questions that Anna had taken Alina's advice and begun to assemble a list of details she could recall about her Scottish parents. She intended to take this information with her to Glasgow and use it in a search for anyone remaining, or any source remaining, that might shed light on the reasons why her family was so divided.

Not that this list was going to be simple. It required much searching of memories long left behind, and Anna had not seriously tackled this task until Lawren's departure.

Now it could be put off no longer. In a week or two she intended to be reunited with Lawren in Glasgow and together they would travel to the Oban house to spend a few precious days together.

Thinking of this, Anna was overwhelmed by longing to see him again. He had only just left her, and yet, the parting hurt in a way that was both painful and satisfying. Emotions she had never expected to feel again had resurfaced once she had accepted Lawren into her world.

Now the thought of being so far apart was almost unbearable. Who would she tell about these feelings? Even on days when circumstances kept them from seeing each other, they would talk for hours on their phones. Lawren had said these conversations allowed him to work while they exchanged inconsequential details about their respective days. He claimed he had never before been able to draw or paint without complete silence around him, which was one of the reasons why he usually worked late into the night. Now, he found Anna's voice so relaxing that he could draft work or let his unconscious brain roam imaginatively, brush in hand, while listening and talking on a Bluetooth earpiece.

Anna derived considerable satisfaction from this confession. She felt as if she was a tiny part of the creative genius of this brilliant artist.

"This is not helping me to get going on the list!" she chided herself. Another deep sigh and she determined to try again to focus on the task at hand.

"Right! Start at the beginning. What do I know for sure and what is supposition?"

With these two categories defined, she felt encouraged to begin.

First, she would write what she knew, and if other ideas were prompted by this, well and good.

My mother's maiden name was Jarvis, so my grandmother was Aileen Jarvis.

My father's name was Angus McLeod. I know nothing about his parents. Possibly he was named after his father ie. Angus McLeod?

My parents met at college. She was studying nursing and he was becoming an engineer, like his father! So that gives me something to work with.

I know they married in a rush because their wedding picture was hardly bridal in appearance.

Why?

They were both young.

World War II was barely over.

There was a <u>scandal</u> brewing.

Philip, my half-brother, filled in this part. Angus McLeod is Philip's father and he was raised in England by his mother, (what was her name?) and Kyle Purdy. Kyle was my father's best friend.

Why would my mother rush into the marriage when her soon-to-be-husband had fathered a child?

Obvious.

She wanted to escape from the situation and avoid disgrace, recriminations, or even the likelihood of my father's closer connection with the girl he had made pregnant.

This makes sense. That is why they emigrated so quickly!

Anna sat back and looked over what she had typed. There seemed to be more questions than definite answers. Suddenly she remembered Lynn, Philip's sister. They had met once when Philip was summoned urgently to his mother's deathbed in a nursing home in Heathfield, Sussex.

Of course! The old lady's name was Isobel. Could it be that all four young people knew each other?

The chances of this were good. Three of them were in the wedding picture and the best man at the wedding married Isobel who was definitely known to my father.

This Kyle Purdy must have been a special young man; taking on his best friend's pregnant girlfriend when the real father had left with his new wife and fled to Canada.

This also explains the problems in Philip's family home; problems that drove him away at an early age leaving Lynn to look after both her father and mother.

No wonder Philip had dropped all contact with his sister. There must have been tremendous guilt in his situation. He was shocked when James and Caroline confronted him with a picture of his real father's wedding with his adopted father as best man!

Of course! This also explains why there was no contact between my father and Kyle. Either Kyle was angry at Gus for abandoning Isobel or, perhaps, he was afraid to give his wife a chance to reconnect with a prior love.

So many missed opportunities to sort things out and make better choices for everyone involved!

Anna had never stopped to think about this complicated scenario before. She was amazed at how much she actually knew, or could surmise, from just a few known facts.

So my parents left for Canada under a cloud and had to start from scratch with nothing and no one to help them. I understand now why they had to work so hard and why my mother was not

a relaxed, stay-at-home lady like Alina's lucky mother. I never thought of it this way before but it could have contributed to the fact that both my parents died too young.

But, what about the grandmothers who were deprived of their grandchildren?

Didn't George McLennan's research, when he was trying to find out about Helen Dunlop,

reveal that her mother had been married twice?

Anna saved her notes and went to her office to dig around

in old files she had transferred from her apartment when she and Alina had bought the condo. As she rummaged around, she could hear Alina humming contentedly while she worked in the kitchen. She seemed happier now that Lawren would be out of the picture for a while.

Oh, she's probably just looking forward to playing hostess to Philip soon.

Anna shook her head to remove the unworthy thoughts and resumed the search.

George's precise notes about Helen Dunlop emerged from the drawer in a red file folder. Anna had chosen the bright colour for all the relevant information, so that one day she could retrieve it more easily.

I guess that day is now, she decided.

Among the papers was the letter from Helen that had been given to Anna when she arrived in Oban for the first time. George had handed her the unopened envelope, following Helen's directive.

Anna picked it up at once, unable to resist re-reading the only hand-written letter from her benefactor, meant for her specifically.

She imagined she could hear a soft Scottish voice as she read the words again.

"I am your aunt, half-sister to your mother, Marion Jarvis McLeod.

My birth name is Aileen Anne Wilson and my adopted name you know."

Just a minute! Anna re-read the sentences again. She had not noticed it before. It was only because she was delving back into the past in this way that the error became obvious. Helen's birth name was Knox, the name of her father who died in the Spanish flu epidemic in 1918. Why would she deliberately write the maiden name of her mother and not that of her father?

Anna knew that Helen had done nothing without a good reason. She had plotted and planned her life, on her own, for many years. Strange that George McLennan had not pointed out the error when she had shared the letter with him.

Could Helen have intended to leave a clue so that Anna would be able to find the dark secret of Aileen Anne's early abandonment? Perhaps the years she spent at Quarriers, as an unclaimed child, had marked Helen so badly that this was the only way she could contemplate introducing the subject? And yet, she must have meant for her past to be discovered.

Anna decided to ask George's opinion about this when she returned to Oban.

Anna shut the red file and replaced it slowly. The saga of Helen's hidden life was a closed file now, in more ways than one. Her present concern was more to do with her immediate family and whether she could discover more about her mother and father when they lived in Glasgow. She realized it was going to be a difficult task and might well result in frustration. Nevertheless she would persevere as far as she could. George's research had proved essential in uncovering Helen's past. Anna could only hope she might be as successful in her similar quest.

But where to start?

Her swirling thoughts were interrupted by a loud crash and a cry of alarm from the kitchen. Anna jumped up immediately and ran to see what had happened.

She found Alina on her knees on the floor scrabbling around trying to pick up the shards of a glass bowl that had fallen from the countertop.

"Stop right now, Alina!" cried Anna. "You are about to get badly cut. Let me help you stand before you get glass in your hands and knees."

Alina seemed disoriented and Anna led her to a chair. "What happened, my dear?" she asked gently.

"I...I don't know. I thought the dish was farther away from the edge and then it suddenly slipped.

I am so clumsy. I am sorry."

"Nonsense! You are the most careful person I know in a kitchen. It's just a silly accident. Don't apologize."

"That's just the trouble, Anna. The truth is, I have had more of these accidents lately and I haven't wanted to worry you about it. I am afraid my eyesight is getting worse."

Shock at this confession sharpened Anna's perceptions. She had been so involved with her own issues lately that she had missed the deterioration in Alina's condition. She had vowed to always be there for her dearest friend and now she had broken that promise at the first distraction.

"I am the one who should apologize! I am ashamed that you have felt you should keep this from me, Alina. Please talk to me and tell me how you have been dealing with this all on your own."

"Oh, it is such a relief to be able to talk to you about it! I haven't wanted to burden you with my worries when you were in the midst of more important concerns of your own."

Alina dabbed at her cheeks with chocolate-smudged hands. Anna felt waves of shame flood through her. She reached over and placed a napkin in Alina's hand so she could wipe her eyes.

"You are my *first* concern, and always will be, no matter what is going on in my life"

She folded Alina into a warm hug until her sobs had diminished and Anna had a chance to calm her own beating heart and determine to make reparations for her neglect.

"Right now we have this time to ourselves. We need to catch up with each other and see where we are. There have been many changes in our lives lately and we have to be honest about the effects, whatever they mean for the future."

"I know you are right, Anna. I don't want you to think I am avoiding the inevitable. Change can be beneficial. You have a new beginning with Lawren and I am happy for you.

He obviously loves you and how could I be anything other than glad about that?"

Anna squeezed her old friend's arm when she heard this. Alina's tone of voice was sincere and Anna knew she meant every word.

"There have been good changes for you, too, don't forget. Philip is a half-brother to me and he has an automatic place in my life and heart. Whatever your relationship to him becomes, he will be in both our lives from now on. Don't you agree?"

"Of course, I do. I must admit I am looking forward to his visit. I want to show him around town and see how Susan and Jake get on with him. I think he will be surprised by the A Plus business."

"He should be in admiration of what you have accomplished there, my dear. Without your talents we would not be living comfortably here together. Quite an achievement for our time of life, I'd say!"

"Well, I most definitely did not do that on my own!" She chuckled, and Anna joined in a laugh aware that Alina had recovered her equilibrium and was ready to discuss the real problem.

"Now, please tell me about your eyesight,"

Alina gulped, then turned to face Anna. "There have been small changes, of course. I have been adjusting to those but in the last month things have been accelerating. I get so frustrated when anything I need has been moved. The reason for my annoyance is because I find it so difficult to find the missing item. I can look for a short while but then my head aches and my eyes start to get much worse."

Anna realized she had been guilty of re-organizing a kitchen cupboard lately without understanding the effect on Alina. She also figured out why there had been finger marks on the doors and hairs in the powder room sink. Alina's eyesight was no longer acute enough for her to spy these small items and do her usual meticulous cleaning.

"Some of that is my fault, Alina. I will be more careful now I know what's happening. Please don't keep things from me again. I want to help."

"I know you do, but can you appreciate how difficult it is for me to admit the truth? It's almost as if I can fool myself as long as I don't have to confess it to someone else."

"You need not be that brave. Everyone who knows you wants to help and support you, Alina. Even Philip. You said you told him about your macular degeneration when you spoke to him in Manchester."

"Yes. I thought it was best to get everything out in the open so there would be no false hopes or expectations."

"That was wise of you and I imagine he had a few confessions of his own to make?"

"Oh, we had a heart-to-heart over a long meal in his dining room. He knows himself quite well. He's a workaholic and a perfectionist but he sees a different way to live now and wants to mend fences with his family in England as well as getting to know us better over here."

"Good. Mending fences and building bridges is exactly what I am intending to do in Scotland.

How could we fail with such good intentions among us?"

Chapter Seven

Lawren Drake slept for most of the way to London's Heathrow Airport. Anna had booked a seat for him in the rear of the plane where a few rows had double, rather than triple, or more, seats. She had suggested his chances of a peaceful night would be greater in that location.

As ever, Anna was right, he thought, when he realized the seat beside him was to remain empty for the flight.

He removed his boots and stretched out across the seats and within minutes of departure had fallen into a deep sleep.

He saw himself walking up a long driveway. Anna Mason was by his side. They were both smiling happily as they contemplated a life together in the splendid mansion they were approaching. Steps led up to a massive door surmounted by a circular pedestal.

The building above soared upward to the sky with sunlight reflected from its many windows.

The doors swung open and a strangely-dressed man stood there gesturing to them to enter.

Lawren went forward into a vast marble hall where a double staircase ascended upwards.

The older man was dressed in velvet and lace belonging to

a vanished era but he beckoned to his visitor to follow him into a drawing room of huge proportions filled with chairs, couches and tables everywhere he looked. The ceiling was high and the walls were covered in oil paintings. Stately men in armour, or flamboyant court dress, were matched by elegant ladies in sweeping gowns with children and dogs at their feet. An expansive park, stretching for miles, could be seen in the background of many of these paintings.

Lawren moved to look more closely at the art work. He tried to decipher the signature at the bottom corner of the nearest portrait, but the letters seemed to swim before his eyes.

Just as he was almost reading the name, D R A K E, he became aware that his host had disappeared from the room and Anna had not followed him into the house.

A sense of panic filled him. He spun around to look for the door but it had vanished.

"Excuse me, sir. We are landing soon. I need you to sit up and fasten your seatbelt. You have missed breakfast but I can get you a snack and some coffee if you would like."

Lawren reacted physically to the hostess' request but his brain was still spinning. It was moments before he could gather his senses and understand that he had been deeply immersed in a vivid dream.

Although he valued his occasional psychic instincts, he was not prone to dreaming at all which made this incident both unusual and disturbing.

The bustle and chatter around him in the plane was less real to him still, than the dream scenario. He set his mind to recall the details of the dream before they vanished into thin air.

A large, impressive house.

Anna by his side.

A man from a bygone era welcoming him in.

The room filled with ancestral portraits.

Was it the name 'Drake' he had seen on a portrait?

What on earth, or in heaven, did all of this mean?

Was his unconscious mind sending him a message?

The act of flying from one reality into another was, in itself, a thoroughly disorienting experience without this strange dream descending upon him.

He looked out of the window to see banks of white cloud as far as the horizon. Dreams were cloud-like, ephemeral events, not meant to be taken seriously. And yet, he could not shake the lingering feeling of panic that the final scene had evoked.

He decided to apply logical thinking to the dream and hence dispose of its effects entirely.

The search for his father's family home was obviously on his mind.

The hope that he would be seen as an emissary from his father, and received gladly, must have been a factor.

Anna's appearance by his side indicated that he wanted to provide a home for their future together.

The portraits were a symptom of his father's declaration that there had once been a distinguished artist in the family.

He immediately felt reassured by this approach. It was only a dream after all.

But why had Anna gone, leaving him alone and trapped inside?

Was this a bad omen?

Was he being warned that the search for Hartfield Hall would be futile?

"Nonsense!" The word exploded from his mouth, alarming the hostess who had returned with a tiny tray wrapped securely in plastic and a small plastic cup of steaming coffee.

"Oh, sorry! I was just thinking out loud." He accepted the breakfast offerings but declined the challenge of unravelling the breakfast pastry, instead, choosing to swallow the scalding coffee in three gulps.

"If that doesn't banish these stupid thoughts entirely, nothing will," he declared to the window.

The clouds had dissipated and glimpses of rural England with its ancient villages, farms and towns could now be seen through the remaining shreds of vapour.

We'll be landing soon.

The quest begins.

Mindful that his father eagerly awaited the results of his mission, Lawren decided to waste no more time on vain imaginings. He checked under the seat in front and found his backpack still wedged there securely.

With no luggage to collect from the carousel he would soon be on his way, ahead of the rest of the passengers. By the end of this day, he planned to have some pertinent information to share with those at home in Canada.

Lawren had forgotten the vagaries of travel in the modern age. Consulting his itinerary he discovered that a cab ride across London was required to connect him with a train station on a line that went directly and swiftly west to his destination in Wiltshire. His father's instructions were vague but he did know the name of the nearest town to the estate he was seeking. Burton-on-Avon was remembered by his father as "a small market town built of golden Cotswold stone with narrow streets and a fine, old, arched bridge over the river."

The details meant nothing to his son who only hoped he could find accommodation for a day, or two at the most. Already he could feel the distance between himself and Anna stretching out uncomfortably.

He wanted to get this business over with and speed north to Scotland to meet up with Anna again.

The train from Paddington was a surprise. Expecting some version of train travel from old British movies, Lawren was pleased to discover a fast modern transport with comfortable seats and clean windows.

He settled down quickly and watched busy city scenes of London gradually give way to countryside and pastoral views. The train crossed over a portion of Berkshire then across most of the county of Wiltshire almost to the border with Somerset. Anna had included a helpful map with his itinerary. Teachers are so organized, he chuckled, reminding himself to thank her during their planned nightly phone call.

Berkshire looked expensive from the large homes and farms that could be seen from the railway lines; a location that seldom, in his experience, showed the finer areas of any town or city.

Wiltshire was quite different and he marveled at the contrasts in house styles, stone boundaries and even brickwork from one county to another. There were small towns and villages from time to time then open fields with strange curved, corrugated metal structures close to the ground scattered here and there. He puzzled over this for some time until the sun came out after the drizzle of rain that had dulled the views since he boarded the train.

The advent of sunshine encouraged the occupants of the metal shelters to emerge and warm themselves. Lawren was astounded to find the inhabitants were pigs; large pinkish brown creatures, rooting around in the grass. He had thought all such animals were raised in pens on farms or in large factory farming situations. He immediately formed a good opinion of a nation whose concern for animal welfare permitted a free and healthy life for its livestock. The thought of the superior pork and bacon from such animals made his mouth water and reminded him how hungry he was. He had eaten nothing since lunch with Anna eons before.

Attendants on these new train systems seemed to be in short supply. Other than a young man who had clipped his ticket and inserted it into the top rim of his seat, he had seen no train staff to proffer food or drink. The few passengers in his carriage were working on iPads or laptops and communicating with cell phones. There had been two family groups who left after about forty minutes. Station announcements came from an indistinct disembodied voice and were followed by a red digital summary on display above the automatic door exit from his carriage.

Lawren calculated the arrival time to his destination and hoisted his backpack well before the train slowed. He waited until the train was almost stopped before standing and making his way to the exit. Watching other travellers had alerted him to the danger of trying to walk on a fast-moving train.

The man ahead of Lawren pressed a button to open the train doors and Lawren was glad he had not had to figure out the system for himself. He jumped down onto a station platform and before he could orient himself, the train picked up speed and vanished down the track toward Bath.

First impressions of Bradford-on-Avon included an antique station that looked like it had been built about a hundred years before. He found the exit quickly and soon noticed a sign reading 'town centre'.

Hopeful that there would be restaurants of some description there, he set off at a smart pace, glad to get moving again after his long periods of inactivity.

This is incredible. It feels like stepping back in time to another century. I had no idea places like this still existed. Only small areas of Montreal or Quebec City have this kind of ancient look to them.

This is an old, old town crowded together within a space where the river meets hills but there are rows of small houses ranging up the hillside there. The view from the top would be spectacular. Oh, there's the bridge my dad mentioned. It's beautiful! The arches and the stone parapets are simply perfect and what's that tiny building perched on one end? Where is my sketch pad? I need to take a photograph of this and come back here later. My fingers are aching to draw.

No, concentrate on the task at hand. Find something to eat and a place to stay. It's already evening by Canadian time. I have to get settled first but there's so much here to look at. How could anyone ever leave here? My parents must have been crazy-in-love! This place is unique.

Lawren practically stumbled onto a tourist information office in a store near a church that seemed to be a mix of French, German and Italian gothic architectural styles. The rain was just starting again and he turned from venturing inside the church to confirm his opinion of its style varieties in favour of staying dry inside the small tourist office and finding some practical information. He could not resist picking up a selection of pamphlets about the town and area which he shoved into an outer pocket of his backpack to peruse later.

"Are you staying in the area, perchance?" enquired a polite voice. The tiny woman who owned the voice emerged from behind a counter and approached Lawren. "I see from your luggage tag, you are from Canada. What brings you all this way to Bradford-on-Avon?"

Lawren looked into a face that could only be described as pointed. Despite her sharp features she had a practiced smile and he needed her help. Ignoring the personal questions he took on the role of poor travelling innocent (not so far from the truth, he thought), and, in response, plied the woman with enquiries.

"Where can I stay without spending too much? I really need a meal also, and a map of the area and if you have bus timetables, that would be helpful or, even better, a place where there are bikes for hire."

She moved into professional mode at once and bombarded Lawren with schedules and advice until his head was spinning. He did manage to catch the name of an inn nearby and after making sure it served food, he asked to be pointed in the right direction. She happily stepped onto the pavement, whipping a handy umbrella over her head, in practised fashion, and indicated a narrow lane off the main street through which he would come to an archway in a wall and beyond that the old inn itself.

Lawren turned back to thank her but she had retreated into her shop like a hermit crab into its shell. Perhaps she doesn't get many customers this late in the year, he thought, as he hefted his bundle of information and stowed it inside his leather jacket, promising himself to buy an umbrella soon or he would be soaked to the skin in this climate.

The rain grew heavier as he walked and a rumble of thunder could be heard. Suddenly Lawren shivered and he began to long for hot food and a warm bed. He had no patience left for wandering around looking for shelter so he approached the inn with every intention of finding it satisfactory.

A wooden board above the entrance declared he was entering The Sailors' Rest. The painted sign swayed in the wind and he caught only a glimpse of the figure of a man with his hand resting on a globe of the world before he dived through a partly-open door and stood inside to get his bearings.

It seemed dark in the interior but that might be because the wooden walls and floor were stained with many years of smoke from an open fire in the small room nearby. He was drawn to the crackling fire, as a moth to a flame, and stood as close as was safe, rubbing his bare hands together and shaking raindrops from his hair.

"Can I get 'ee somat to drink sor?"

Lawren jumped at the unexpected voice. He had heard no footsteps approaching.

"Not at the moment, thanks. What I need is some food and a bed for the night."

"Right, sor, I'll see what I can do about tha', but lunch is off and we don't serve owt now till the evening. Pub grub only, I'm afeered. Follow me and I'll show you a room."

Lawren's mouth dropped open. This man sounded like a character from Dickens and looked the part too! He was wearing a long leather apron and his shirt sleeves were rolled up over muscular forearms.

His hair owed its deep, dark colour to a dye bottle and his mustache drooped at both ends like a smuggler from bygone days. Once more Lawren longed to grab a pencil and draw but he quickly followed the landlord up a creaking staircase and along an uneven hallway thinking to himself that he had wandered into the set from a 1940's movie melodrama.

Wait till I tell Anna about this!

Despite his trepidation, the room that was offered was adequate and had a small window looking out to the rear of the inn where he could see parked cars. *Good! I am not alone here.*

The landlord opened a door into an adjoining bathroom that was the same size as the bedroom.

"I'll be leaving this 'ere door unlocked for you, sor. Normally it's a shared bathroom but the gen'leman who was on the other side left this mornin'." He looked curiously at Lawren's backpack which he had laid down on the bed in an act of possession, and continued, "Ah, you be from far parts, Oi see." Rubbing his chin with a not-too-clean fist, he decided to take pity on the traveller.

"My Mavis might be able to fetch a tray for you, sor. That's if you decides to stay with us awhile?"

Lawren agreed with alacrity. Venturing out into the rain again was not an appealing thought and the bed looked very welcoming.

'Good, then. Just come downstairs when you be ready and you can sign the register. I'll talk to my Mavis."

Lawren did not know whether to laugh or sigh after this encounter. He had a quick wash in the spacious, but cold, bathroom, with its black and white tiled floor and walls. There was a huge bath in one corner against the shared wall and a quantity of thin, but large, white towels folded over the edge.

"No shower, I see," he murmured. "Not quite the Holiday

Inn, but definitely a part of the different qualities of England, I suspect. I can't wait to see Mavis!"

"Oh, Lawren! I am so glad to hear from you. How are you getting on? Where are you now and what have you found out?"

"I can't tell you everything, my darling. It would cost the earth! But I must say it's been a fascinating adventure so far. I am staying at an old inn straight out of Dickens, if not Shakespeare. Mine host and his wife Mavis are a study in contrasts. She's a buxom wench about twenty years younger than her husband but they have been kindness itself to me so I am fed and warm and looking forward to a good night's sleep."

"Excellent news! What do you think about the town?"

"I haven't seen all of it yet but so far it's quaint and old and beautiful. If I can't get time to sketch here I must take pictures. You won't believe how ancient it is."

"I wish I had come with you to see it all. When will you visit your uncle?"

"Haven't had a chance to look for the house yet, Anna. That's one of tomorrow's challenges. I mean to start out early and maybe I'll be heading to Scotland soon."

"I leave here day after tomorrow, as planned. I'll wait for you in Glasgow."

"I can't believe how much I am missing you, Anna. I want to talk to you every minute of the day.

Love you!"

"Love you more! Goodnight my darling."

"Goodnight my love."

Chapter Eight

The next day dawned bright and dry although Albert, as the landlord was called, warned Lawren, "It promises rain later, sor."

Over a hearty English breakfast served in the bar, a meal that Lawren calculated would save him money as lunch was impossible after the amount of food he had already consumed, he asked Albert if he knew the location of Hartfield Hall.

Albert hesitated only a moment and shook his shaggy head saying, "Me and Mavis has been here for about five year now. We come from Somerset so we don' know the area over well, yet. This here business don' allow for much time to wander aroun' the county. Ask in the town. Someone'll know where it is." Albert provided this information while lifting Lawren's dishes and swiping the table with a cloth. His advice was delivered over his shoulder as he disappeared behind the bar and into the kitchen where 'his Mavis' could be heard singing along to the radio as she worked.

Well, I had better go back to the information centre. None of the maps I picked up had a name like Hartfield. It may take a local, long-time resident to help me out.

Backpack over his shoulder, he walked swiftly down the

lane, breathing in the cool fresh air and feeling ready to conquer any problems on his way to find his father's heritage and get back to Anna.

The information centre was closed at this early hour but he knocked twice on the door just in case, and was rewarded with the sight of a familiar face peering around the 'closed' sign.

The click of a lock signalled that he might be in luck.

Hmmmm.........A good start to the day's adventures.

"Oh, it's yourself, young man. Come away in. I was just sorting out a delivery of guide books and leaflets. Can you lift this box up for me? Thank you. Now, did you find the inn all right? Good. You look much refreshed this fine morning. What can I do for you today?"

Her narrow, sharp-featured face with beady eyes resembled a robin listening for a worm under the earth and Lawren knew he would have to satisfy her curiosity despite wishing to keep private family matters to himself.

"Well," he began, "I noticed many exceptional places in the pamphlets you gave me. Wardour Castle, Stonehenge, Avebury and Salisbury Cathedral are all in this county."

"Of course," she interrupted. "There's six thousand years of history in these parts."

"Yes, I am sure you are right but I only have a brief time and I need to find a place near here called Hartfield Hall."

"Oh, yes, *Hatfield House,* home of the Marchioness of Salisbury. Her gardens are famous for their magnificent designs. I think it is still open to the public. I'll check on the computer and make sure for you."

That doesn't sound right.

"Excuse me! I think you have the wrong name. It's *Hartfield Hall.*"

"Dear me! My hearing is not what it was, I'm afraid. Hartfield Hall.

Now, I know it is around here somewhere. Just let me look in a guide book for a moment."

The moment stretched into several and Lawren grew impatient to be on his way. He picked up one of the books stacked on the counter top and consulted the index to speed along the process. After trying several guide books, it became clear that the house in question was not to be found.

"That's strange!" she said, "I am sure I have heard about it. Perhaps it's in an older edition."

She scurried off to a curtained area behind which Lawren saw a tiny office where piles of dusty books competed for space with tea-making facilities.

He could hear impatient noises drifting out from behind the curtain and a volume or two struck the floor before she emerged triumphantly with a small, worn booklet in her hand.

"I *knew* I had seen it! Here we are; Hartfield Hall, the country seat of the Drake family for several hundred years. It's about five miles from Bradford-on-Avon, north-west by this map although it is out-of-date, I fear. Your best bet is to follow the high street out of the town, keep the river on your left and head toward Trowbridge and ask again there. A taxi might take you or you could ask at the bus depot. Do you have business there, young man?"

"Thank you for all your help and for opening the door to me. I'll be out of your hair now and let you get on with your work. Goodbye!"

Lawren escaped swiftly. He had enough information to go on with. Obviously Hartfield Hall was not as well known today as his father had believed.

His steps quickened once he was walking through the town following the path of the river. The cost of a cab ride was out of the question, and a bus might be difficult since he was not sure of his exact destination.

He could probably walk the five miles although a bike would make things easier. Just at that moment he spied a garage off the main street and decided to try his luck there. A five pound deposit and a copy of his debit card secured a somewhat-battered bicycle but it was a racing model with the multiple speeds which might be necessary in this hilly area.

He asked if any of the garage staff knew about Hartfield Hall but was met with blank stares.

Strange and stranger!

This thought was blown away as soon as he straddled the bicycle and felt the wind in his face. For the first time since arriving in England he felt at home. Reminding himself to keep to the left, he applied muscle power and soon left the quaint streets of the town behind.

This is more like it! It's great to get moving again.

He pulled the skip of his baseball cap down toward his nose so he could ride fast without fear of it blowing off. He breathed deeply of the crisp air and noticed the trees were nearer to Fall here in England than they would be back in Ontario in the month of September.

The blue sky was scattered with clouds and the scent of wildflowers and bruised apples made his nose twitch as he laboured up the hill, steering close to the road's edge whenever cars and trucks came lumbering up behind him then roared past without leaving him any room to negotiate.

The first chance to catch his breath and ask for directions came when he had ridden an estimated three miles distance from Bradford-on-Avon. The river could be glimpsed from time to time below his present altitude so he knew he was heading roughly on the recommended route.

He came across an area where a motorcyclist had stopped for a drink by the side of the road. A half-moon-shaped parking place had been carved out of a field and on it a white van was dispensing hot drinks and sandwiches. Lawren took the opportunity to seek help.

After paying for a scalding polystyrene cup of instant coffee, (*why were the drinks in England so hot?*) he ambled over to the cyclist who was straddling his bike and reading a newspaper.

"Do you know the area?" enquired Lawren.

The man looked up and replied, "Should do, mate. Lived here all me life."

"Can you direct me to Hartfield Hall, by any chance?"

"Hartfield? Hartfield? Here Fred, you ever heard of a Hartfield House in these parts?"

A debate commenced between the motorcyclist and the van driver in language that was just below the level of Lawren's understanding. Eventually a decision was reached.

"Sorry, matey. No clue! Try up the road a ways."

Lawren emptied the rest of the awful coffee onto the grass verge and threw the crumpled cup into a waste basket helpfully provided by Wiltshire county council. He set off again with the feeling that he was on a wild goose chase and that he could not just wander off into the countryside forever without a definite destination in mind. Telling himself that Trowbridge would assuredly be his last stop, he began to look out for a house near the road where he could ask his question once again.

After another twenty minutes or so, a farm appeared on the horizon. Lawren rode up to the gate in a fence and waited there while a woman in a headscarf finished pulling weeds from her front yard and looked up.

He did not venture into the yard because a large dog had been eyeing him suspiciously since he pulled off the road.

"I'm looking for Hartfield Hall." Even to his own ears, his words sounded defeated. He expected another negative answer and started to pull up the collar of his leather jacket in preparation to turning around. He was beginning to wonder what on earth he would report to his father on his return to Canada.

"Yes." The reply was non-committal. It could mean anything.

"Do you know where it is?"

"Foller this track about two mile. You'll see it." The woman stared at him as if he must be mad but Lawren was so relieved to finally be close to his destination that he wasted no time in accessing the path that wandered up the hillside past the farm. A sign read; 'Footpath. Right of Way. No horses.'

As it said nothing about bicycles, he forged ahead. So intent was he on trying to avoid the ruts and stones in the narrow path that he missed hearing the woman's last comment, flung over her shoulder as she dumped her weeds on a large mound and headed back indoors.

"You won't like it. None of us do."

The quality of the track did not improve as it passed through high wooded banks. There were pools of mud that had to be avoided and a sandy ridge, liberally pockmarked with holes, disgorged a family of rabbits when he arrived at their warren. Their fleeing feet sent a shower of wet sand down onto his head and he almost capsized.

Take it slowly. You can't risk breaking a leg so far from the main road.

After that surprise, he proceeded more cautiously and eventually the track opened out and paralleled a paved roadway about one car width in size. When he looked ahead from the paved area he saw a house in the distance silhouetted on a rise.

At last!

Excitement and satisfaction rose in him. He was instantly transformed from doubt into delight.

He sped along the road keeping his eyes on the house which grew larger as he approached. At first no details were obvious. It seemed to be a tall, grand, central edifice with wings at a lower level fanning out to each side.

He could see chimneys standing out against the skyline and a species of plant trailed up the walls on one side of the house. He wondered if it might be a Georgian design style but columns and windows now appearing could indicate Palladian. In any case, such an old building had, no doubt, undergone a number of renovations as new families over the centuries updated their home.

My father lived here as a boy. This should have been his inheritance, and perhaps, mine also. Will I meet a relative here who will welcome me to the family?

As he continued to seek out detail, something odd began to happen; while initially he had seen only the overview, he now discovered unexpected signs of deterioration. There were parts of the roof where slates or tiles were missing and bricks had fallen from one exposed corner. The façade was painted in a light brown wash of some sort and he could now detect what could be patches of damp, bleeding through. Up close, it was obvious that windows were missing or cracked.

Can a house in this condition be occupied? What is going on here?

He slithered to a stop on the pockmarked remains of a driveway circle in front of the entrance to the house and stood there gasping with effort and shock.

For a split second the exterior of the dream house he had seen on the plane flashed before his eyes, superimposed on this wreck of a building. He laughed out loud at the flagrant contradiction of the imagined ultra-luxurious dream mansion and this parody.

How utterly ridiculous! Am I on a fool's errand here?

His laughter doubled him over until the tears escaped and ran freely down his cheeks.

"Here! What's your game?"

Lawren's head snapped up at the sound of a rough male voice.

"Get out of it! Get away from here!"

Lawren quickly scanned the first floor of the house to find where the voice was coming from. He had a sudden sense of vulnerability. He was on private property, no matter what its condition. If this person had a gun, he was not in any position to defend himself.

A head emerged from a window and Lawren saw the

enraged expression of outrage on an old, wrinkled face. The man was shaking a stick at him from the comparative safety of a ground floor window that had seemed, on first sight, to be screened by a potato sack, or some such thing.

No gun then. But why am I finding only old, weird people in this country?

Lawren gulped and straightened up rapidly, pushing his hands to the front of his body in the international signal for 'don't shoot'.

"Hey, Man! Cool it! No threat here, I swear. I didn't mean to alarm you. I'm just looking around.

As the old fellow, whose head was encased in a brown cap, did not advance from his safe position, Lawren ventured to ask a question. After all who else was available to advise him about the mystery he was confronting?

"Look! Is this really the old Hartfield Hall? I couldn't find a sign anywhere but they told me in the town it might be around here."

There was a silence as the man disappeared behind his drape again. Lawren waited for a response and was just about to leave in disgust when the man emerged through the front door and growled, "Who's asking then?"

"I'm Lawren Drake. I've come all the way from Canada to find this damn place. I expected an estate and a mansion house and instead I got *this!*" The pent-up emotion of the last 24 hours was evident in his disappointed tone. He shook his head and turned away for the last time.

This old guy must be a vagrant or a caretaker of some kind. I don't want to tackle him in either case.

There's no telling what he might do if provoked.

"Wait! Come closer! I want to see your face."

Well, I do not want to see yours, you old tramp!

"Stop! I,............... I think I knew your mother."

A jolt of adrenalin flooded Lawren's body. If this old man was telling the truth, he must give him the chance to explain. If he left now, he would never know for sure.

Leaving the bicycle lying on its side with wheels spinning, Lawren slowly climbed the stone steps toward the figure, now clad in a long black coat that had definitely seen better days. Lawren stood still and submitted to an inspection from a pair of pale blue eyes, but held his muscles at the ready should a rapid retreat be required.

I can be out of here in seconds if necessary. He could never catch me.

Instead he heard a deep sigh and the words, "Her eyes, right enough. I never did see eyes like those on any other person. You'd better come inside. There's rain on that wind."

Lawren was still taking in the statement about his mother's eye colour. No one could have known he got his golden eyes from his mother.

No one; except a person who had actually known his mother.

The old man shuffled along in his heavy coat and boots and led Lawren into the room he had been occupying. Drawing the sack over the gaping window he beckoned to a broken chair and sat himself down on a three-legged stool beside an open wood fire set in a metal basket raised off the floor boards with bricks. It was a small, damp room that might have been a storage area once. It had cupboards set against the walls but everything Lawren could see was now in poor condition.

He sat down gingerly on the broken chair and waited for an explanation.

The old man chewed the inside of his cheek and thought deeply.

Lawren waited, conscious of the long ride home, the pending rain and the inevitable darkness.

Does the bike have lights? Does the bike have good brakes?

Finally the old man spoke. "You must be the son of master Edmund."

At these words, all thoughts of inheritance and prosperity vanished from Lawren's mind. The family home was a disaster, the family, clearly, not in residence and the entire trip a waste of time and money.

And yet, there was information to be gained here. Denying his first instinct to flee, he decided to find out this man's relationship to his mother, and, if possible, what had happened to Hartfield Hall and the remainder of his father's family.

"How did you know my mother?"

"She was my daughter," came the quiet reply.

Chapter Nine

Lawren watched as a light grew deep within the pale eyes of his companion. It was as if thinking of the past had returned life and energy to him. He sat back carefully and let the old man talk.

"Your mother came to us during the war. She was just a child then; sent far aways from the London bombing like many other children in the dark days of 1940. Folks don't care to remember it now but the capital was bombed every night except one between September 7 and November 13 in 1940. Can you imagine what a terror that must have been?

Margie says to me, 'Dan, we ain't got kiddies of our own. We must help those that do. We'll take one of the little uns.' That was the kind of woman Margie was. Always thinking of others. Always.

In those days this was a fine, big estate. I had a steady job as gardener and Margie was a cleaner who helped in the kitchens betimes. We had a tied cottage to live in where I still live on my own…… for now, at least.

The Drakes were country gentlemen and I watched young Edmund and his brother Henry grow up.

None of that there snooty London nonsense of sending the boys away to school. No, they grew up on the land and learned their lessons from a tutor with plenty spare time to see how the estate farm was run. They was always respectful of the farmhands and the workers. Your father had ever a kind word for me and helped me pick fruit in season although most of it went into his mouth, the little devil!

Young Sylvia arrived in Bradford-on-Avon station with a big luggage label attached to her coat by a safety pin. Margie took to her right away from the first minute she saw the wee lass with her pale face and her skinny little legs. She understood how strange it would be for a city girl finding herself in a big place like this far from her family in London. She just wrapped her arms around Sylvia and held her tight through the tears, and there were many tears. It was weeks before the little mite would enter the big house here. I let her sit beside me in the walled garden when I was planting or working the soil.

She was afraid of everything at the start. She would call out to me when a bumble bee got too close and she was amazed at the butterflies. It was while she was chasing a big yellow butterfly one day that she ran into your father and near knocked him down. They laughed right hard together and they were fast friends from that moment on, though two more different children you never could see. Still, they says opposites do attract, don't they?

Years went by and Sylvia was settling down well. You would hardly recognize the lovely girl she was then, compared to the waif she had been. Her yellow hair grew long and thick and those golden eyes gleamed with health and happiness. She ran in and out of the big house and she was a pet to all, high and low.

The war still raged on in Europe but Hitler never set foot on these shores thanks to Churchill and our brave armies fighting for freedom on land and sea. It was like we was living on an island here in Wiltshire. Just far enough away from the south coast to be spared the worst of the bombs and with our own food supplies here for everyone around who needed help.

But war can damage lives even from a distance.

The letter came to our cottage from the war department and at first me and Margie didn't know what to make of it so we kept it to ourselves.

It said Sylvia's whole family was wiped out in March, 1943, in the Bethnal Green disaster. One hundred and seventy-three souls were killed on their way to shelter in the underground station in London's East End after a bomb alert warned them to flee from their homes nearby. Dozens died on the stairs to the lower levels where they thought they would be safe.

Damnation take those bloody Germans!

There was only one thing to do. We never told Sylvia what had happened. We just let time go by until she had almost forgotten she had ever known another place. She called Margie 'Mum' first, then she called me Dad and the truth is we were as like a real mother and father to her as anyone could be.

When she was sixteen, Sylvia was taken on in the house as maid. Everyone loved her gentle ways and pretty looks; Edmund more than most. I suppose we should have known what was happening but we still kept the picture of Sylvia as a child in our hearts until it was too late.

Edmund was warned off by his father and even sent away to college for a year. That only made it worse.

He was given the choice of breaking off his romance with Sylvia or being forced to leave Hartfield Hall forever. Margie and me thought that was cruel. A blind man could see how much they loved each other.

The fights between Edmund and his father got more and more terrible until Sylvia threatened to leave the county and go away down south to bring peace back. That were the last straw for Edmund.

The two young folk, pride of their families, eloped one night with only a couple of suitcases. Edmund, your father, had made his choice and it was a hard choice I am sure. Hard for everyone.

Sylvia left a letter for me and Margie and, I suppose, Edmund did the same for his parents. I never read that one.

Give the girl credit, she wrote to Margie for years so that's how we knew where she was but we were under strict orders never to tell anyone at Hartfield Hall where she and Edmund had gone or all news would stop. We knew about your birth and your early years. It was strange not to be able to celebrate your childhood successes in school and art studies but it weren't worth the risk.

After the letters stopped we knew Sylvia had died. There was nothing we could do. In the law we had no real claim on our girl.

We never got to say goodbye. It near broke Margie's heart.

My Margie would have loved to see you, my lad. She would have wept over your beautiful eyes, just like Sylvie's.

Just like our lovely Sylvie's."

Silence fell in the room again. Lawren was lost in imagining his mother here as a child. He could not absorb everything he had heard. *How much of this did his father know? Why was he hearing this for the first time?*

Dan was wiping his eyes with the cuff of a shirt that hung down from his coat sleeve. Clearly, Margie was gone and the old fellow was alone.

After a few minutes, Lawren asked softly, "So what happened to Hartfield Hall?"

"Well now, Master Henry, your uncle, took over the estate when your grandfather died but he was never fitted for the work. The war years had weakened the country and things started to go wrong. Some around here said Henry gambled, but I saw no signs of it until precious heirlooms from the house began to go missing and estate staff were laid off. Soon after, parcels of land were sold. No one knew it then but a big developer was buying up every speck of land that came up for sale. When there was nowt left but a ring around the house itself, we knew it was all over.

Sir Henry and his family sold the house and took off for Australia. Australia! Can you believe it? No true Drake him! The gardens and forests fell to weeds and waste. All my decades of hard labour vanishing in a few short years.

Since then things has gone from bad to worse, as you can see, young Lawren. The developer moves in next month. Soon all this land'll be covered with little houses as far as the eye can see and this dear place, Hartfield Hall, will be gone forever, knocked to smithereens by a wrecker's ball."

Into a pregnant pause, Lawren asked, "Why are *you* still here, Dan?"

He shook his head wearily. "Leaving this land will be the end of me. I doubt I'll survive until there's a new house built for me. My cottage is still there for now and I'll be in it till they carry me out.

Too many memories to leave now. Too many memories; good and bad.

I come here most days just to keep an eye on the old place. There's not much left, but no lad with a match is going to burn it to the ground while I'm around. I am right sorry you didn't see it in the glory days, Master Lawren. It was magnificent then."

An idea seemed to strike him and he slowly pushed himself up from the stool and grabbed at Lawren's arm. "Come with me! Come along!"

Lawren was happy to move after sitting listening for so long. He followed the bent back of old Dan into the stately front hall where they had entered the house. Dan pointed upward with his stick and declared the upper levels were unsafe due to roof damage.

"The rain gets in up there now. Anything that's still there

gets ruined. My legs won't carry me up those stairs. There's nothing I can do about it."

Dan sucked his teeth in frustration then, remembering he had a visitor, he nodded to Lawren.

"Look in here. It's what's left of the Grand Salon."

Lawren went into the high ceilinged room with ornate fireplaces and wall sconces still in place. The tall windows were tightly shuttered but he could make out dusty carpets covering the floor and a few remaining large pieces of furniture showed what must have been an elegant room in its heyday.

Dan was roaming around pulling dust sheets over couches and sighing at signs of deterioration.

Abruptly, Lawren was transported to the dream place he had seen on the plane. He felt dizzy as the dream transposed itself over the vestiges of the salon in which he now stood. Vibrant colours sprang into life around him like a CGI effect in a movie. The room was twirling rapidly while he glimpsed a fire in the grates, silken-patterned fabrics, glittering chandeliers and crystal everywhere, and a family with two boys seated at a gaming table playing cards and laughing together.

As swiftly as the images had arrived, they disappeared in a swirl of colour and the sad, dull room was restored.

"Dan!" he gasped, holding on to the nearest chair. "Were there ever portraits on the wall here?"

The old man turned in surprise. "Indeed there was. You can just make out the outlines where the huge frames lay against the wall for many, many years. Some was painted by a Drake of bygone times, I think, but most were more recent paintings of Drake families. Some of the best ones went to museums in Wiltshire, if you should want to see them, and one is in the British Museum, or so I'm told."

The portraits I saw in the dream were once in this room! What just happened to me? Was the dream a warning not to come here?

Lawren was shaken by the vision he had seen. He felt the need to escape from this place and integrate the overwhelming new information he had received into his former life picture. His entire family experience in Canada was changed forever. He now had a completely new perspective on his parents, their origins, and their choices.

This is overwhelming! I feel shattered!

He reached inside himself for a reality check and it came with a glance at his watch. Hours had passed since he had found the way to Hartfield Hall. He must leave soon. He looked over at the old man shuffling around in his past life and mumbling to himself.

How sad to be the last person to remember the glory days. When everything you loved has gone there's nothing left to live for.

"Dan, I have to leave now. I can't thank you enough for telling me about this place. I will speak to my father when I get back to Canada and tell him what you have said. I know he will be immensely grateful to you for all you have done, both in the old days, and especially now."

Tears sprang into the faded blue eyes and the wrinkled mouth drew into a line that showed how hard it was for Dan to hold back his emotions. He managed to force out a few words before closing up the doors to the salon and heading back to his small room and his dying fire.

"Master Lawren, tell him I am grateful that he loved our Sylvie so well and sent you back to see me this once before I go."

Lawren swallowed his own deep emotions and reached out to pat the old man, slipping a twenty-pound note into his trembling hand. He turned and fled at once through the outer door. He felt he might collapse in grief if he stayed one more minute.

The promised rain must have started to fall when he was inside the house. It was a light, persistent rain that took a while to penetrate but still managed to soak through clothing nonetheless.

Lifting up the bicycle, he took one last look at Hartfield Hall and saw a faded stone shield high above his head on a pediment that surmounted the front entrance. It had a simple pattern of a diagonal line with a circle, or perhaps a star, on either side. It was difficult to make out anything more in the fading light of the afternoon.

I meant to take photographs of this place for my father. I can't do that now. Better that he keeps whatever good memories still exist for him.

The problem of what to tell his father was added to the list of problems he was now accumulating but his first priority was to concentrate on the road back to Bradford-on-Avon. Darkness was falling swiftly and he was acutely aware of the dangers on these wet and busy English roads. His heart thumped with a combination of fear and dread that he might never get back to safety. He began to realize that safety meant Anna and home.

There was something alien in this society where the class system could intervene in the lives of young people in love. He determined to learn from this experience. He would waste no more time establishing a viable life with Anna. She had always asserted that finances were not a crucial component in any relationship between them. She was so right.

The bicycle sped downhill faster and faster but Lawren Drake scanned every inch of the road ahead of him for possible hazards. Fortunately the hired bike had both lights and brakes that functioned reasonably well. He was annoyed with himself that he had not had the sense to check this out before leaving town but he could not have known what this day held for him.

Nothing now would be allowed to impede his journey back to The Sailor's Rest.

It seemed like hours of travel in darkness before he saw the lights of the town. He was shaking with cold from the chilly wet wind on his face. His hands on the handlebars were frozen into a deathlike grip.

He noticed that most shops on the high street were closed for the night so he bypassed the garage. Albert's pub grub should be available at this hour and his mouth watered at the thought of hot food and a warm fire to thaw out his body. Thawing out the shocks to his mind was another thing entirely. He could only think that talking today's events over with Anna tonight might help that dilemma. A wave of longing swept over him. Anna would soon be waiting for him in Glasgow.

Anna.

Her very name sounded like home to him.

There was one more urgent need before he left Wiltshire. There were drawings pushing restlessly against his mind. He must take the time to record his impressions on paper. It was the only safe way to relieve his mental stress, or at least some of it.

What a day! What a strange and unsettling day.

Chapter Ten

Fiona Jameson was frustrated. Her Land Rover had developed a broken axle and she was confined to Oban until the local garage could effect a repair.

This won't look good on my record. I am sure I did not cause this to happen.

She fussed around her old cottage near the seafront but it took only an hour to tidy and polish everything in the tiny place.

Inactivity was foreign to Fiona. From the time her dear Granny took over her care when she was left an orphan by the sad deaths of her parents, Fiona had understood how essential it was that she should contribute to the household expenses. She did odd jobs for neighbours and helped around the house until she was old enough for babysitting duties. She always had a part-time job somewhere in the community and that was her introduction to many people in Oban.

She waited tables at restaurants and shelved books in the library and in summer she helped out with any tourist-related activities that needed an extra hand. Everyone knew Fiona as a hard
worker who arrived on time and did whatever she was asked to do without complaint.

As soon as she was old enough to get her driver's license she invested every penny she had saved and took on an older driving partner in a taxi service business. They leased a car at first and got a

good deal from the local garage because of Fiona's reputation.

Schoolwork often got short shrift as she built up clients by posting lists of prices and services in doctors' surgeries, legal offices and the veterinarian's premises. It didn't take long before seniors in the community, who did not drive, were calling on Grant during the day and Fiona at night, to take them to appointments and events.

When local businesses began to employ them for last-minute deliveries, they knew they had a viable business. After her Granny died, Fiona owned the cottage and had the security of knowing she could support herself no matter what else happened in her life.

It was through her taxi business that she met Anna Mason. Fiona always thought of that as a lucky day.

Anna quickly became a valued customer but, more importantly, she became a mentor and friend to Fiona and was responsible for coaching her through her secondary school exams.

"I would never have made the marks to get into the university if Anna had not come to Oban," she mused as she watched leaves blow across the road that separated her cottage from the shoreline.

"I can't wait to see her again and tell her all about my new career."

This thought reminded Fiona that she should press her uniform jacket so it would be in top condition whenever the Land Rover was ready to take to the road. Sitting for hours driving around on supervision duties did nothing for the smart appearance required of Wildlife Officers.

She immediately fetched her jacket from the closet and set up the ironing table in the kitchen. She always smiled during this task remembering the many hours she had watched her Granny iron her school blouse and press the pleats in her skirts. It was one of those times when they could talk together and her grandmother would share stories of the days when Fiona's mother was a child in this very cottage.

Granny had taught Fiona the importance of preparing the garment to be pressed. Check for spots and stains, examine cuffs and pockets for lint or handkerchiefs, use a lightly-damped clean cloth and make sure the iron is hot enough for steam.

Fiona went through the list of instructions in her mind as she always did. She found a used tissue in a pocket and a crumpled card the size of a business card. At first she thought it was one of her own cards.

Although Grant had taken over most of the work now she was employed, she still maintained the habit of handing out her cards whenever the opportunity arose. She was about to toss the card into the kitchen bin when she saw the name.

> Gordon Campbell
> Estate Manager
> Glenmorie Castle

There were two phone numbers and a fax number on the card and a symbol that looked like a deer's head.

"What?"

It took a moment before she remembered the card handed to her on her exit from the castle. Busy days had gone by and the truth was she had forgotten that she had promised to call and arrange a time to return and speak formally to the game-keepers about the Scottish wildcat project.

"Oh, heavens above! Did I call him a stableman and he's the one in charge of the estate? And he's a Campbell! He could be related to the Duke of Argyll himself. What have I done?"

She quickly finished pressing the jacket and tried to calm

her mind. During the probationary period she was acutely aware that any negative report could look bad on her record. She needed to fix the unsatisfactory first impression she had left at the castle and she needed to do it now!

The Land Rover was out of commission. Where could she borrow a vehicle?

She found her mobile phone and dialed the number on speed dial for Grant.

"Oban Taxi Services, Grant speaking."

"Are you on the road, Grant?"

"It's yourself, Fiona! What's the problem, lass? I wasn't expecting to hear from you. How's the new job going?

"Grant, I need to know right away where you are and where the car is?"

"It's right here by the house. I've no jobs until the school run in a couple of hours or so. What's wrong Fi? You sound mighty upset about something."

"Oh, Grant, I need to mend fences. I've made a big mistake and I need to fix it as soon as possible."

"I take it you don't mean that fence-mending literally? A mistake? That doesn't sound like you, Fiona.

I thought you liked the new life out on the moors all the day long?"

"I do! It's just difficult to keep all the balls in the air at the moment. My work car has broken down. Will you meet me at the Columba Hotel? I'll drive you home then return the car as soon as I can."

"Don't worry yourself, Fi. Leave me in town. The wife has a shopping list for me as long as your arm. I'll get it done in Tesco and you can collect me there."

"Oh, thanks Grant. That'll save me time."

"I'll be expecting to hear all about this emergency, Fi."

"Never you mind about that! Just get into the car. I'll be waiting."

The changeover worked out as planned and Fiona settled into the familiar driver's seat thinking of the many hours she had spent driving the big People Mover car in all weathers. It seemed like a long gone past life. Now she had other priorities and at the moment getting to the castle was the most important of them.

There was a bit of a line-up waiting to cross the Connnel Bridge so she had the chance to call ahead and announce her arrival. A cool voice, that might have been that of Gordon Campbell, stated he would be available to discuss the matter with her.

"Thank heaven, he's there!" she declared to the sheep in the field. "I'll not sleep a wink if this mistake isn't fixed today."

Risking a traffic violation, she roared all the way up the divided highway and along the snaking driveway to the castle, parking beside the double gate into the stableyard.

As she was not strictly on official business, she was wearing jeans and an old blue sweater her Granny had knitted. She ran her fingers through her brown hair and found an elastic band on the floor of the car to tie it back in the ponytail she usually favoured. She hoped her more casual style would make it easier for the estate manager to forget his first impression of her.

She found him in an office attached to the last horse box at the end of the stable block. The sign outside had the same name and job description as his business card with hours of operation added and the deer's head in a much larger and more detailed illustration.

Clearing her throat and straightening her shoulders for possible battle, Fiona prepared a smile and opened the office door.

Gordon Campbell looked up as soon as she entered, then stood and extended his hand in welcome.

His dark hair was combed in a side part, his face and hands clean, and his clothes, the tweed jacket with leather patches over twill trousers, were much more indicative of the attire belonging to an important man on the estate.

"So glad to see you again." The identical phrase emerged from both mouths at exactly the same time and caused both of them to stop in surprise.

"Sorry about that!" It happened again, and Fiona dissolved in helpless laughter followed closely by Gordon Campbell's deep chuckles.

"You go first," he managed to say.

"No, *you* go!" replied Fiona. "I have to wipe my eyes before I can speak sensibly."

"Fine! Whatever you want. Please sit down for a minute. I really am glad you came back. I feel we got off on the wrong foot the other day and I want to make amends."

"No, please! I am the one who needs to explain myself. I took a very inappropriate, righteous attitude with you. I admit I thought you were a stablehand, but that's not an excuse," she rushed to add.

"There I go again! I apologize. You probably guessed I was new at the job."

He hid a smile behind his hand and politely denied her inadequacy.

"Look! Let's forget all that and start again. Is it a deal?"

Fiona nodded her head in gratitude and took her first deep breath since entering the office. He was being very understanding and now that the ice was truly broken she could explain herself more effectively.

"My name is Fiona Jameson and I have just qualified with the Scottish Wildlife Services. As you could tell, Mr. Campbell, I am trying to find my way around the properties in the area and establish connections with landowners and managers like yourself. This is a job I relish immensely. I knew I was meant to do this as soon as I began to take the courses and I mean to spend the rest of my working days in protecting and preserving the best of Scotland for future generations."

God help me, I've gone too far and bored the man into a semi conscious state! He looks stunned! What am I doing? Shut up Fiona! He has no interest in hearing your life story.

"I *am* pleased to meet you. May I call you Fiona, and please call me Gordon?

I feel I know you already, Fiona, as my lawyer in Oban is George McLennan. He speaks highly of your reliability and skills in photography. I am sure this new position can only add to your reputation."

Thank you George! There's free babysitting coming your way for this.

"I'm thinking you are not here on official business today, Fiona?"

She tugged at the neckline of her sweater. Sunshine had darted into the office from between a line of trees nearby and Fiona blamed her sudden sense of heat on the warm autumn rays.

"That's correct, Mr. Campbell ………Gordon. My Land Rover is out of commission at the moment. I borrowed the car from the taxi business I share and I need to return it soon or Grant will be late for an appointment."

There I go again! Too much information! What is wrong with me today?

Gordon Campbell stood up and advanced around his desk to stand in front of Fiona.

"Right you are! I won't keep you much longer, then. I just want to tell you that I have discussed the wildcat project with the estate staff and they are in agreement that this is an important step in maintaining the welfare of the wildcat in Scotland. Thank you for bringing it to our attention. Please come by whenever you are in the area, Fiona, and if I can do anything at all to help you in the future, let me know. I admire what you are doing. It's a vital job."

Another handshake was exchanged, and Fiona found herself walking back to the car wondering what had just happened.

I thought things were going quite well considering all my stupid remarks but then he turned all official on me and rushed me out the door. Maybe he can't spare the time to chat with a mere girl like me. He looks to be about thirty, perhaps. Probably married with a gaggle of weans about his feet but I didn't notice any family photographs on his desk. He was very nice to me all the same. I think he was cuter with his hair all flopped over his forehead and his temper riled up. I wish I had worn something smarter for the meeting but I had no time to think about that.

Fiona's practical Scottish side asserted itself and she concluded, as she reversed the car and headed down the driveway with the tower castle in her rearview mirror;

At least he doesn't sound as if he will contact head office about my rudeness. I've mended that fence, I am pretty sure. I wonder if I'll ever have cause to come back here again. I would love to see more of the estate and meet those gamekeepers. They might not want to talk to the likes of me but I bet they have some amazing stories to tell.

Gordon Campbell watched the neat figure of Fiona Jameson retreating toward the double gate. He ran his hands through his hair in frustration, causing the tidy, longer locks to descend over his forehead.

She was such a bonny lass with that youthful enthusiasm and glowing good looks. Why couldn't he have built on the comfortable first moments they had shared in the office? Instead he had hustled her out the door with not a word about another meeting.

He never seemed to meet any women at all in this job. Only hunting, fishing types ever arrived on the estate and all the workers were men, even the chef. The 'daily' woman came and went like a ghost, leaving food behind for his supper. He had never yet seen her to thank her.

He knew about the range of social events in Oban through reading the weekly Oban Times but he rarely managed to organize a visit there to participate in any of them.

He decided to be more proactive in the near future. At this rate he would be an old man hobbling around the castle on his own forever. If there were more lovely females like Fiona Jameson around he would have to make a sincere effort before it was too late.

A word or two with George McLennan on his next business trip to town would not go amiss. George might have some connections, or some ideas of suitable occasions where he could meet people. It wouldn't be a bad idea to ask George some discreet questions about Miss Fiona Jameson. He had seen no rings on those strong fingers.

He returned to his desk and the piles of accounts and calendar dates to be scheduled. Autumn in the Highlands was the busiest time of the year. He must be dreaming to think a social life was possible for him, never mind a romantic life.

He could hear the beaters approaching the stableyard with the sturdy highland ponies that carried game down from the hills for the hunting parties. From the sound of the chatter, they had had a good day.

He pushed the paperwork aside and went out to greet them. Ensuring the estate was able to pay its bills was his main concern. All other matters took a back seat today, as they did every day.

It was his life.

For a moment he envied the young Fiona who would spend her days out on patrol in all weathers, not stuck in an office for most of the time like he was.

He hurried out to greet the paying customers with the subtle female scent of Fiona's hair lingering in his nostrils.

"So how did your fence-mending visit go, Fiona?" Grant's face and voice expressed deep curiosity. Obviously he had been thinking over the unusual emergency situation while gathering the groceries for his wife.

"Ach, it's not as bad as I thought, Grant, don't you worry about it."

Grant was not about to let this interesting event go by without more information. He continued to quiz Fiona while they transferred the shopping from his cart to the back of the big car.

"Who was it you were so anxious to see, again?"

Although she was reluctant to give Grant fuel for the fire of curiosity, she did wonder if he might have any knowledge of Gordon Campbell.

"Well, I had business up at Glenmorie Castle with the manager, Gordon Campbell."

"Oh, yes!"

Clearly, Grant was expecting more details before he would divulge any gossip.

"He seems like a nice man. Hard working and quite young for the responsibilities he has on the estate." *Help! 'nice' man! That's the death knell to any decent description!*

"Do you know anything of him at all, Grant? He didn't sound as if he had much of a brogue. I'm thinking he might be upper class Scottish or one of those English incomers." Fiona realized she had broken down and asked the question directly. She was not going to get anything out of Grant without some degree of honesty. He knew her from childhood.

Grant picked up on Fiona's interest immediately but he was determined to tease her a while longer.

"I may have heard a thing or two around town about him."

"What have you heard then?" Fiona slammed down the rear door of the car to punctuate her words.

'He arrived when you were away at the university that first year. He took over the job after old Hamish retired to live with his daughter in Aberdeen. His legs were giving out on him and he couldn't manage the stairs in the castle. That's why the new office was built in the stableyard."

Never mind old Hamish! What about Gordon Campbell?

'I think your Mr. Campbell is a nephew of the Duke himself; some relationship of that sort in any case.

He doesn't get into town much but a few local folk speak quite well of him."

"Oh, and what do they say?"

Having stretched Fiona's patience to the limit, Grant gave in and told her everything he knew.

"He's a fine gentleman, by all accounts although a bittie lonely up there in the castle with no women around. He moved here from Carlisle or is it Melrose? One of those border towns anyway. He didn't have much in the way of luggage, they say, so I fancy he was not expecting a wife and family to join him.

Does that help you, Fiona?"

"I'm sure I don't know *what* you mean Grant. Shouldn't you be heading to the school about now? You don't want to keep those kiddies waiting."

Waving her hand casually as she turned away, Fiona knew she was hiding nothing from her partner.

The word about her interest in Gordon Campbell would be spread all over Oban in no time flat. Just as well the man in question would not hear that word. That might be extremely embarrassing.

She walked briskly through the parking lot and headed back to her cottage.

I fancy a meat pie and beans for supper tonight and I'll be calling the garage first thing tomorrow about the Land Rover. It's time to get back to work. I need to start watching out for the arrival of the Greenland White-Fronted geese now that they will be receiving special protection.

A light rain had blown in from the west picking up moisture from the sea. Fiona marched along with a smile on her face impervious to the droplets accumulating on her hair and on her sweater. For some reason she did not notice the weather.

Chapter Eleven

Anna had booked a room at the Jurys Inn in Glasgow where she had stayed before. It was not the most glamorous hotel but its central location was convenient for all the places she might want to go on this short visit.

She felt a nagging sense of frustration and impatience that had nothing to do with the bustling streets and colder weather of a big city. She had not come to Glasgow on holiday. Her mission was to try to track down information about her parents' life before they had emigrated to Canada.

Her frustration arose from the fact that Lawren would not be joining her for several days. Hearing about his disappointing attempt to find the former home of his father in Wiltshire had upset her terribly. At this distance she could not do anything about it other than to keep in touch daily by phone. What she really needed was up close and personal contact with him. The week they had been apart was stretching into a decade in her mind. She was still amazed at how quickly her relationship with Lawren was developing into a necessity for her wellbeing. She frequently cautioned herself not to get too lost in the needy side. She knew this was a female tendency and a contributing factor in the failure of her marriage to Richard.

"I am not that naïve young girl any more," she lectured her image in the hotel's mirror. "I know the pitfalls of loving too soon and too unwisely but time is against us at this point in our lives and I don't want to waste a single minute of it."

She turned back to packing her slouchy black leather handbag for a day out. She had to keep herself busy otherwise worry about Lawren would undo her resolve. She pictured him exploring Wiltshire and drawing busily as a distraction from the failure of his hopes about the family mansion there. She knew he had fostered dreams of tracing his father's English family and perhaps acquiring the finances his own artistic endeavours had always made so elusive.

This was another worry for Anna. She blamed herself for his wild goose chase. If he had not been so concerned about the disparity in their living standards, the journey into his past would not have assumed such importance.

She sighed for the umpteenth time this morning and smiled briefly, remembering the strange word that was one of her mother's favourites when she was upset about some delay or other. The Scottish side of Anna always seemed to come to the fore when she was hearing Scottish voices around her.

"Well, I hope my search for family information will be a tad more successful than Lawren's has been.

I will try the Mitchell Library and the Records Offices today. The City Hall in George Square is my first stop. It's close to Strathclyde University's Technical College and I won't return to this room until I have some evidence to work with."

So saying, she hefted her purse with its burden of paper, pens, small change for copying machines and an assortment of gloves, scarves and a mini umbrella. Nothing would impede her progress this day; not weather, or fatigue or distractions. She let the heavy door slam behind her and marched down the hallway to the elevators with determination in her step.

Many weary hours later, an exhausted Anna Mason dragged herself into a restaurant near the entrance to The Prince's Square. She had had every intention of walking the short distance back to her hotel but part way down Buchanan Street her feet gave out and she knew a rest and some sustenance were essential if she was not to faint from overexertion.

The lunch-time crowd had gone and only one table was occupied by two women whose heads were close together signifying that secrets of some kind were being shared over large glasses of wine.

Anna cast around for a secluded table with comfortable seats and when she found one she was prepared to be ignored by waiters until she had divested herself of coat, scarf and shoes and spread out some of the copies she had obtained during her day's search.

It took only a few moments of scanning the documents to confirm what she had already believed. There was information to be gathered if you knew the right sources to approach. A librarian at the Mitchell had been most helpful once Anna's years as a teacher and librarian in Canada had been casually mentioned. It turned out that Sheila's auntie lived in Toronto and Sheila herself was an admirer of the Toronto Public Library System to which she gravitated on frequent visits to Auntie Mary.

That connection established, Sheila proved to be a fount of knowledge about accessing records of births, deaths, marriages and assorted related professional records which she magically produced from distant computer terminals located all across the city and even in Edinburgh.

Anna gladly paid the nominal fees and collected up sheaves of paper. She took a distinct, black, British cab from the library to George Square after she felt the weight of her handbag. One thing she did not want to miss was the interior of Strathclyde University. It was where both her mother and father had studied in their late teenage years and most likely where they had first met.

As soon as she saw the entrance close to George Square, she remembered dropping Fiona off at this very spot when she sat her high-school equivalent exams. Strange, she thought, how a place has a role to play in people's lives over a generation or two, and across oceans.

The university was not noticeably different in style from the Ontario Institute for Studies in Education or, for that matter, the newer buildings at London's Western University. It was set at the foot of a steep hilly street and Anna remembered Lawren's description of The Glasgow School of Art which must be nearby because of a similar setting. There were, however, no Art Deco touches inside here that she could see.

She decided to bypass the crowded information desk and sidled over to the walls to read some of the bronze award plaques. She was casually scanning names while listening to the hum of young voices in the foyer and thinking how similar the buzz was to any large educational institution anywhere in the world; ambitious young people with their lives ahead of them and plans to make for the rest of the school year that had recently begun.

Suddenly her attention was drawn to a familiar name on one of the boards.

Distinguished Service Medals Awarded to Students of The Royal College of Science and Technology in the wars of the 20th Century.

Listed alphabetically was the name Kyle Andrew Purdy. Army Corps: 1941-46.

Two things struck Anna at that moment. First; that this must be the Kyle Purdy who was her father Angus' best friend, and best man at her parents' wedding. Kyle Purdy had married Isobel who was Philip's mother, although he must have known that Philip's father was Angus McLeod.

So, he was a decorated soldier, a man of some compassion, and a man from whom Philip had fled at an early age.

Second; the university must have had a different name in those days and perhaps an entirely different appearance.

One thing was certain. She had found the place where the family drama had begun long ago.

Anna considered this a good sign. A name from the past had appeared before her eyes. So far she had reason to believe that this search was not going to be as problematic as she had initially feared.

Encouraged by this new coincidence, Anna set off, down the busy pedestrian way that was Buchanan Street, on her journey back to the Jurys Inn. With each step, the bag she was carrying grew heavier and her feet, in the most sensible shoes she owned, were beginning to throb.

"It's that trans-Atlantic flight to blame," she murmured, as she gave up at The Prince's Square.

Once settled there, she was confronted with the evidence she had hoped for. Reams and reams of it!

She pushed the pile aside and coughed loudly until a waiter caught sight of her in her secluded spot.

The only food available at this time of day was afternoon tea, so Anna ordered that and returned to her bounty.

Where many others would be overwhelmed by such a task, Anna Mason pushed up the sleeves of her wool sweater and began to organize the papers into piles. This required the use of an adjacent table which she co-opted without delay. These convenient round tables allowed for an efficient use of space and a few steps in stockinged feet permitted quick access. Order was made from chaos in a remarkably few minutes by adopting a naming category after the pertinent names were highlighted in neon yellow by a marker from the depths of Anna's purse.

"Will I set the tray down on a *third* table for you Madam?"

Anna had not noticed the waiter standing by her side until he spoke up.

"Yes, that would be most satisfactory," she replied, crisply. She did not apologize and decided to give him a good tip if he refrained from further implied criticism.

A brief break to consume scones liberally spread with strawberry jam and fresh butter, washed down with several cups of tea, brought Anna back to table one, refreshed and ready to summarize her findings.

Her mother's side of the family had died out in Scotland. Simon's family and Anna were the only remaining McLeod relatives in Canada. Philip was, of course, a half-brother to them but as he did not claim the McLeod name or have any children of his own, that line was not likely to supply any further descendants.

The most exciting news of the day's research was that her father's family had produced another son around the time when Angus had left Scotland to live in Canada. This younger son was named Ross and he was something of a celebrity in Glasgow as he had acquired a reputation as a builder of homes of distinction in the outlying districts of the city.

Anna stopped to take in this new information. Ross McLeod was her uncle.

She immediately wondered what, if anything, he knew about his older brother and the Canadian branch of the family. She was filled with the desire to see this unknown uncle and find out if there was a resemblance to her own father.

At the same time a rage smouldered within her. It would be a risk to contact this man and she might be rejected by him, but that very fear was what had held back previous generations. Helen Dunlop's mother erased the memory of her lost, adopted child and never sought her out. Anna's mother once ignored a plea from Helen to make a connection. Both Anna's parents turned their backs on Scotland and their families there, because of the taint of scandal. Angus McLeod obeyed his wife's demands and never tried to reach his son, Philip. Simon and Anna grew up without the knowledge of their heritage.

Now Lawren's tragedy was added to the list. His parents fled to Canada rather than be split up by a domineering father.

As the catalogue of tragedies paraded before Anna's inner eye, she groaned in exasperation. It was too late to mend the errors of past generations but she was utterly determined that this folly would end with her, and end soon.

No matter what the result, she would seek out, and meet with, Ross McLeod, her uncle.

The next thought that occurred was that the uncle would need to be alive for this noble task to be accomplished.

Anna chuckled at her own foolishness and she felt the tension release.

Was he still alive? If so, he would be considerably younger than her father. The necessity to answer this question, sent Anna back to the piles of papers arranged around the three restaurant tables. She lifted the tea tray, now considerably lighter since its contents had been consumed, and placed it on a fourth table leaving room for the appropriate copies to be perused.

She quickly shuffled through the birth certificates looking for the name, Ross McLeod, and found out that he would be in his early seventies. Not old by today's standards and not far from her own age.

She had not asked for a death certificate, so that issue was still in limbo.

What if he had married? This avenue might be productive in more ways than one.

A marriage certificate was finally unearthed and indeed, Ross had married a Joyce Armstrong in the nineteen sixties.

Would they have had any children? If so, they would be

first cousins to Simon and Anna. How wonderful if Anna found cousins not much younger than herself who would be a new link to Scotland for the rest of her life!

Brushing aside all thoughts of possible rejection, Anna turned back to the biography of Ross McLeod she had thrown down as soon as she had read the brief details about his building company, McLeod & Son.

Of course! That was a major clue she had missed. There *must be* one son at least.

Now she scanned the rest of the page and to her joy discovered a list of the children of Ross and Joyce.

Praise be! That lovely librarian at the Mitchell will get a free weekend in London, Ontario, for this excellent work, whenever she's next in Toronto!

Anna's hands shook as she read.

A son; Rory.

A daughter; Jocelyn.

A son; Murray.

A daughter; Heather.

"Madam, we need to be setting up these tables for the evening meals, if you don't mind."

"I don't mind one little bit," said Anna, with a happy smile on her face. "There will be a handsome tip for you, young man, if you can help me carefully gather up all this paper in the piles you see here."

No further incentive was required. In mere minutes the papers, clipped together in sections, were safely stowed in Anna's capacious handbag and she was dancing out into Buchanan Street with renewed energy. She was already planning what she would tell Lawren that night during their phone call. He was due a good surprise for a change.

Back in the restaurant a comment was directed to the man polishing glasses behind the bar.

"Here, did you see that, Andy? They Americans are a weird lot all right but who cares when they tip this well. *She* can come back here any time and bags me her table. OK, pal?"

Anna woke the next morning with a headache and a fierce appetite. She had talked for too long on the phone the night before but she had desperately wanted to share her good news with Lawren.

By the time they had made their reluctant goodbyes, she was much too tired to eat, contenting herself with a squished chocolate bar she found in her purse, then falling into bed without taking the time to brush her teeth.

"Ugh! I feel awful and I look even worse! Thank heaven Lawren isn't due to arrive in Glasgow for another day. I have a lot to do before then and the first thing is to shower and brush my teeth!"

Once she was feeling fresher, Anna had to deal with her rumbling stomach. She had sampled the breakfast that came with her room cost on a previous visit to the Jurys Inn and she knew she could eat to her heart's content, sampling anything she wanted from the buffet. She collected a pen and writing pad from the bedside table, checked that her room key was in her pants pocket and, on an afterthought, picked up the phone book on her way out the door.

The restaurant was full of chattering guests when she arrived, but as there was a large tour bus idling at the side of the road outside the hotel, Anna knew things would quiet down soon. She chose a table in a far corner and waited. Sure enough, the place emptied like magic when the departure hour arrived. No tourists would take the risk of being left behind when their luxury coach took off for castles, mountains and lochs.

Anna sauntered around the buffet tables while the staff dutifully replenished fruit, yogurts, toast and coffee. A chef was stationed in the centre to dispense eggs, bacon and sausages but Anna poured herself piping hot coffee, set it on a tray and filled a large bowl with cereal and as much fruit as it would hold. The milk in Scotland was more like cream compared to the 1% variety she was used to in Ontario so the end result was like a luxury dessert.

The cereal took the edge off her hunger and the coffee perked up her spirits. Ignoring the plentiful local newspapers in favour of her pen and paper, Anna began to make a list of everything she needed to do before Lawren arrived.

- Contact Ross McLeod if possible and ask for a meeting.
- If he is unavailable for any reason, try to find his children.
- Call Alina and ask how things are going with Philip.
- Call Simon and update him.
- Tidy the hotel room before Lawren arrives.
- Wash hair and find a nice outfit.
- Remember to take a camera.

A quick re-read of her list made it obvious that she was distracting herself from the main objective. All the other items were dependent on a successful meeting with her uncle and that had to take priority.

"Right! This requires serious sustenance!"

She returned to the buffet and filled a large, warmed plate with two fried eggs, tomato, two sausages, mushrooms, and a slice of brown toast complete with butter and marmalade. She eschewed more coffee for fear of having to search for a washroom all morning, and chose instead a decaf tea.

Surprisingly, the feast did the trick and Anna left the breakfast room with renewed determination. Crossing the reception area, whose automatic doors revealed a blustery, rainy day on the Glasgow streets, she retreated to the café bar with windows looking out to the River Clyde. It was empty at this time of day and she could use her phone without disturbing anyone or being overheard.

The first order of business was to look up the phone number of McLeod & Son, builders.

She found a large advert in the yellow pages with a typical black and white, grainy picture of the two principals smiling broadly. She examined this closely and could not come to any conclusion as to a resemblance between Ross, Rory and her father, Angus.

There was nothing to do but call the office number supplied in the advert.

With fingers perspiring slightly, she called.

"Good morning. What can McLeod & Son do for you today?" It was obviously a young woman secretary who answered. Anna cleared her throat and replied, "Is it possible to speak to Mr. McLeod senior or to his son?"

There was a slight hesitation, then the cheerful voice resumed, "Mr. Ross McLeod is at the building site this morning but Mr. Rory McLeod is available. May I say what you wish to discuss?"

This was the tricky part and Anna had not prepared an answer. She said the first thing that came into her mind. "It's a family matter. Please tell him my name is Anna McLeod Mason."

"So, not a business concern then?"

"No, but it is important, and I do not have a great deal of time in which to make this contact."

The line switched to some background elevator recording and Anna twisted in her seat while seconds ticked by. If she missed this opportunity there was no telling how long it might be before she could bring herself to try again.

"A family matter, you said?" Anna started to breathe again when the male voice came on the line.

"Yes, thank you for talking to me. You must be Rory McLeod? I have reason to believe we could be cousins. My father was a brother to your father. I did not know this until just yesterday and I am here from Canada and in Glasgow for only a short time. Is it possible for us to meet? I am anxious to find out if we are indeed related."

Anna had rattled through this speech at a fast rate in case Rory, if it were he, should put down the phone in the midst of her impromptu speech.

"You'll forgive me if I am a little hesitant, Ms. Mason? Are you sure about this?"

"Yes, I am pretty sure. I don't have written proof with me at the moment as I was not expecting this turn of events when I began researching family history. I can have documents sent through the internet, if you wish."

There was a long pause and Anna began to nibble at a hangnail. *Say yes! Say yes!*

"Well, I don't see what harm it can do to meet. Can you make your way to my mother's home and I will join you at lunch time?"

"Thank you so much." The relief was clear in Anna's tone.

What followed were details of an address. The location meant nothing to Anna but she carefully copied down the information for a cab driver. She imagined the interesting calls that were now speeding on their way between Rory and his mother and also, to his father.

Anna had time for a quick wash in her hotel room before she collected together some of her paperwork and found a coat and umbrella. A cab was ordered after a call from the convenient, dedicated line on the corner of the reception desk.

Just a few steps from the hotel entrance and she was safely inside the cab out of the wind and rain. She handed over the paper on which she had copied the home address and sat back to see where she would be heading.

The cab driver was one of the rare, silent Scots so she had time to look around as they sped through the city. The city centre's stately Victorian buildings and busy one-way system began to merge into more leafy streets and upscale houses. Anna looked for clues as to the area they were entering but was not successful for a while. Rows of shops with unusual names and fancy restaurants distracted her until she saw the entrance to a large complex of buildings and read the sign: Glasgow University Campus.

"What area is this?" she asked.

"Kelvinside, Miss. We'll be at your address soon."

Anna felt the rush of excitement begin to die down inside her and stark reality begin to take its place.

Images of Helen's sad story and, more recently, Lawren's crashing disappointment haunted her. There was no way of knowing what lay ahead in the next few minutes. She would have to prepare herself for the worst case scenario. That way she would be armoured against the pain of rejection.

Chapter Twelve

Elegant red sandstone apartment buildings near a park, gave way to individual houses on a rise overlooking a river below. The cab drew up before a gate inscribed with intricate, wrought iron letters. Beyond this imposing entrance was a short driveway leading through well-established garden beds punctuated by handsome feature trees. The house seemed huge as it rose above the gardens. Its front doors were graced with stained glass windows.

Anna swallowed and prepared herself to be quizzed extensively. A family who lived in such a home would not take kindly to a stranger from far away insisting on a relationship. She must assure them as soon as possible that she wanted nothing from them other than information.

As she stood at the door, so deep in thought that she had not yet found a door bell or knocker, the doors opened and she was confronted by a small woman with a huge welcoming smile, who promptly dusted off her floury hands on her apron and beckoned Anna inside without enquiring as to her identity.

"Come away in! I've been baking as you can see. Ross

loves my cheese scones and if I don't get a batch done every morning there are complaints before bedtime."

The woman, who Anna presumed to be Joyce McLeod, led the way into a spacious kitchen and pulled out a tall stool at a marble island counter. She went directly to a coffee machine, that Anna recognized as a very expensive Italian model, and poured two cups, which she then placed on the counter side by side with a tray of brown and white sugars, cream, milk and an assortment of pastries.

"Oh dear, I didn't even take your coat yet! Awful weather, isn't it? I guessed, with you being a North American, you would prefer coffee, but I can whip up tea in a second."

Anna shrugged off her coat and placed it over the next stool in line at the counter noticing that there was plenty remaining space for a large group. She was thunderstruck at this welcome and temporarily unable to think of a response.

Her hostess recognized her discomfort and immediately launched into an explanation.

"I know I'm chattering away here. Ross says I'm like a runaway train once I get started!" She laughed uproariously and Anna could not resist an open smile at her honesty.

"The fact is, my dear, I am quite nervous about meeting you. It's been some years since we found out about my husband's older brother and to finally meet his daughter after all this time……….well! I am a bit gobsmacked and that's the truth!"

She stopped dead and a silence fell which allowed Anna to focus on her face for the first time. She was a lovely woman crowned with silver-grey, abundant hair springing from her forehead with the same energy of the woman herself. She had a cheerful face that welcomed smiles and was blessed with the fine complexion of the Scot who has lived in a moist climate.

Relief flooded Anna's heart and she reached forward and did the only thing that seemed appropriate. She wrapped her arms around the woman and hugged her close.

"Joyce, I can't thank you enough for this warm welcome to your home. I had no reason to believe you would be so generous as to accept me so fast. I confess I am on the verge of tears now. Finding my father's family when I had no idea there was anyone left has been very emotional for me."

"Now don't you cry, Anna! You'll set *me* off and the children all complain that I am the original waterworks. They won't go to a weepy film with me no matter what I threaten, or promise."

Anna smiled again and wiped her eyes. This happy woman, so aptly named, was what her own mother should have been if her life in isolation had not been so difficult.

"Joyce, may I drink this delicious coffee now? The smell of these cheese scones is driving me crazy!"

"Of course! We have a lot to catch up on before Rory arrives for his lunch. Help yourself to anything you want and I'll fill in some of the details for you."

As Anna sipped coffee and tasted a marzipan concoction with a checkered pattern of pink and white cake inside the sweet edging, Joyce's voice filled the kitchen and turned the dull morning light into a rainbow of understanding in Anna's mind and heart.

"You see, Anna, Ross was born a few months after your father and mother left Scotland for Canada.

I fancy your Dad never knew his mother was expecting. In those days a late-life baby was not so welcome in a family and a woman would have kept it quiet in case something went wrong with the pregnancy. This is what made Angus' father so angry when his son confessed that he had made one girl pregnant and was running away with a different girl. Can you imagine the shock of it all? His wife was expecting a child. His son had fathered a child at the same time and was prepared to leave that girl in the lurch and flee far away.

Of course, we never knew any of this when Ross and I got married. His father was what the Scots call 'a hard man with a drinking problem'. Angus McLeod's name was never spoken in their home and Ross grew up thinking he was an only child. It was much later, when Ross' mother was in failing health that we found out the true story.

I want to tell you that story, Anna, if you can stand it."

"Oh, please do, Joyce. I have been living in the dark for so many years and now you are shedding light on so many forbidden areas for me."

Anna settled back and listened as her Aunt Joyce filled in a lost part of Anna's family history.

"Ross and I took Catherine, his mother, on a tour of Scotland one autumn. It was what she had begged for and we all knew it was for the last time. She longed to see the sights and sounds of her youth. We were travelling up the west coast and we came over the hill above Eilean Donan, the lovely MacRae castle at the joining point of three sea lochs.

It was a dull, cold day but Catherine insisted she was strong enough to climb up to the battlements. We had her well wrapped up against the weather. I held tight to her one arm and Ross clung to the other. I'll never forget what happened there.

A shaft of sunlight pierced the clouds and the sea turned from grey to bright blue in a second. Something about the scene gave her new energy. We were almost turning back to the warmth of the café nearby when Catherine stopped at an archway and tears began to run down her cheeks.

'He's away over there', she said, clinging on to the railing with a death grip we could not break.

Ross looked at me and I knew he was wondering if his mother had lost her mind.

She carried on talking as if we were not there at all. She said she had come to this very spot for years and looked out towards Skye and the Atlantic Ocean. It was the closest she ever came to where her son had gone.

Ross was shocked to the core to hear this, but that was nothing to what happened next. She cried out the name

Angus. 'Angus, come back home!' in a pitiful, broken voice just full of loss and longing.

We took Catherine to the restaurant and Ross got her a dram to warm her up. She was cold like a statue. Once she had broken the silence of all the long years she told us everything that had happened back then. It came like a flood held back behind a giant dam.

It was the war years, of course, and things were difficult for everyone. My father-in-law, your grandfather, had flat feet and was not allowed to be a soldier. He resented this and let his temper control his feelings. He was a hard worker, of course, an engineer who helped build many structures in Glasgow but it was as if he had built a high wall against the memory of his first son. He would never allow Catherine to talk about him. I think she must have suffered a lot in silence and in the end, she could not keep that silence any longer.

She died soon after. I think she had unburdened herself at last and passed on the secret to her second son, leaving it up to him to decide what to do about it."

Joyce McLeod took a breath and a sip of coffee, leaving Anna to try to calm the wild beating of her heart.

Another story of family misunderstanding and separation was being presented to her so soon after she had heard Lawren's sad tale. Her mind jumped again to Helen Dunlop's traumatic life. What was wrong with all these people who did not understand what family meant? The closest ties of all had to be those within a family group. The deep and familiar anguish of not having a child of her own, swept over Anna. Had she been fortunate enough to raise a child herself, nothing in the world, and *no one* in the world, could have come between them.

Was it because women were subservient to men, the sole breadwinners, in the old days? Anna's mother had a career as a nurse and she had been insistent that Anna follow in her footsteps. Having a career to fall back on had, undoubtedly, saved Anna's sanity when she and Richard divorced. Could she ever have accepted their marriage break-up with some shreds of dignity, if it had meant poverty as well as emotional devastation? Regardless of her ability to earn a living, Anna knew she had come perilously close to throwing herself on Richard's mercy, despite his infidelity. She almost begged him to choose her and repair their relationship.

The scenario this presented was not something Anna wished to dwell upon.

She could see Joyce's story was almost concluded so she asked a question that was now boring into her brain. "Joyce, what did your husband decide to do about his mother's confession?"

"Well, you have to understand that this news came to us only a few years ago. We were both heavily involved in Ross' business, the children's busy lives and his father's final illness from alcohol abuse. We decided to sit on the information and only try to find out what had happened to Angus and his wife in Canada."

"So you found out about Simon and me?"

"Yes. Your parents were both gone. You were teaching in Ontario and Simon was living with his family in Alberta. That's about it. We never expected to find you on our doorstep. Which makes me wonder, what brings you to Glasgow now, Anna?"

It was time for Anna to turn the tables of the conversation and try to condense a long family story from the perspective of the other side of the Atlantic.

Before she could begin, Joyce's head swivelled toward the entrance hall.

"Hold that thought, Anna! Rory's here at last. I'll just get us all a sandwich and heat some pasta and we can sit down in comfort. Oh, don't worry! Rory has known about you and Simon for years."

Joyce slipped to the other side of the marble countertop and busied herself with food preparations, leaving Anna to stand and meet her cousin Rory.

He came into the kitchen like a force of nature, rubbing his hands together and tossing his auburn hair to one side. He was tall, similar in height to Anna and Philip, and Anna guessed that his height came from his father, rather than his mother. He had a ruddy complexion, although that could be because of the cold wind outside, but he also had the identical beaming smile of his mother.

"Anna! Well, I never expected to be meeting a long-lost cousin today. I apologize for not arriving sooner. With Dad out on the site today, there were several things, and people, I had to deal with before I could leave the office. Has my mother been looking after you? I imagine she's been filling you in on the family secrets. I hope you are not too shocked?"

"On the contrary, Rory, I was about to divulge a few secrets of my own!"

"Leave the lass in peace for a minute, Rory! Take Anna over to the window and get her a drink. She'll be needing a pick-me-up after all that's happened already."

Rory quickly complied with his mother's request and settled his cousin on a high-backed chair at an oval table set within a tall bay window overlooking the front gardens. He fetched a chilled bottle of white from a wine fridge and placed a set of crystal glasses at the ready.

By the time Anna had tasted the wine and savoured the fine vintage, Joyce had arrived at the table bearing plates of sandwiches and a steaming bowl of pasta. On her instructions, Rory collected two bowls of pasta sauce from the countertop and an assortment of plates and cutlery.

Anna could see that this was a familiar routine for mother and son. It appeared that Rory either lived in this spacious home with his parents, or was a frequent lunch-time visitor.

After her substantial hotel breakfast, Anna was unable to do justice to the food on offer but she made up for it by attempting to answer Rory's questions about when she had arrived, where she was staying and what her plans were.

To answer this last question, Anna decided to start at the

end of her story by introducing the topic of Lawren, and the whole sequence of events that had led to her property in Scotland.

"You see," she began, "I knew nothing of Scotland before Helen's legacy. When I decided to keep the Oban house my life changed for the better in every way possible. It's a long story but it was there that my artist friend, Lawren Drake, became my life partner. He arrives in Glasgow tomorrow and we will travel to Oban within a day or two. My brother Simon and his family are staying at the farmhouse at the moment. It will be the first time they have met Lawren. They are due to return to Canada soon."

Rory and Joyce exchanged a glance at this news. Having found a new branch of the McLeod family, they were reluctant to miss the opportunity to meet all of them.

"I am thinking *we* have plans to make Anna, but first let us bring you up to date on your Scottish cousins. Rory, you start."

"Right you are! You might need to take notes, Anna. There's a whole tribe of us now!"

Anna's eyebrows twitched at this announcement. She hoped she could keep track. The day had presented so many surprises already.

Joyce disappeared for a moment and returned with an armful of framed family photographs. As Rory spoke, she pointed out her children and their families.

"I am the only unattached one of the lot, Anna. Blame it on the building business. I have been involved since leaving school and I expect I will take over from Dad one day soon."

"The sooner the better!" breathed Joyce.

"Jocelyn is next in line. She's the real redhead of the family and as you can see she's passed that on to her children. Ginger tops the lot of them! What they make of that in France, I can't begin to guess!"

"Jocelyn, has a real talent for languages," explained her mother. "She has worked for the foreign office for years as a translator and met her husband there. They live in Paris now with the two boys."

"Next, comes my brother, Murray. He's the brainy one."

Joyce elbowed her son in the ribs in annoyance at this characterization.

"Well," continued Rory, "you must admit he's the one who followed in Grandpa's footsteps and became an engineer, and a very successful one. His advice and expertise allowed Dad and me to forgo the expenses of employing a firm to supply that kind of help."

"Och, I'm sure Anna doesn't want to hear all that stuff, Rory! Tell her about the children."

Joyce found a picture of Murray's family and proudly presented it for Anna's inspection.

"What lovely girls they have," exclaimed Anna, when she had admired the large house and gardens in the background of the photograph.

"Last, but never least," continued Rory, "is Heather, the baby of the family. She causes more trouble than all the rest put together. She's living with some rocker in England, would you believe? We don't see much of her these days."

"You have a wonderful family, Joyce. They have been very fortunate to be brought up in this beautiful home."

Laughter greeted this statement and Anna wondered what she had said wrong.

"Oh, goodness me, Anna! This house would have been much too hoighty-toighty for our bunch of rapscallions. We lived in Dennistoun in Glasgow's east end when they were young. It was a big, fourth floor flat on Whitehill Street and I can tell you climbing those stairs with prams and shopping and babies in arms was no picnic. By the time Ross had the cash to buy this place, Jocelyn and Murray were gone and Rory and Heather were the only ones left at home. We had all the space and no one left to fill it, you might say."

"Oh, stop, mother! Anna doesn't need to hear ancient

history! The poor woman's eyes have glazed over. Give Anna a chance to catch her breath, won't you?"

Anna laughed. She had been delighted to be immersed in this family story and taken into the fold like a lost lamb. She had to search through her memory for a feeling this comfortable. It was certainly far different from her own childhood. Cozy times at Alina's home would be the nearest she could come to a comparison.

A cell phone chimed out and Joyce got up to fetch it. She answered "Yes!" enthusiastically to the caller then turned back to her guest. "That was Ross. He's on his way here. Rory, you've to get back to the office *toute suite*, your Dad's leaving for the day."

"Okay dokey, Mum! I'll see you again, Anna. It's been great to meet you!'

With that, Rory left the kitchen and the door slammed behind him in short order. Anna thought it would be quite a challenge to manage an energetic family of the size of Joyce and Ross'. No wonder what was happening far away on the other side of the Atlantic was not of much concern in their busy lives.

She stood up and helped clear the table of dishes. Joyce commented that Ross would have eaten on his lunch break at the building site. She insisted that Anna stay until her husband arrived home as he was very anxious to meet her.

Anna was not sure how much more excitement she could stand in this one day but her Aunt (strange to think of this), had been so welcoming that it would have appeared ungracious to leave at this point.

While Joyce loaded the dishwasher and wiped down the countertop, humming along to a song on the radio, Anna stood at the bay window and admired the long view downhill to the park. She had been standing there in a daze for a minute or two when she suddenly realized that a figure of a man was approaching the front door of the house.

Joyce must have heard his footsteps on the stairs for she

went to meet him. Anna could hear a whispered conversation taking place in the hall outside the kitchen, then Joyce walked back in, followed by a stranger.

A shock hit Anna like a tidal wave. This man, her Uncle Ross, was so like her own father that her mind flipped back to days before he had gone to live out his last years with Simon in Alberta. Their farewell scene was suddenly vivid in her mind. She had driven him to the airport and loaded his luggage onto the

weigh-in belt when her father had turned to her and given her a rare bear hug that forced the air out of her lungs. "Take care of yourself, Anna, my dearest. Remember, family is how we survive."

At the time she had not understood his urgency or the meaning of his remark, but standing here in this Scottish home, facing his own brother, with the knowledge of all her Dad had missed in his life, she finally grasped the meaning. She, too, had missed much but that was all going to change.

These are your folks, Dad, and I claim them for my own.

Chapter Thirteen

❦

Seeing Ross McLeod for the first time gave Anna such a thrill that she moved forward into his open arms without a thought for the unusual circumstances of their meeting. She realized this behaviour was not typical for her. In the last hour, or perhaps it was since she had fallen in love with Lawren, she had become a much more giving person. Hugging did deliver comfort and acceptance and these were feelings she truly was experiencing on this amazing, once-in-a-lifetime day in a beautiful Glasgow mansion.

Her Uncle Ross, still so like her father Angus that it was hard for Anna to drag her eyes away from his face, insisted that she sit down with him and Joyce, and tell them what her life had been like as a child in Canada. Anna complied with this request. Little did this big strong man in the dark suit, white shirt and tie of an executive realize, but he could have asked her for anything in the world at this moment.

"Before I say anything," she began, "you both must understand that in the last few years I have re-evaluated my childhood in light of what I had discovered about my mother's side of the family. Today's wonderful events and the sobering information you have shared with me, Joyce, are still raw to me.

I don't doubt my feelings about my mother and father will soon undergo another transformation."

Ross and Joyce nodded sympathetically and Anna felt encouraged to continue.

"My parents worked very hard to provide a good home for Simon and me. Like many other immigrants, they had to establish themselves in their professions. My Dad was an engineer like his father before him, as I now know, and he used to show me the bridges in London, Ontario, that he had designed and supervised.

He had a particular affection for one of London's oldest bridges, named Blackfriars. We would sit together on a bench in the park nearby and watch the traffic cross the River Thames. He could tell me things like the stress on the bridge from the sounds the vehicles made on its wooden surface.

I remember moments like that, and stories he would read to me when my mother was on night duty at the hospital, but the truth is that he was most often absent from our lives.

My mother was not an easy woman. She had high standards of cleanliness and punctuality and an obsessive need to see her children succeed in life. I think she was often lonely which is not surprising considering how far she was from what you Scots call 'kith and kin'.

The relationship between my parents was not always smooth sailing. I accepted everything as normal then. Children know no better, but there were tensions and sometimes savage arguments in hushed tones at late hours.

I now think the fact of my father's infidelity, the reason why they had married so fast and left the country so quickly, was a constant pressure on both of them, for their own separate reasons. My father felt guilty and my mother harboured anger for a long time about leaving so much behind. All of these tensions combined with financial strains and the needs of two growing children pushed them further apart as the years went by.

Simon and I married within a year or two of each other,

leaving my parents with no one at home to act as a deterrent to their expressions of dissatisfaction. My mother grew more and more bitter, even after she had retired from nursing. Dad belonged to a bowling club and spent many afternoons and evenings there, rather than at home. He eventually became an expert at the sport and travelled throughout Ontario to various competitions with his bowling team buddies.

You will probably find it significant that Scotland was not a topic of conversation in our home. Perhaps it was too painful for them to recall all they had once known and left behind them. Neither Simon nor I knew anything of grandparents, aunts and uncles, or cousins. We never questioned that our small family didn't celebrate with relatives from out of town like our friends at school so often did. We had no photographs of ancient elders in our home. Again, we never thought at the time that this was strange.

At first, Dad would go to Calgary to visit Simon and as his family with Michelle grew, Mum went there also for a week or two in the summer. I think she enjoyed that carefree time."

Anna stopped and looked around for a glass of water to moisten her dry throat. The next part of her tale would be difficult. Joyce, ever the attentive hostess, noticed Anna's need and fetched a bottle of sparkling water from the fridge.

"If you want to stop there, Anna, it's perfectly fine with us. You can continue another day. "

"No, I want to finish my story now. If I have learned one thing lately, it is how little we can count on the future. This won't get any easier if I wait."

A few sips of water and a brief glance out of the window to calm herself, gave Anna the courage to go on as concisely as she could.

"My marriage ended in divorce and I had no children to care for. My teaching career transitioned into work in the public library system so when my mother took sick I was the one nearest, who had time to nurse the one who had always nursed others. She was not a good patient. My father did what he could to help but she often pushed him away. I did my best for her but I am afraid my own fragmented emotional state was not the perfect preparation for the demands of a sickbed.

The serious infection she had contracted in hospital work took over her weakened system and she died peacefully in hospital, under the loving care of those nurses who knew her best.

Dad soon moved out to Calgary and stayed happily with Simon's growing family taking some furnishings from the London home which was then sold. I moved into a small apartment."

"Oh, Anna, my dear, weren't you lonely then?" Joyce's voice contained a wealth of fellow feeling. She had never known an empty table or an empty life and could hardly imagine what her new niece had suffered.

"I was lucky, Joyce. I had a wonderful group of friends who always supported me and they were there with me all the way. In fact, it was through their intervention that I took up the challenge to stay at the house in Oban I told you about before."

A quizzical look from Ross to his wife, and her reassuring nod, indicated that she would fill in the required information later.

Ross took this opportunity to ask Anna how she had found out about her father's side of the family.

"I can tell you that!" interrupted Joyce. She could see Anna's approaching exhaustion and gladly supplied the information. "It must have been recent because Rory told me on the phone that Anna knew nothing until a day or so ago. You can see she's still in shock, Ross, and it's no wonder at all."

"It's thanks to an astute research librarian at the Mitchell Library that I am here today."

"Well, we are beyond glad that you found us, Anna. Believe me, you will not be forgotten now.

If you agree, we will immediately consider you, and Simon of course, as additional members of our close family. You are welcome here at any time."

Before Anna could find adequate words to reply to this generous gesture, Ross spoke again.

"Anna, let me add to that. You are the last link to my lost brother Angus. Ever since we discovered your existence, my heart has been heavy with worry about you. Joyce will tell you that I had made myself a promise to fly to Canada and track you and Simon down, no matter what it cost me in time or money."

He turned to his wife with a satisfied smirk that twisted Anna's heart anew. It was an expression so like her father, yet one she had completely forgotten about, that she could hardly believe it.

It felt as if her father was brought to life here in this comfortable kitchen and she was being gifted with the chance to fix their relationship through this wonderful man, his younger brother Ross.

"What my dear Joyce, did not know until this very second, is that I have already bought the tickets for both of us."

Joyce jumped up and threw her arms around her husband's back. "Does this mean you have finally decided to retire, Ross McLeod?"

"Of course it does! I knew you wanted me to do it."

"That's as may be, but you kept that secret close to your chest and you surely made me wait for it, you rascal!" She thumped his back with her fists and tried to circle his broad shoulders.

"Let me down woman! You'll be giving my niece a bad impression of us!"

Anna thought that could never happen. She could not have dreamed up the events of this perfect day if she possessed the most fantastic imagination in the world.

. . .

She left in Ross' car after exchanging phone numbers with Joyce and thanking her profusely for her extraordinary welcome. Anna was silent on the ride back to her hotel but her uncle seemed to understand that her heart was full. Perhaps he felt something of the same.

His parting words were to assure her that they would keep in touch and she should call on any of the family should she or Lawren need any help whatsoever while in Glasgow.

"We have a lot of catching up to do, Anna but I can understand that you need time with Lawren at the moment. This is not goodbye. Now that we've found you, we'll not be letting you go."

She waved until the car turned right, around the corner into the Broomielaw, but the truth was that she could hardly see the car. Her uncle's final words had unleashed the torrent of emotions that she had been barely able to control all day. She wept like a child while standing outside the hotel; rain mingling with her tears. It was a feeling of being cherished like a child again that had broken down the barriers of adulthood.

Not even with Lawren had she been able to let her emotions go like this. It was disturbing to be so out of control and yet, at the same time, it was such a feeling of release, as if years of trouble and loneliness were being washed away and a lighter, happier Anna was being born.

At once she thought of Lawren. She could not wait to show him this new Anna with all the barriers melted away. She glanced at her watch and counted the hours before he arrived at Glasgow Airport. He had asked her not to meet him there but to wait at the hotel. They had decided not to talk on the phone until they met again and Anna was glad of this. She could not see how to tell him what had just happened to her. Hopefully, by tomorrow she would have processed enough to be capable of speaking rationally about it all.

She realized she would have to talk to Simon and to Alina first, and those conversations would give her a framework into which she could fashion a story of some sort. It would be like a practice run.

Somehow she was reluctant to return to her hotel room for either of these conversations. She was too full of fleeting feelings to settle there in the midst of luggage and all the signs of temporary occupation. She walked to the street corner and peered into the windows of the café. As she suspected, the booths and tables were filling up with customers in the late afternoon. She did not want to share her news with any of these strangers. Where could she go on a rainy afternoon in the dusky light to get the privacy she required?

Ahead of her, across the busy road was the embankment of the River Clyde. She remembered the first time she had walked that hidden pedestrian way and the buildings that had risen high above her, so impressive against the skyline. There was a church she had seen there. Churches in Britain were often open to the public for private prayer or contemplation. She crossed Jamaica Street without another thought and headed to the Cathedral entrance. If the doors were open to her she would go inside. If not, she would return to the distractions of her hotel room.

As she reached the entrance, a woman in a headscarf, emerged from the doors and popped open an umbrella almost in Anna's face. She must have been deep in thought as she hurried onto the pavement and never noticed or acknowledged Anna's presence.

Since she now knew the Cathedral of Saint Andrew was still available to passersby, Anna stepped carefully inside and found the huge interior space empty of parishioners but full of pews, tall windows, carvings, pillars, plinths, plaques and memorials of all kinds. Anna sank into the nearest pew. Her back was aching. Previous experience told her that this pain was not caused by overexertion, but simply by stress.

"Even wonderful and unexpected events can be stressful in their way," she murmured, rubbing her back as she gazed around the cavernous building. Not a sound of the traffic passing in the street filtered through these great stone walls.

Strangely, although she had entered with the intention of finding a quiet place in which to use her cell phone, Anna discovered she had lost the desire to do so. What now seemed more urgent was simply to sit still and try to absorb the healing peace of this ancient place.

In moments, the feelings that came to the fore were not stress-related but rather, feelings of gratitude.

"I am probably in the right spot for that," she thought. "What am I most grateful for?"

It was difficult to know where to begin. She was not on her knees with clasped hands, but as she sat there, in silent prayer, she found there was so much gratitude in her heart.

I finally understand more about my parents past lives here in Scotland and I can accept their choices.

I have found a whole new family of cousins and their families stretching into the future when once I feared I was childless, and the last of my line, other than Simon's brood.

My Samba friends and my dear, dear Helen have helped me reach this place in my life.

Now, I have Lawren too, and that is the most marvelous of all.

My life has expanded beyond Canada to another home in Scotland and the friends I have there.

It is all amazing and totally unexpected and I am so, so grateful for these benefits.

Anna had no sense of time passing as she sat there. Finally she came back to the present and noticed that the lamps lighting the church had dimmed. A man approached with the air of a person who knew he was going to disturb someone but could do nothing about it.

Anna did not wait to be ejected. Her damp shoes and rain-speckled coat were contributing to a feeling of chill in her bones. She hefted her purse and fled out of the church door, glad that the hotel was close by. Tea, and lots of it, was required. Then she would decide what to do next.

Twenty minutes later, Anna was sitting cozily on her hotel bed with the quilt up over her chest and three small cups full of tea by her bedside. She had already consumed one cup from the tray with the first packet of biscuits and now the second was just at the right temperature to be gulped down quickly.

Warmth was seeping into her bones at last and a sensation of tiredness came with it.

She may have closed her eyes for a moment but she was jolted awake by the jarring noise from her cell phone on the bedside table.

What? Who? Where am I?

She reached for the phone and watched as it slid in slow motion to the floor. Pushing back the bedclothes and bending down to retrieve the phone awakened some of her senses but it was still a dozy Anna who managed to croak out, "Yes?"

"Oh, Anna, I am sorry to be calling so late. I've been trying all day and I got worried."

"Alina! Don't worry. I think I am fine. My cell was turned off for most of the day. I've

been meaning to call you anyway."

"That's good. I need a chat with you, too. Philip is at a meeting in City Hall where they are discussing ways to rejuvenate London. He saw this in the news and decided they needed his

advice about heritage buildings. Honestly, he is full of surprises, Anna, but this gives me a

chance to tell you what's been happening here."

Anna could tell her friend was off on a roll and she need say nothing much in response. This suited her fine in her half-awake state and she contented herself with just enough in the way of approving noises to make Alina think she was listening fully.

"*I have to confess you were right about being alone in the condo. Philip could never cope*

with you and Lawren here at the same time. He has been a different person since we've been

on our own. I suspect even his housekeeper in Manchester intimidated him in some ways.

We've had long talks about our future plans and he came up with what I think is a brilliant

idea, Anna, but first I'll tell you how it all came about.

He was in the middle of telling me a story concerning house designs. Everything he is truly interested in involves buildings in some way, I've discovered. Anyway, he was describing this house he designed for his sister Lynn and her husband Stavros, on this Greek island. You met Lynn once before didn't you? Well, he told me how Stavros decided to split his retirement years between Greece and England. They have family in England still. I think it was while he was going over the arrangements the couple have made for renting their island property and working together on some archaeology projects that he had his brainwave.

No! I won't make you wait any longer! Philip thinks we, that's he and I, should buy a vacant condo in the Rosecliffe complex and live here together for part of the year.

Can you see how great this would be, Anna? You and Lawren would have privacy. There would be space for Lawren to set up a studio. We could continue with our A Plus business concerns.

We could go to Oban as couples together or Philip could rent it for both of us. Philip could return to England when he wants to work on some project and if I travelled with him we could rent out our condo."

Anna's brain moved into high gear near the end of Alina's long recitation. What? Move out? Buy property? Presumably

Philip could afford to do this. He must have developed a deep liking for Canada's version of the original London in a remarkably short while. This was all happening too fast.

Any thoughts of involving Alina in the events of Anna's day in Glasgow vanished from her mind. There was enough to deal with right here.

"Hold on a minute, Alina. Do you seriously want this commitment? I thought you were unsure

about a life with Philip. How did things escalate so quickly? I haven't been gone for a week yet!

Surely you are not rushing into this because of me?"

"No, no, Anna! It's not like that at all. Philip is a different man here in Canada and he really wants to make a go of a relationship with me. It's not a wild romance like yours, at least not yet, but I can actually see a point when that may well be possible for us.

Anyway, Anna, I know this is a lot to dump on you all at once with Lawren's stuff weighing on you as well."

Anna just shook her head at this comment. Alina had no idea how much had already been added to the complexities of her life on this day and with Lawren arriving soon she had more than enough to occupy her brain. Alina's eager voice continued before Anna could say any more.

"I'll leave it with you to think over and you can tell me what you feel about this after you and Lawren have a few days peace in Oban.

Oops! I see it's very late in Scotland. Apologies again, my dear. It's been so good to talk with you.

Night, night! Anna."

Anna heard kisses blown through the phone before the line went dead.

This was a different version of the Alina she had known for so long. If Philip could effect such changes in her friend with this lightning speed, anything else might be possible. But, buying a house together? That was a big change for both of them.

Anna had finished the rest of the tea while listening to

Alina's tale. She felt she had reached overload. Both her brain and her bladder were full.

"I must get up and go to the bathroom," she said sleepily, but the thought disappeared for the time being, as sleep claimed her again.

Chapter Fourteen

"Anna, you're shaking like a leaf. What's wrong?"

"Oh, Lawren, my darling, I'm just so glad to see you!"

"Very flattering, I'm sure, and I am more than glad to see you again. It feels like an age since we were together in London but you don't fool me that easily. Something is wrong. Tell me."

Anna stepped back from the powerful embrace that had occupied their first minutes together in her hotel room.

She wanted, more than anything, to unload the mental burden she was now carrying, but first she needed to hear if Lawren had told his father about events in Wiltshire.

"I promise I will tell you everything that's happened, Lawren, although you will find it hard to believe.

Can you wait till later for that? I want to know how the rest of your time in England worked out."

Lawren looked skeptical about the delay. He could tell Anna was holding back a worry of some kind. And yet, he knew her well enough to realize there would be a good reason for her reticence.

All at once the small hotel room seemed constricting. He had a sense of claustrophobia. Anna had been living here alone for several days now. He felt, against his arm, the bulk of a package of folders in his jacket pocket, and remembered his idea.

"Look, Anna, let's get out of here! It's a bright day for a change and there's so much to see in Glasgow. I collected enough information at the airport to keep us occupied for weeks. We'll go and have a day out and clear our heads of everything for a while. What do you say?"

Anna said yes, emphatically, and knew at once it was the exact thing she needed. How wonderful to be with someone who not only understood her moods, but who knew precisely how to change them for the better.

"Let me find my walking shoes and my raincoat, just in case. Have you eaten? Breakfast is over in the restaurant here, but we can find lunch or something nearby if you want."

"No! I am in charge today. I want you to relax and enjoy yourself. No worries. No negative thoughts. Just the two of us on holiday. We'll be tourists with nothing but time on our hands. Agreed?"

Anna's response was to jump up from the chair where she was pulling on her shoes and then lead Lawren in a jig around the room to express her happiness.

In a minute they were dancing along the hall laughing like children on an unexpected holiday from school. No one saw them kiss in the elevator or noticed when they ran hand in hand for the exit doors.

"Where to now, oh mighty tour guide?" said Anna.

"Ah, follow me, my dear!" answered Lawren, in his best Rasputin impression.

And she did.

It had been a wonderful, magical day. The best of all the good days since Anna and Lawren had been together. He had promised her a holiday and that was what he delivered.

They started out at Kelvingrove Art Gallery and Museum,

a large and imposing building. The structure stretched out to either side and looked vaguely reminiscent of a Russian Palace with towers and pinnacles. The rich, red sandstone and the name Kelvingrove reminded Anna of Ross and Joyce's house. Their house must be close by. She almost told Lawren about her visit there but decided to wait. Nothing should spoil his delight in showing her the city.

The lobby entrance impressed with marble floors and soon opened up to a balconied hall reaching two stories high into a splendid ornate ceiling. A display of life-sized, stuffed, tropical animals captured Anna's attention immediately. It took a moment or two before she saw, suspended in the space above her, balloon heads of people bobbing gently up and down as the air currents changed.

Anna had looked up at these in delight and noticed each one was different; some laughing and smiling, others grimacing or frowning. Lights from beneath illuminated the floating heads and made them come alive.

Before she could comment on this effect, Lawren was pulling at her hand. He seemed to know exactly where to go next. They climbed the first set of wide stone steps. Everything was stone of one kind or another which had seemed to Anna to be sensible, given the number of feet presently walking or scampering from exhibit to exhibit. The voices echoed in the space and gave even more lifelike qualities to the bobbing heads. She wondered if these were meant to represent real Glaswegians.

When they turned left into a wide area and Anna glimpsed massive paintings set in galleries against the outer walls, she knew why Lawren had been so anxious to get here. She watched him transported in wonder as he gazed in turn at the works of Dutch and Italian masters. He was obviously in his element in this setting.

Anna tiptoed to a bench in the centre of the French Art gallery and waited. Eventually he found her and sat down beside her.

"You have chosen one of my favourite paintings," he said. They sat together in front of Claude Monet's *Vetheuil*, lost in the endless sky and cornfields until Lawren had his fill and jumped to his feet again.

"You must see this!" he called, as he ran ahead, leading the way down the stairs to the main level and to another gallery almost directly beneath the one they had just left.

When Anna saw the title, 'Mackintosh and the Glasgow Style' she remembered his previous enthusiasm about The Glasgow School of Art and knew she was in for a rare treat. Although she could appreciate the elegant design of Charles Rennie Mackintosh's paintings and furniture, Lawren's knowledge revealed aspects she would never have recognized for herself. For example, *The Wassail*, by the artist, might have remained to Anna's eyes as an interesting study in vertical lines had Lawren not pointed out that these were stately, elongated figures clad in cloaks at a Christmas celebration.

They skirted through some minor exhibits on the same level, of which the Ancient Egyptian was of the most interest to Anna. She was able to provide some of her own knowledge there, thanks to her recent visit To Egypt. It was hardly possible for her to believe that when she and Alina had explored the Nile she had not even known about Lawren's existence.

A tantalizing aroma of fresh-brewed coffee soon attracted them to the lower level where the ceilings were of normal human height and lines of children chattering excitedly indicated that this was an educational wing. They headed straight to the restaurant and waited only a few minutes before being seated in a long hall with tall windows down one side letting in bright daylight.

Lawren declared he was ravenous after all that culture and he proceeded to order from the extensive menu. A variety of appetizing dishes soon appeared on their table and Anna discovered she, too, was hungry.

It was during dessert, a delectable slice of treacle cake smothered in hot custard sauce, that Anna asked once again about Lawren's father. "I know you set rules for today, my darling, but if you can bear to tell me, I really do want to know."

A replete Lawren relented. "I don't want to bring the atmosphere down a notch, Anna, so I'll start with the positive notes." Anna quickly understood that there were negative things to relate also, but she did not interrupt.

"As you know, I felt so low after my visit to what's left of the Hartfield Hall my father remembered, that I set out to explore some of Wiltshire before heading back to London. I was able to get trains or buses everywhere. The public transport system in England is excellent. I saw Stonehenge and, even better, I think, Avebury, where the public can walk all around, and between, the giant stones of the circle without any barriers."

"I am curious about how did you felt there, Lawren?"

"I'm not surprised you ask that question, Anna, and you are right. It was a very strange feeling for me. I imagine my psychic antennae were working overtime in that ancient place. I kept thinking there was someone watching me but every time I turned around to look, I was alone.

I didn't stay too long there. I went to the ruins at Old Sarum which is where the modern town of Salisbury was founded. From the hillside you can see the spires of Salisbury Cathedral and the old town wall. I tell you Anna, we must go back there some day. I could have drawn and painted for weeks it was so stimulating to my imagination."

Anna could see from his excited manner that this was an understatement.

"Did you know there are white horses carved out of some of the hillsides? The whole county is chock full of medieval towns and ruins. I spent an hour or two in Laycock Abbey just wandering around thinking of what life must have been like there for monks and priors. I did some sketches too."

He stopped to sip from his mug of coffee and Anna reached forward to touch his hand. Their matching silver rings clinked gently together and both of them smiled at the sound.

"Did you tell your father about all this?"

"I tried to." He looked down at his empty plate and ran his finger around the rim to collect the last of the delicious custard. Anna knew he was stalling but she remained silent.

"He really wasn't interested in anything other than the family house he had sent me to visit. I didn't know what I would say until the last possible moment and then I lied."

"What else could you do? You could hardly shatter the dreams of an elderly man at this point in his life."

"I know, but it was not easy to lie to my father. I told the truth about his older brother having emigrated to Australia and that made it easier to accept the fact that the house he had loved was now being sold to another owner. Of course I said nothing about the appalling condition of the building or the housing estate that will soon occupy the land but I did distract him with the information that I had spoken to Dan the gardener."

"What did he think about *that* news?"

"Oh, Anna, I was glad I did tell him. It opened up a whole host of stories from his boyhood and how he and my mother met and the happy times they had when they were first in love. He completely forgot about the financial issues he had sent me to explore and drifted off to sleep recalling the gracious home and grounds that will forever be intact in his memory."

"Lawren! That is the best possible outcome from this sad journey. You did the right thing for him."

He sat up straight and shook his head from side to side briefly as if to remove all negative thoughts for now. "And, my lady, I have something else to show you and then there will be shopping for you and a splendid high tea in a restaurant so amazing you will hardly believe it can exist at all."

"What? Eat more? I'm full to the brim already!"

"That's why the shopping expedition is necessary! I expect you to explore each and every little nook and cranny at top speed. There are countless more sights on Clydeside we could see, of course, but we'll save those for another visit. I want you to have energy left for the remainder of the evening back at the hotel."

Lawren winked at this disclosure and Anna felt a hot blush rise up from the pit of her stomach into her face. Had she dared, she would have suggested they cut the afternoon schedule short and head back to the hotel right away. For now, she was unsure of her sexual power in their relationship but some day, she thought, it would be fun for her partner to find out.

They accomplished the shopping expedition in Byres Road after a sortie along Sauchiehall Street. Anna duly entered every boutique and vintage store while Lawren looked at art and antique shops and carried the accumulating pile of Anna's purchases until called upon to offer his opinion.

She had a wonderful time, made all the more delightful because she had never before had the opportunity to shop with such an appreciative male. Richard had hated shopping of any sort and Anna's rare expeditions had been with Alina, or others of the Sambas. There was something very reassuring in having a male on hand who would give an immediate 'thumbs up or down' to a dress or hat or purse.

She could see him mentally composing outfits for her and she knew whatever he recommended would be flattering to her colouring and her figure.

While Anna was deliberating inside a shoe store on whether she should purchase a wedge-heeled red leather pair, Lawren rushed in and said, "Get them! They're gorgeous! I'll be in the church at the top of the road. Come and find me there."

Anna paid for her purchase wondering what was happening now. Lawren had never spoken about a church affiliation. Perhaps this was a building of architectural interest. She emerged from the shoe shop into a cloudy skyscape. The day was moving toward night already.

She found the church easily as it was well illuminated, and she entered with just a hint of trepidation. *What next?*

Lawren came rushing forward as she arrived. He was as excited as she had ever seen him. His golden eyes were lit from within and his face glowed.

"Look up, Anna. Look up!"

At first she thought they were still in the Kelvingrove Museum. Against the night sky there were vivid paintings and designs on the curved dome of the glass roof.

"What is this?" she asked. She was reading inscriptions in each section. Questions followed by answers. 'Where are we going?' 'Our seed returns to death.'

The central figure was huge and stylized under the question, 'Where are we?'

A very good question under the circumstances, Anna thought.

"This is the work of Alasdair Gray," said Lawren. "I have read about this Auditorium in what was the Kelvinside Parish Church. It's now called '*Oran Mor*' and I never expected to find myself here. This is one of the largest pieces of public art in Scotland by a man who was a painter, author, playwright and goodness knows what else. Isn't it magnificent?"

Anna had to agree. She thought she was standing in another art gallery inside a church until the sounds of cutlery on plates drifted toward them accompanied by delicious smells. It soon became apparent that the body of what was once a church had been converted into a handsome restaurant. Lawren had obtained a table in one of the side aisles, by some means, although the centre area, once the nave, was almost full of customers. They were seated near the round windows, set into the walls at a low level and lit from within so that the inset circular patterns, filled with multi-hued glass, were gleaming despite the darkness outside.

"This is the most unique place for fine dining that I have ever seen" breathed Anna, looking around in amazement. Lawren was grinning like a Cheshire cat at her delight.

Suddenly she had an idea. "I'll be back in ten minutes, Lawren. Order anything you like."

She disappeared back to the Auditorium, carrying the shopping bags, and asked for the ladies' restroom.

There was no way she was going to sit in that splendid restaurant with all those elegant people, in the flat shoes and raincoat she had been wearing all day. She quickly found the red shoes and a black, ballet-length skirt Lawren had selected for her. With a sparkling black belt tying the outfit together over her white cashmere sweater, she felt appropriately dressed for the occasion. She found a pair of gold and garnet dangling earrings to make the effect complete. A rapid comb through her hair and a touch of bright lipstick and she was ready to glide back to the table with her head held high.

Lawren's look of approval said it all. She did not need to hear the words. She felt them in every inch of her body.

Anna was never able to recall the food they ate. It was a light meal but the feast was before their eyes rather than on their plates.

As the coffee was served, Anna thought the time was right to tell her news.

"I promised to tell you what happened yesterday, Lawren. It won't take long to tell but it is the most incredible and unexpected thing."

Lawren's attention which had been veering among, the setting, the food and Anna, now returned to her face with rapt interest. "What?"

"That's it exactly. One of the questions painted on the roof here is 'What are we?' Well I have discovered something more about what I am. I am a niece of a Scottish family. My aunt and uncle and an extended family of cousins live near here in Kelvinside."

"How did this happen? When? What's been going on? We spoke on the phone a couple of nights ago and you mentioned nothing about this. I know you can work fast, Anna, but this is supersonic!"

His joke took the tension out of the situation and Anna was able to relate the events of her meeting with Ross and Joyce and Rory without the emotional tug that her previous thoughts and memories had caused. Lawren asked a dozen questions, some of which she could not yet answer. His concluding remark made Anna realize afresh what an amazing man he was.

"It's a pity we are leaving early tomorrow. I would like to meet this new family of yours, Anna. They sound like a wonderful group and I am grateful for the way they have accepted you."

"Well, we will soon meet Simon and some of his clan in Oban. Perhaps it's best that you get to know the McLeods slowly. I don't want to overwhelm you."

Before Lawren could reply to this, a waiter appeared at their table with a tray on which two glasses filled with an amber liquid were balanced. Anna's eyebrows signalled surprise and her companion whispered that he had ordered the whisky when she had made her quick change earlier.

The glasses were carefully placed in front of them and the waiter said, "*Slainte mhath*".

"I've heard that Gaelic phrase in Oban. It means, 'Good health'. Am I correct?"

The waiter smiled his approval and was about to leave when Anna asked, "What does *Oran Mor* mean?"

"To be sure, it is 'the great melody of life' madam." With that he was gone.

Anna and Lawren clinked glasses and toasted each other.

"To our good health and to the continuation of *our* great melody of life," offered Anna.

"Perfect!" replied Lawren. "Now, drink up, my lovely lady! The night is still young."

Chapter Fifteen

It was a somewhat sleepy couple who made it just in time for the 9:30 am departure of the train to Oban. Lawren had elected to take the train rather than to drive north, as he had heard Anna's account of her first trip to Oban and he wanted her to relive that experience with him by her side.

The train was not very busy, so they sat comfortably, linked together, half-asleep as the train travelled through the precincts of Glasgow. Once outside those limits, however, Lawren was glued to the windows and the spectacular views. His questions came fast as he sought the names of the mountains, valleys and lochs that were revealed in an endless parade. Anna did her best to supply the required information. She smiled inside as she remembered her own first journey and the same need to know what she saw and where she was. This was Lawren's chance to see the land-based interior of the Scottish west coast. Together they had experienced some of the western isles on their trip to Iona but the heather-clad hills and tumbling waterfalls of Argyll and Bute had their own, unique, wild splendour.

When he stopped to take a breath again, he turned to Anna and his expression reflected her own feelings.

"It's simply magnificent!" he said.

"I know," she replied, and she squeezed his hand to show her understanding.

"But, look at the people in this carriage," he continued, quietly. "The man over there is asleep and that family seems to be having a picnic. The two young men are watching their phone screens and ignoring the scenery completely and that girl has her eyes shut and her ears plugged with headphones. What's wrong with these people?"

"I suppose even the most gorgeous views in the world are commonplace to those who have seen them many times before," suggested Anna. "By the way, can you hear the music the girl is listening to?"

"I can hear some of it? It must be very loud. Would you like me to ask her to turn it down?"

"Oh, no!" insisted Anna. "It sounds familiar to me but I can't remember why. I must have heard it before somewhere."

As the hours drifted by, Anna could not help comparing the comfort of Lawren's presence and the prospect of their holiday together in Oban with the trepidation of her first journey north and the feelings of uncertainty that had been her constant companion on that occasion.

How her life had changed in the interim! It was difficult to absorb the differences and yet she was so much more confident and happy than she could ever have imagined on that prior trip.

How had it all happened?

She knew now that by accepting the challenge of coming to Scotland and attempting to live in Helen's old farmhouse, she had awakened something within herself that had lain dormant for decades. The Anna sitting comfortably with Lawren was a new creature. Had it not been for her willingness to accept new experiences and take chances, she would never have been able to overcome her natural fears about a new relationship with a younger man. She had learned that age has nothing to do with the life force. Her old-fashioned ideas had been swept away when she opened her heart to Lawren and now the future, however long or short it might be, was something to be welcomed and cherished in every way possible.

Thoughts of the future reminded her that there was at least one other piece of information that she had not yet shared with Lawren. She waited until the train was passing one of the long lochs and gently nudged Lawren's arms to get his attention.

"Lawren, I heard something interesting from Alina on the phone."

"Oh, what was she saying?" His eyes never left the view but his tone of voice indicated that he was paying attention.

"She's thinking of buying a condo in our Westmount complex and living there at least part of the time with Philip."

Lawren's head snapped round and he looked into Anna's eyes to make sure she was not joking.

"Really? What would make her do that? Does Philip agree to this idea?"

"I imagine he does agree. They have some elaborate plan to spend part of the year in Manchester, part in Ontario and part in Oban. Philip got this idea from his sister Lynn and her husband the Greek professor. Apparently they are in the process of working out a similar plan for their retirement years."

Lawren frowned and his eyes darkened. "Is this something you would consider Anna?"

"Which part? Living in two countries? I am doing that already. Buying a home? Philip is in a position to take on that expense but I think it would be an excellent thing for us to have the condo to ourselves.

What do you say?"

"I don't believe I have a say in this, Anna. I don't have

now, nor am I likely to have anytime soon, the finances to consider that kind of lifestyle."

Anna raised her fist and pretend-punched his shoulder. "Now, don't you start that again, Lawren Drake.

I thought we had dealt with those issues already. What we have, we share."

"I may have allowed you to think I agreed, Anna, but that was when I had a possibility of inheriting money from my father's family. No chance of that now."

"The situation has not changed as far as *I* am concerned." She raised her left hand with the ring on her middle finger catching the light from the train window. "Remember this? It's a promise, isn't it?"

Lawren's heart melted. How could he forget that moment in the firelight when the word 'soulmate' was first spoken between them. He touched her hand with his and pressed them together until the matched set of rings made the gentle click of silver on silver.

"I won't listen to any apologies from you, sir. I know you are a proud man and I respect that, but I value your love far more than any amount of money."

There was nothing more to be said on the subject.

Lawren kissed her hand and Anna snuggled contentedly into his shoulder. He was not, however, finished with the topic. There were mitigating factors in this possible home purchase that Anna might not have considered. If he could not contribute financially, he could always think ahead and save his lady from future problems. For the remainder of the journey his mind was busy with prospects and plans while Anna dozed against his side.

Grant met them at the Oban station and quickly disposed of Anna's case and Lawren's backpack.

When they were comfortably settled in the back of the large car, Anna looked around at the seafront of Oban and heaved a glad sigh. "It's like coming home! This is our first time arriving here together, Lawren, but I hope it will be the first of many times."

Once they had left the town behind, Anna asked, "Well, Grant, what's the news?"

Grant chuckled and replied in his soft Aberdeenshire voice, "I dinna ken if you'll have time to hear it all, Ms. Mason, but I'll at least start you off. No doubt the ladies of your acquaintance will fill in any gaps."

"That sounds intriguing, Grant. What's been happening?"

"Now then, there's the new Phoenix Cinema on George Street where the Disney film 'Brave' had its premier performance. A Waterstones bookstore has opened. One of your Highland knitting ladies has won a speed-knitting contest and beaten the holder of the Guinness Book of Records in the process.

And, you'll mind the fuss there was last November 5th when the Guy Fawkes fireworks display went off in a blaze in a mere fifty seconds instead of twenty full minutes? Well, some lad watching, put the whole

fiasco on the internet and now everyone wants another big Obang, (that's what they're calling it), this year, only it's to be all done in ten seconds, if you can believe it!"

Lawren and Anna were laughing out loud at Grant's offended tone but Anna stopped when he finished his recitation with this piece of news. "Aye, I thought there was another thing, Fiona's got a boyfriend."

"Tell me you're not kidding, Grant?"

"Not a bit of it! It's true as I'm sitting here. Mind you, she's not exactly shouting it out from McCaig's Folly up above the town. I'm thinking I'm one of the few who knows. It might be best not to say anything, Ms. Mason, until she tells you herself."

Anna thought this was good advice. Fiona was a private person who would not appreciate her personal business being a topic of speculation for all and sundry. She would wait, with whatever patience she could muster, until Fiona chose to reveal the information.

Whoever he is, I hope he's a worthy opponent. Fiona is not one to trifle with and I will appoint myself 'in loco parentis' if required to do so.

There was a welcoming committee assembled at the front door of the McCaig Estate Farmhouse.

Grant had called to alert Simon as soon as the Glasgow train had pulled into the Oban station.

Anna eagerly waved out of the car windows as they came over the rise in the track and saw the house. She tried to point out her family members for Lawren but had to give up as she was too excited to wait until the roll call was done.

Lawren settled the bill with Grant and carried their luggage up the path watching Anna greet her brother and his wife, Michelle. The older couple were the easiest to identify. He was not sure who the trim woman with thick, bouncy hair might be, but the young girl waiting beside her was obviously a daughter. His keen eye assessed Anna's brother and determined he must be more like their mother than their father. He did not have Anna's height and colouring, but his upright posture spoke of the same early training.

He stood back until the first round of hugs and chatter had been completed. Although Anna had said she did not see enough of her brother because of his busy life as an environmental engineer in Alberta, it was clear they had a great deal of affection for each other. The kind of banter that is shared by close family members had already commenced between them. Something about Simon's beer belly was being commented on by Anna. Michelle, a small, round woman with grey hair and a warm smile, took the chance to step forward and offer her hand.

"Never mind those two! It's always the same when they get together. You must be Lawren. It's great to meet you at last. We are so happy that Anna has found someone who appreciates her and I must say, we are astounded at the painting you did for her. This is Donna, our daughter, and beside her is Ashley, our granddaughter."

Lawren smiled and shook hands with the three women. Ashley seemed shy and hid behind her mother's shoulder but she held his gaze and almost started to speak to him before changing her mind and leaving the conversation to her elders for now.

"Just leave the case there, Lawren. We prepared a meal for you in the kitchen. There's nothing like travel to give you a good appetite, we always find."

Anna threw herself into his arms before he could follow Michelle. "Oh, Lawren, forgive me for deserting you. Blame Simon; *I* always do!" She turned back to her older brother who was laughing and shaking his head at her antics.

"Hi, Lawren. Good to meet you. Are you sure you know what you are doing with this one?"

Lawren did not know an appropriate response to this challenge so he let it go with only a lopsided grin as his answer. Clearly, Anna was a different, lighter person within her family group. He still had a lot to learn about her and the next few hours would be instructive.

Michelle proved to be an excellent cook and an experienced hostess. Anna praised the relay of succulent dishes she managed to produce from the ovens of the Aga.

"Well, I didn't know for sure what Lawren might like so I covered all the food groups just in case," she confessed. "You can freeze some of the leftovers and save cooking time for the rest of this week. We'll all be off to Glasgow tomorrow and you two will have the place to yourselves."

"But, I thought you were staying here for another day or two," said Anna. "We don't want you to rush off on our account. There's plenty of room."

A look was exchanged between husband and wife and Simon resumed the conversation. "We have had the most wonderful time here Anna. Everything you told us about Oban and Scotland is true. We'll be back for sure and the rest of our Calgary gang will come too. There's something Michelle and I have to tell you and something else that you need to know." Simon paused for effect and Anna interrupted.

"All right! That's enough of the mysterious hinting. What's going on?"

"Patience, my dear sister! Patience! You know, that virtue you never did find the time for?"

Anna threw him a glance and Simon moved on speedily. "Michelle and I are moving from Alberta to Prince Edward island."

This announcement stunned Anna to immobility. Her mouth fell open.

"I know it's unexpected, but with retirement overdue, we decided to get as far from the rat race as we could, and spend our declining years close to the ocean and the fresh air of the Atlantic coast."

Michelle continued as soon as Simon drew a breath. "Simon won't tell you, but he is tired of struggling with the oil sands projects and their environmental impact. It's been a good living for us and the family, however, and now we want to do something for ourselves. We've bought a large cottage near the shore between Victoria and Charlottetown, so the girls, their brother Ken, and all the grandkids, can come and stay any time and, of course, now that we know how wonderful it is here, we can hop across to Scotland when this place is free."

Anna blinked rapidly as she attempted to absorb this unexpected information. She could see that Simon was waiting anxiously for her response so she gathered her thoughts together and answered with delight. "This is great news! You will love the milder winter in PEI and Lawren and I can visit you there when the family are busy working. One thing I have discovered since coming here to Scotland is the difference it makes to live near the sea. This is a decision you two will never regret. Well done!"

She nodded to Simon and asked, "Is there any wine? I feel like a toast is required."

"My thoughts exactly!" responded Simon. He disappeared into the larder off the kitchen and emerged with two bottles in hand. "Red and white; take your pick and let's get started on that food. You first, Lawren. You are the guest today."

Lawren obediently filled his plate. Eating might save him from the questions that would surely come at this meal. He was not certain he was ready to open up to Anna's family until he knew them a lot better.

It was much later in the afternoon when Anna remembered that Simon had hinted there were two pieces of information he had to share.

Lawren and Ashley had ventured up Helen's Hill together as she wanted to show him the patch of blackberry bushes that had provided the pie he raved about at lunch.

Anna was sitting in the garden lazily watching their progress up the steep hill. The sun was shining on the front of the house as well as on the hill, but she was in the shade and the cool air forced her to get up and return to the house to find her brother.

"Simon! Where are you?"

His reply came from the lounge where he and Michelle were making up the pull-out bed for the night.

She found them there and fetched the duvet that kept the bed cozy.

"I'm glad I caught you two together. Listen, are you sure you need to leave Oban so soon?"

"Absolutely! There's a special reason why. I meant to tell you about this at lunch but we were having too much fun eating and drinking to introduce the subject."

"Is this the other thing you mentioned?"

"Right! Sit down Anna. We got a call from Ross and Joyce in Glasgow."

Anna at once felt remorse because she had not had the chance to fill her brother in on the events at the Kelvinside house. "I am sorry, Simon. You must have been shocked to hear from them. I did not warn you they might call."

"Don't worry, sis. They explained everything. They said you had given them your Oban info and mentioned we were here."

Michelle reassured Anna with her interpretation of Ross and Joyce's personalities. "They could not have been nicer, Anna. They welcomed us to the family and spoke very highly of you and they insisted that we stay one night with them before we return to Canada. It seemed to us a really good chance to meet them in person. It's not every day of the week you discover a whole new branch of the family, especially in yours and Simon's circumstances."

"You're right of course, Michelle. I thought they were extremely kind and considerate. We had a good, long talk about family matters and, honestly, I felt at home with them after only a few hours. I'll be keen to know how they seem to you when you meet face to face."

Simon had been listening to this exchange and now he moved from the end of the bed and sat on the arm of his sister's chair. "Isn't life strange? To suddenly find we have a living, breathing Aunt and Uncle, not to mention a whole clan of cousins, after all these years of believing we were alone in the world. What would Dad have said if he had known about a younger brother?"

"That's the sad part, Simon. Our father and mother deliberately chose to separate themselves from any connection to Scotland. I can't help thinking how much they missed."

"Well, that's not going to happen to us. Agreed?"

"Agreed! There's no excuse now that we'll be closer together in the future. We'll start by planning our next reunion before you leave."

The brother and sister exchanged a high five and did it again with Michelle.

Anna had one more important thing to say.

"I am so glad you brought Donna and Ashley here. I want everyone to share this place with us. There were sad times here for Aunt Helen once, but with every laugh and each happy moment, it seems to me the sadness is lifting and there's a new beginning for all of us."

Much later that evening when silence had fallen at last on the farmhouse, Lawren and Anna lay in bed whispering, in that intimate couple's prelude to sleep. Moonlight streamed through the window and laid moving patterns on the bed and the floor. The painting above the fireplace was in deep shadow but it was that subject that prompted Lawren to speak.

"I like Ashley. She's quite bright for a teenager. She asked me a number of interesting questions about my painting of you and your Aunt Helen while we were up on top of the hill."

"Oh! What did she want to know?"

"It seems she has been studying the portrait while they have been here. She says she sees things in the borders and the background of the painting that I never intended."

Anna came fully awake. "What kinds of things?"

"She is convinced there are clues about where the castle is and she sees printing on the book with words about Helen's family. She is somewhat obsessed with the subject and asked me a lot of questions."

"What did you tell her?"

"I told her to ask you. I suspect she is writing information down, for what purpose I don't know. It is an interesting story, you must admit, particularly for a young person who loves mysteries."

"Do you think she is slightly psychic like you, Lawren?"

"I doubt it, although I haven't ever encountered anyone with the kind of vibes I have. I do have a feeling you will have an e mail correspondence with Ashley when she gets back home."

"I won't mind that at all. If she wants to write about Helen, I will encourage her, although she will have to use different names and dates, of course. We could have an author in the family. I don't think Helen would mind, do you?"

The question remained unanswered. Lawren had drifted off to sleep.

Chapter Sixteen

"I know it was a very short visit, Lawren, but what did you think about my family?"

"Do you want the truth?"

Anna was sitting on the kitchen window seat, hugging her sweater close to her for extra warmth and stroking Morag, who had hardly left Lawren's side since they had arrived at the farmhouse. The weather had broken overnight and the sky was obscured by rolling dark clouds. The temperature had dropped significantly and rain was beginning to drip down the huge panes of glass.

Lawren's question seemed to bode ill, but Anna needed to know what he felt about her brother and sister-in-law. She realized there was a lot for him to adjust to lately, especially since he had been living a solitary life until she had met him a comparatively short time ago.

He brought a cup of coffee over to her and sat down on the wide cushion. Morag immediately claimed a spot on his knees and purred happily. The kitchen had that strange quietness that follows the exit of a large and voluble group. Simon's rented car stuffed with people, luggage and souvenir purchases had rocked down the path and out of sight on the way to Glasgow at an early hour in the morning.

Anna twined her fingers around the hot cup and waited to hear Lawren's verdict.

"First, you are lucky to have such a good relationship with your brother, Anna. Perhaps it is because you don't live in each other's pockets or maybe just because you are alike in many ways.

Secondly, Simon is extremely fortunate to have found a wife who is so compatible with him. It's obvious they are two halves of a whole. They complement each other perfectly and I can tell their home life is happy and filled with children, grandchildren and family concerns.

I would really like to meet the rest of their children one day as Donna is a great recommendation. She is quiet and observant and dotes on Ashley without restricting her in any way. I saw her tear up last evening when Ashley was talking about how much she loves this house and Scotland. It could mean that she loses her daughter to another land some day but her main concern was that daughter's happiness."

Anna was astonished at Lawren's perceptive analysis of her family. His comments explained why he had been content to sit back and listen last night as the group related their adventures and joked about the big changes to come when they moved to PEI.

In a way, Anna was alarmed at his acuity. What would he say if she dared ask his honest opinion of herself? How did he truly feel about the fact that neither of them could expect to share the full family life that Simon and Michelle had created together? For a brief moment she deeply regretted that she and Lawren had not met in their youthful years.

"Does it make you sad to see a close family like that? Believe me it's ten times more chaotic when all of them are in the same room."

"No, it's a wonderful thing to behold, my dearest, but I am more than content with only we two …….. and Morag of course!"

. . .

It had taken a day or two of solitude for them to relax. It had been a rollercoaster ride of emotions for both of them since they had left Canada. The current inclement weather kept them indoors where they were happy to read, talk and plan for the future.

Lawren had given thought to Alina's announcement about buying another condo in the London complex. He introduced the topic one afternoon when they had retired by the lounge fire with glasses of wine and a selection of cheeses to spread on oatcakes.

"I want to suggest an alternative to Alina's idea about purchasing a condo with Philip."

Anna immediately gave him her full attention. She wondered what Lawren's concern would be. Their brief previous conversation on the topic had not caused him to express any great interest.

"I've been thinking about Alina's situation with her eyesight. Your condo is set up to give Alina many aids to help her if her macular degeneration becomes a serious handicap. The kitchen has a number of improvements like the bright tape on counter edges and the dishes with circular rings of colour. The cooker, too, has special knobs for limited sight and the phones have enlarged numbers."

Once again Anna was astonished at Lawren's powers of observation. He had never mentioned any of these items before, but he had obviously been noticing everything.

"Another thing is her garden. She loves those hostas and a new place might not have the shady yard they need."

"What are you getting at, Lawren?"

"Well, I've been thinking it would be much easier for us to move and Alina to stay put where she is most safe and comfortable, that's all."

"But that's a brilliant idea and the most generous thing I can imagine. I know you two have not always seen eye to eye about things and this could be the gesture that changes the situation for everyone."

"You mean you think it would work?"

"Of course it would! I could be close enough to help Alina if she should need it and we could continue our business projects together. Yet, all four of us would have the privacy we need whenever we need it. It would be a fresh start for us, Lawren. I'll get Alina onto the real estate agent as soon as possible. She might even have an available condo unit in mind already."

She stopped abruptly as a new thought occurred to her.

"Wait! Did you mean we should buy in the same condo complex or in another location further away?"

"No, I like where you live. It's convenient when you have to travel and it's as quiet and well-maintained as anywhere else in the city. Besides, your warehouse for A Plus is not far away."

"True enough! What did you think about Alina's suggestion of a studio for you in the condo? There would be plenty of room."

"I would rather keep my studio for now. Everything I need is there and the downtown location is useful. My father has already moved into the retirement residence he spoke about and he seems more than pleased with the facilities so I don't have to worry about having him so close. I see now that extra space will be needed for family visitors in the future."

Lawren hesitated for a moment then went on. "I am still concerned about finances, Anna."

"Now, before you get started on that, I have a few things to say. Philip has plenty of money and he can buy my half of the condo. That leaves only one half to fund and I can easily afford that. I would like you to choose furnishings, Lawren. What we have is too feminine for your taste, I'm sure. We can do that gradually as you wish. There's plenty of time."

Lawren was well aware that Anna was trying to save him from embarrassment with this furniture-buying scheme. He also knew it was useless to try to make her understand his reluctance to be what his father would call 'a kept man'. The situation made him even more determined to make a success with his painting.

On reflection, he realized he might have lacked a certain impetus to succeed before. His simple needs did not require stringent efforts to earn money and he had basically lived like an impoverished student for many years. Things were different now. He was a woman's avowed partner, a member of a large family group and, who knows, perhaps more in the near future. If he was to be able to hold his head high in that future, he would have to start soon to earn a more than respectable income.

The phone rang allowing him to avoid answering Anna's implied question. She got up from their comfortable perch and walked over to the wall signalling with her eyes, curiosity about who might be calling on such a wet day.

"Hello!"

"*Hi Anna! So good to hear your voice.*"

"Yours too, Bev. How are you all?"

"*That's what I'm calling about. Look, you two lovebirds have had enough quiet time together. It's time to catch up with the rest of us exiles. Jeanette is on her way over here with the baby and Alan is coming to the farmhouse to collect you two in ten minutes. No excuses! Tell Lawren to bring his drawing pad.*"

"Yes, ma'am!" replied Anna, with thinly-disguised laughter in her voice.

"*Can't wait to see you, too! We'll be ready!*"

Lawren borrowed a long Barbour coat and happily went off with Alan to see how Duncan was working out with his sire, Prince, in sheep herding skills. The pair was becoming renowned in the area and Alan wanted to show off.

"In any case", he murmured to Lawren, "You'll never get a word in sideways when these women get together. You'll be better off outside and the rain looks to be tapering off now."

Bev and Anna had a lot to catch up on. It seemed like life

was accelerating for both of them and there was much more happening than there used to be in the lives they led previously, in London.

Once Anna's relationship with Lawren had been approved and the news of her discovery of an Uncle Ross and Aunt Joyce had been announced, to Bev's great surprise, the focus turned to Bev's updates.

"I have to tell you how much I enjoyed meeting Simon. He is a fine man and that Michelle is something else entirely. She came over here and helped out with a batch of baking for a women's group that booked the country cooking facility in the tea room, and she even gave me a recipe for cranberry scones *and* she's going to send over the cranberries!"

"I know; she's amazing! Simon is lucky to have her. They have a wonderful family life and soon they will be living in PEI. Isn't it great!"

Anna paused to take another sip of Bev's Canadian-style coffee which she kept especially for her friends.

"Now, what about *your* family, Bev?"

"Well, Eric is doing great here, I am happy to say. He has loads of friends and he loves the country life although he is still a computer nut like his older brother."

"That compulsion did James no harm, remember? He is invaluable to A Plus and has several other business clients, I understand. How is he doing? Any romance on the scene?"

"I think you mean, Caroline? I suppose you could call it a kind of romance. They see each other occasionally when she is in England but she works overseas a lot in emerging economies and refugee camps."

"So she is focused on her career?"

"James admits she has a big future ahead of her. She wants to start an NGO then venture into politics. She is a world-changer, if there is such a phrase. James is betting she'll be the next female Prime Minister in either Britain or Canada, or possibly both!"

"Wow! Now, there's an ambition for you. Only, I do hope

she will consider a personal life also. I think it can be lonely all by yourself at the top."

"I imagine so, Anna, but there's at least one guy who is willing to follow her there, if she doesn't wait too long."

Both women thought about their own lives and how important timing had been for them and also the benefit of having someone special to come home to.

"Speaking of waiting, shouldn't Jeanette be here by now?"

"Right! There's something I want to ask you about before she arrives."

Anna could not think what Bev was referring to but she waited for the explanation.

"We, that is Alina, Maria, Susan and I, would like to add Jeanette to the Samba group, if you agree.

One surprised heartbeat later Anna responded. "It's a wonderful idea. I only wish I had thought of it first."

"Great! In case you were wondering about the name change, we thought we could call ourselves SAMBAJ. It has a nice exotic ring to it."

"I love it! Jeanette is a Canadian originally, of course, so that fits perfectly but, I must tell you, Bev, that I have had thoughts of my own about the future of Samba. This group of close friends has been such an influence on all of our lives that it should not die out when we are beyond the point of being able to give each other that help any more."

"I hope that point does not come for a very long time. What are you getting at Anna?"

"I've been thinking we should do exactly what you suggest and incorporate some younger members to bring new life into the group. Jeanette is a perfect candidate to start with and possibly we could ask Fiona. It could be an International Samba group without worrying about the extra letters. Hey! Maybe one day Caroline could join us if she isn't too busy running the world!"

Laughter filled the kitchen and neither woman heard Jeanette arrive with baby Annette in a carry seat on her arm.

"All right, you two! What's going on here? Anna come and get your wee namesake before she breaks my arm."

"My pleasure, Jeanette! Oh, you have grown so, my darling girl. Come and sit with your godmother for a while. I have things to tell you."

Jeanette and Bev exchanged a fond glance as they watched Anna settle Annette on her knee and gently wiggle her arms out of her velveteen coat, talking all the while in that soothing voice that women naturally adopt when talking to babies and small animals.

"That's Annette occupied for a while," said Jeanette, with a sigh of relief. "Now it's up to you, Bev, to fill me in on what's been happening here. I am behind in all the gossip and it's not fair!"

By the time Bev had told Jeanette all the news, including her admission to the Sambas, Lawren and Alan had arrived back and the reason for Bev's request to Lawren to bring his sketch book was revealed.

Jeanette informed him that George was anxious to start on the family portrait painting that he had commissioned months ago on Lawren's first visit to Oban. She asked if it would be possible to begin preliminary sketches right away while Annette was sitting so calmly on Anna's lap.

Lawren agreed, and added that he could do the portrait in two separate segments; one with Jeanette and the baby and the other with George and Liam blending them together at a later point.

"Oh, that sounds excellent!" exclaimed Jeanette. "We were worried that you might not have enough time to get ahead with the painting on this visit with Anna taking up all your waking hours, as she does."

Anna would have protested loudly at this, but she feared the baby would be alarmed. Jeanette had already figured that out so she smiled to show she was only joking.

A search began, to find a spot in the house where the light was suitable for Lawren to sketch by.

Anna handed over her warm and sleepy charge and she and Bev resumed their conversation while Alan heated up one of Bev's famous home-made soups and sliced bread for the group.

"What's this I hear about Fiona? Is it true she has a man in her life? How did that happen? She's just starting in her new job and seems so anxious to succeed."

Bev revealed the little she had heard and finished the short recitation by suggesting Anna speak to Jeanette. "Apparently George knows more about the young man than anyone else in town and undoubtedly he has passed on information to his wife."

Anna had to be content with this delay. Little did she know that in George McLennan's Oban office the young man in question was being grilled about his intentions, at that very moment.

Chapter Seventeen

"You are perfectly within your rights to tell me to mind my own business, Mr. Campbell, but my wife and I consider Fiona to be one of our family, ever since her Granny died, and we care deeply what happens to her."

George stretched his neck and shrugged his shoulders in discomfort at having spoken to a client in such a manner. Truth be told, he would never have chosen to introduce the personal element into his business dealings but Jeanette had insisted that *they* were responsible for looking after the young woman in lieu of her parents and family. The words she had said were burned on George's brain.

"We would hope someone would do the same for our two should, God forbid, anything occur that would remove them from our care."

Tears had fallen as Jeanette gave this speech and the sight of those tears had undone George to such a degree that he had made the promise now being fulfilled in excruciating embarrassment for him.

He raised his eyes to see how his comment had been received by the handsome young man seated before him across the width of his desk.

Gordon Campbell appeared totally confused by this turn of events. He had made an appointment to discuss updating his will, and, out of nowhere, the previously-reserved solicitor, Mr. McLennan, had launched into a statement about a young woman he had met only a couple of times.

"Hold on a minute!" he protested. "I take it you are talking about Fiona Jameson? I hardly know her. We met over estate matters and I invited her to go to the pictures in Oban with me out of politeness and because I don't know many people here in the town. Are you saying someone has reported to you that I have done something to harm Fiona?"

Gordon jumped to his feet and scraped the chair back over the floor as he continued to speak in an increasingly aggrieved tone. "I have heard the rumours about small towns and the gossip mill that exists there, but this is simply ridiculous. I can assure you, Mr. McLennan, that Fiona is safe from any further meetings or dates with me. I hope that satisfies you, sir."

Before George could summon up a single word to refute his client's impassioned accusations, the young man had stormed out of the office and clattered down the stairs at such speed that the secretary came rushing in to see what had happened to her boss.

"Are you all right, Mr. McLennan? Did that man assault you in any way? He left in such a hurry, I was afraid you might be lying in a pool of blood on the floor."

George found his voice soon enough to reassure his secretary of his continued health but as soon as she had left he was engulfed in horror at what he had done. Not only had he insulted a new client, and newcomer to the town, but he had also ruined whatever chance there had been of a relationship between Fiona and the fellow.

His first impulse was to blame Jeanette. Then he realized he would have to tell his wife about this sad incident in order to assign blame to her. In the process he would, no doubt, be required to listen to her complaints at the way in which he had mishandled the entire situation.

This prospect did not appeal to him at all.

Best to keep quiet for now, and wait to see if things work out on their own.

Fiona had been excessively busy catching up with work assignments since her Land Rover had been restored to full operational status. She set out early each morning to fetch the vehicle from the main car park in town where she had special permission to park overnight. The narrow road between her cottage and the sea path left no room for private parking of any kind.

She usually enjoyed the short walk. It allowed her to sample the weather and look over the sea shore before any but the sea-going fishing trawlers disturbed the calm of the day. Occasionally she would spot some wild life as the early mist gradually lifted over the water. Recently she had the thrill of seeing a sea eagle soaring on its eight feet wingspan and silently scanning the shore for fish. She had stopped still and removed her camera from her deep uniform jacket pocket and slowly brought the viewfinder to her eyes. She could see why the sea eagles had been named 'Flying Barn Doors'. They really were enormous creatures with distinctive white tail, yellow legs and yellow 'meat cleaver' bill. This one was an adult at almost three feet in length and must be one of the group of sixteen birds introduced back into Scotland from Norway in 2010.

She had carefully depressed the button and snapped the first picture then continued to shoot while the eagle was in sight, without taking the time to see if her efforts were successful. Experience had taught her that if she took a sufficient number of photographs some would usually be suitable for enlarging.

In addition, she would occasionally find something in a

picture she had not intended to capture and that one was always the very best shot.

She smiled at the memory. An enlarged photograph of that recent morning's eagle encounter was now hanging on Callum Moir's veterinary surgery wall and, she had been told, receiving rave reviews.

There was nothing unusual to see this particular morning. In truth, she was more focused internally than on the exterior world.

There was the slightly annoying situation with Gordon Campbell. She thought they had made quite a nice connection when they had gone to the Phoenix Cinema. They had laughed at the same places in the film and found agreement, over a cup of coffee in the nearby restaurant, about the more stereotypical parts of Disney's interpretations of Scottish accents and traditions. She had noticed one or two side glances at them from the locals as they sat chatting but surely that was not enough to discourage him.

Gordon had politely escorted her to her cottage door afterwards although any of the Oban population could have told him she was more than capable of fending off any late night drunks by herself.

They had shaken hands at the door and he thanked her for her company. It all seemed perfectly pleasant and appropriate. And yet, no phone call; no note; no anything in the week since.

Had she done something to put him off? She reran the evening in her mind once more and could find nothing on which to pin this disappointment. Not that she was well experienced in such situations. She could have missed a crucial moment when she had said or done something 'off-putting' as Granny would say. The trouble was that her inexperience gave her no clues to work with.

Ach, well! I have other things to concentrate on today. If Gordon Campbell is too snooty to want to spend time with me, it's his loss.

She climbed into the Land Rover after checking the tires,

then she turned on the windscreen wipers and watched as the mist and dew scattered from her view.

As the powerful engine warmed up, she glanced over the checklist on the clipboard on the front seat beside her.

Keep a lookout for:
a) Greenland White-Fronted Geese. Now protected by international agreement.
b) Red squirrels in the area, particularly near housing estates.
c) Grey seal cows feeding pups on rocky shores. Note numbers.
d) Watch for flocks of swallows gathering.
Meet:
1) Scottish Natural Heritage officer, Kenneth MacNeil, at 1:00pm sharp in the Fort William office for an interim review.
2) Party of American tourists who want to hear about the recent work of the John Muir Trust in Skye. 3:30pm.
Contact Labour Party member of the Scottish Parliament, Rhoda Grant, by phone link for additional comments and information for the American group.

As she glanced over the list of the day's activities she wondered if it would be too forward of her to stop in to see Gordon Campbell on her way home from Skye to Oban. She was in two minds about this and thought she would decide later in the day depending on how things went for her.

She had a folder of report copies for Kenneth MacNeil but he should already have access to everything she had been doing since she started in the job. She felt reasonably confident that he would have nothing negative to comment on. She pulled back her shoulders and took a deep breath as she headed north in the car.

Attitude is everything! Not over-confident, but self-assured; that's the ticket!

. . .

The mental trick must have worked well, for Fiona had a positive report from Kenneth MacNeil, who was acknowledged as a difficult man to please in the Wildlife Service corps. He had actually stated that Fiona Jameson might make a name for herself in the future if she carried on in this way. She was elated to have this support at the beginning of her apprentice year and it confirmed her belief that her whole life had led up to this career choice.

She drove across the bridge linking the mainland with the Isle of Skye in a great good humour and soon found the party of Americans in their hotel in Dunvegan. They greeted her warmly and occupied the first fifteen minutes with exclamations of delight about Skye's rugged mountains and the lovely children they had met who were responsible for building a dry-stone wall as part of their school project.

Fiona's purpose was to supply information about John Muir. The Americans had already visited Dunbar on the east coast of Scotland and spent several hours in his birthplace there; a modest three-storey house on the High Street which had been expertly converted into a museum.

She judged that the Americans knew as much as she did about the Scot, born in 1838, who was more famous in the United States than he was in his native land. When she had learned about John Muir in her university courses, she, and most of her class, were amazed at what this lowly young man had accomplished. His work as the pioneer of conservation was extraordinary and resulted in a campaign to preserve the Yosemite Valley in California and subsequently the Sierra Club movement in the states, of which the current group of visitors were avid members.

"I cannot believe the power and determination of that young man," enthused one of the women.

"He had a stern, religious father who would have beaten down any youngster, and yet he escaped from his home as often as he could and found solace in the beauty of the countryside around him."

"Quite true, Hildy," commented another of the ladies who sported a hair style in a strange shade of lilac. "John Muir has had an enormous influence on the national parks system in North America and now we have learned that in his own Scotland, the Trust in his name continues his work to preserve wild lands and wild places such as we have seen here on Skye."

As expected, Fiona could not add much to the group's knowledge but she had a role to play in encouraging them to contribute to the John Muir Trust itself. Monetary awards were given each year to deserving projects in Scotland. Fiona had seen the difference made to the walkers' path at Sandwood Bay after Trust money had been spent to restore its former beauty.

It took only a few minutes talk with the MSP, Rhoda Grant, to persuade the Americans to part with a large cheque from their John Muir U.S. chapter.

Fiona answered questions about her role as a wildlife officer and showed a selection of photographs from her camera's memory. One of the women wanted Fiona to send her a print of the sea eagle and left contact information to enable her to do so.

A damn fine day was Fiona's concluding thought after she bade farewell to the ladies.

Crossing over the bridge again, she thought about the significance of bridges in life. They formed links between mainland and island allowing people to pass over easily in any weather but they also permitted connections between families to be formed. She had stopped in, briefly, to the McCaig Estate Farm House to welcome Anna's brother and family to Scotland and that visit had reminded her how important Anna's role was in forging links. Were it not for Anna's arrival in Oban and her influence on local events and people, Bev would never have married Alan Matthews, several island women might not have had profitable jobs with A Plus, and Fiona herself would not have found a friend and family in Jeanette, George and the children, as well, of course, as the vital role Anna had played in her own life.

These musings led Fiona to reconsider Gordon Campbell. What if he was meant to be a linking-type of person in her life? If she ignored that possibility she might be affecting her own future and that of others as yet unknown to her.

She rolled down the windows and took a deep breath of the sea-salted air.

It's not normal for me to be thinking this way. I must be influenced by these enthusiastic women from across the sea who have brought my softer side to the fore. I have always prided myself on independence. I often claimed I could do it all by myself and, for most of my life, that is exactly how I have survived.

As soon as this thought occurred, Fiona realized it was not the whole truth. Her Granny had supplied the orphaned child with a loving home for years. Much of her 'independence' was encouraged by that wise woman who knew she would be long gone when her granddaughter was still a young woman with her way to make in the world. Undoubtedly her work ethic came from Granny who never let a waking hour go by without some useful task accomplished. The very cottage Fiona lived in was thanks to her Granny's generosity. The taxi business that had kept her solvent had been supported by her driving partner, Grant, for many years. Clients like George McLennan had actively promoted her services and, of course, introduced her to Anna Mason.

How could she pride herself on her independence when, in fact, she had leaned on the strength of so many people?

A wave of shame swept over her and she acknowledged that a little humility was required.

In this chastened frame of mind, Fiona decided to pay a visit to Glenmorie Castle on the off chance that Gordon Campbell was working indoors rather than out on the moors.

After all, it's on my way home. It can't do any harm to offer an olive branch of peace. Or should that be a branch of heather?

• • •

It did not take long to find the Castle driveway. As she approached the stately tower house a flock of white doves from the nearby dovecot circled around her Land Rover and Fiona took this as a good sign related to her thoughts about olive branches and peacemaking.

She opened the stableyard gates and walked through the cobbled yard toward the estate office. The light was dimming as the day wound to a close and she saw lamplight spilling onto the cobbles near the entrance. *He must be there!*

Her heart skipped a beat and she wished she had taken the time to tidy her hair and put on some lipstick. *Too late now!*

Gordon Campbell looked up from the paperwork littering his desk and saw the outline of Fiona Jameson at his office door. He was genuinely surprised to see her but after a long, hard day with a party of inexperienced hunters who had almost shot one of his prized retrievers and scared off every deer and grouse in the entire area, he lacked the mental energy to send her packing. He would not, however, let her escape without understanding how she had embarrassed him in the town.

He opened the door for Fiona and at once she felt a chill in the atmosphere that had nothing to do with the deepening dusk.

"Well, this is a surprise! I hadn't expected to see *you* again, Fiona."

"Why not? I was passing this way and thought I could check up on the wildcat project."

The convenient lie had come swiftly to Fiona's mind when she sensed the atmosphere. This visit might be short and not so sweet after all.

"Now you're here, you might as well come in."

Fiona bridled at this less-than-polite invitation. She almost turned on her heel and made a quick exit but her pride would not allow this attitude to go unchallenged. She decided to get right to the point.

"You seem to be upset with me about something, Mr. Campbell. I would prefer if you came out with it. I am not an admirer of snide comments."

Gordon was taken aback by this frontal attack. The women in his family were never usually this confrontational.

He hummed and hawed for a moment then spoke in a more conciliatory tone.

"You may not like snide comments, Miss Jameson, but I greatly dislike being a subject of speculation in the town. I have no idea what information about me you have spread around to all and sundry but a portion of that at least is derogatory."

Fiona was shocked into temporary silence by this statement and by the tone of voice that still contained a sense of deep hurt. She scrambled in her mind to find the right words to refute these baseless accusations and could find no suitable words at all. The result of her mental confusion was a verbal stutter and a facial expression that could not conceal her total disbelief.

"I,…….. I,………. I'm afraid I have no clue what you are talking about, Gordon. I am not one to spread gossip or innuendo. In fact I have spoken to *no one* about our date and I am completely innocent of spreading anything derogatory about you, even if I knew anything like that."

Despite her attempt to keep control of her feelings, Fiona could feel tears forming in the corners of her eyes. She turned away abruptly and reached out for the door handle. Escape from this painful situation was the only thing left that made any sense to her.

She was a few yards away from the office and stumbling over the cobblestones with bleary eyes, when she felt a strong hand on her shoulder.

"God help me, Fiona! I am so sorry for accusing you. Obviously there is a massive misunderstanding. Please forgive me and come back inside."

She tried to keep her head down so he would not see her

tears but he gently put a finger under her chin and raised her face to his then, even more gently, wiped the tears from her cheeks. It was this unexpected and tender action that undid the intrepid Fiona Jameson.

The next thing she knew, his arms were around her and he practically carried her back across the yard and into his office where he deposited her on his chair with clucking sounds of concern that would have done justice to a mother hen.

Fiona recovered her composure and felt a feeling of déjà vu. Wasn't this what had happened the first time they met? Misunderstandings and confusion had reigned then also. Was that a good omen for the future?

"Look! I can make us a cup of coffee," he suggested hesitantly. "It's just instant, I'm afraid, but a hot drink might help right at the moment."

Fiona was not sure anything would help but as he busied himself with boiling water and spooned coffee out of a large jar, she had time to gather her thoughts. Strangely, the little domestic scene in the office was reassuring to her. So much of her life in the last years had been solitary. Even the university experience in a residence hall had been isolating. Her prior life had been so different from that of her classmates that it was difficult to make friends. The simple act of having a man make coffee for her seemed, now, to assume huge importance.

She accepted the stoneware mug with the chipped edge and turned it around in her hands while she composed her next statement. She had a feeling it was going to be something significant.

Suddenly, two futures rushed up to meet her. One was a life alone and the other offered companionship. She did not know who the companion might be but her choice now would be the key turning point toward, or away from, that destiny.

"Gordon, I am going to be honest with you. I don't play games the way some females seem to do.

I enjoyed our evening together and I would like to see you

again sometime. I know you are new to the area and if you wish, I can introduce you to people you might be interested in, if that is all you want from me. I have many acquaintances in Oban but I am basically a loner. I don't apologize for this.

I suppose it is the result of life patterns forced on me."

She took a deep breath and continued.

"Don't hesitate to send me on my way. It's your choice. Despite the display of weakness you just saw, I can take the rejection. Don't worry about that."

This confession was made while Fiona looked deep into her coffee cup and now she prepared to rise and leave without exposing herself to looks of pity or embarrassment on Gordon Campbell's face.

She consoled herself with the thought that it was best to bring contentious issues out into the open right at the start of a relationship and not to harbor false hopes.

She would go with some dignity left.

Fiona never made it to the door.

She was turned round roughly by two strong hands. A stern voice instructed her to look at his face.

"You have done me the rare honour of being honest, Fiona Jameson, and I will do the same for you.

But not here.

Follow me!"

Chapter Eighteen

He took her arm and steered her across the dark stableyard to the oak doors leading into the Castle.

Neither one spoke as they ascended the stone steps to the upper levels of the building and entered a reception room of huge dimensions that served as dining hall, living room and display area in which the family coat of arms of the Campbells was proudly displayed above an imposing fireplace, and ancient weapons were arranged around the walls between the noble racks of deer antlers.

The baronial hall was a history lesson at a glance.

Fiona was intrigued rather than afraid at this turn of events. She gazed around at tartan fabric on the high-backed chairs and saw stuffed animals in glass domes and wondered why Gordon Campbell had brought her here.

Her unspoken question was soon answered.

He indicated that she should sit near the fireplace and as soon as he had set light to the wood and coal inside the grate, he stood in front of the fire with his head barely reaching the mantel and looked up toward the barrel ceiling as if challenged to be as honest as Fiona had been, but afraid he might not be able to continue if he watched her face.

He began slowly then gained speed as he warmed to his

subject and realized he would not be interrupted by his listener.

"I am the only son of a large family in which there have been girls for generations. My birth was welcomed with jubilation and my future set before I could talk. I don't recall any choices being offered.

My task in life was to be the long-awaited son and heir, inheritor of the proud name of Campbell, protected and cherished by a horde of sisters and female relatives and expected to do my duty in all respects.

My father was a clan chief on the Borders of Scotland. He ran a tight ship, as it were, and employed a large staff of experienced men and women whose families had served Campbells faithfully for close to a hundred years. He was an ex-naval officer with high standards and expected to be obeyed without question.

I did as I was told.

Like many Scots of a certain standing in life, I was sent to England to be educated among the upper classes; those who would soon form the ranks of policy makers and financial wizards of Britain. It was a liberation of sorts for me. I met young men whose wealthy, tolerant upbringings were very different from my own and whose main ambitions in life were to escape the shackles of adult supervision and break free to indulge themselves while they could. Within the university student population there was a palpable sense of a looming deadline. Beyond the end of formal schooling, nothing existed for them other than the twin pillars of duty and death.

I truly tried to disentangle myself from my early conditioning. I went to bars and nightclubs. I accepted invitations to country houses far more elaborate and impressive than my own. I was presented with a series of eligible sisters and fashionable women who attempted to initiate me into their society.

Perhaps it was memories of my own sisters that got in the

way. I was patently unable to treat women as casually as seemed to be required of me.

For a while I drank and danced with abandon until the night I found myself alone on a terrace gazing at the moon sailing above me. I was waiting for an amorous young lady to join me with more drinks; drinks I did not need. I suddenly had a moment of clarity. I was once more falling into an old trap. I was doing exactly what was expected of me with no thought for what I really wanted to do.

I left the garden and the lady behind me and drove all night to Scotland. I needed time to sort out who and what I truly was. I calculated I had a day or two before all hell broke loose behind me. For that brief period I slept in my car and drove wherever the road led me.

Eventually, a calm descended on me as the vast empty spaces of Scottish moor, loch and seascape began to teach me what in life is important. *I* had to be the one in charge of my fate. *I* had to choose for myself.

I remembered a Campbell Castle where a cousin lived and turned the car in that direction. My cousin had gone but the position of estate manager was vacant. I had no official training for the post but I had watched my father manage his properties for years and I had walked the Borders' hills, dales and forests with dogs, hunters and fishermen since I was a boy.

The name helped of course. I took the job and began to learn what it is like to work every hour of the day trying to establish a new persona. It was damnable hard work, Fiona, and it still is. I have little or no time to relax but I love every minute of it and at last I know where I was meant to be.

I am my own man now."

Fiona had not dared to move a muscle while the fascinating story unfolded before her. She had a dozen questions to ask but kept quiet as Gordon appeared to be steeling himself for yet another confession.

"There was only one thing lacking in my new existence,

Fiona. I think, *I hope,* I found it in you the first moment I set eyes on you."

Fiona gasped as his words electrified her. Gordon Campbell immediately turned those solemn grey eyes on her and reached for her hands.

"Not what you expected to hear, I am sure, and quite possibly far too much information, but I had to make you understand why I reacted the way I did. I need a serious lot of coaching to be the romantic highlander you deserve and I want you, Fiona, to be my coach."

No man had ever bared his soul to her as this man had dared to do. His very vulnerability shattered her defenses. There was only one true response.

She rose to meet him and for a few moments, as their lips merged, no words were necessary.

When they moved far enough apart to study each other's face, they saw amazement and acceptance mirrored there, and also the beginning of the inevitable questions.

"Can two independent individuals from entirely different backgrounds come together like this, so quickly?" she asked.

"I can't wait to find out!" he answered. "But there are two important tests you must pass before we can be sure."

Fiona would have been worried by this demand had not his eyes glittered with amusement.

"Bring them on!" she challenged.

What on earth could he ask her to do?

"First, you must let down your hair for me."

"Simple enough," she said, as she pulled the hairband out and let her straight brown hair swing forward around her face.

He did not ask, just ran his fingers through her hair with a deep sigh of satisfaction.

"I have been aching to do that, Fiona Jameson.

Second, and much more difficult, you must declare whether or not you love dogs."

She couldn't resist laughing at this strange request. "I may not have found a man I loved before now, Gordon Campbell, but I can assure you that cats and dogs love me without reservation and the feeling is mutual."

She thought about Sylvester and Morag, the animals at Callum Moir's vet surgery, and Alan Matthews' two Border collies and smiled confidently.

"Good! My own dog, Hector, is on the floor above. He stands guard for me each night outside the bedroom door."

"Excuse me! Are you inviting me to inspect your sleeping quarters?"

She produced a show of mock horror despite her secret delight that this brand-new relationship was moving forward at warp speed. She had a lot of catching-up to do in this area.

He did not deny the invitation so Fiona pushed the agenda even further.

"Is it possible you are asking me to spend the night with you, sir?"

"Well, only if Hector approves of you of course!"

Fiona briefly considered displaying more maidenly shock and horror but she was overcome with the sheer, bold assurance of his statement and contented herself with a fist attack, parried at once by his superior boxing skills.

She eventually retrieved her hands from his grasp and removed her uniform jacket, laying it carefully across a chair back. No official business would be conducted here this night.

A small portion of her brain issued an alarm that she was allowing the situation to move so quickly to a serious stage of commitment, but she shushed it into oblivion. Her Granny always said, 'When your heart speaks, lassie, aye follow where it leads.'

After all, how many young women had the chance to see what a grand Scottish towerhouse bedroom was like? More importantly, how many young women had heard a moving and personal life story that rivalled anything a groom might declare to his bride on his wedding day?

She decided to let whatever was to be, be determined by

fate. No one else was involved in their situation. No one else could be hurt by their decisions. They were alone together in an age-old castle with stout defenses. These thick, stone walls were accustomed to keeping secrets and sheltering the inhabitants from harm.

She would trust herself to this castle and this man.

Anna Mason was alone in the farmhouse cedar closet upstairs when she heard the faint sound of a telephone. Lawren was out at the barn retrieving his easel and brushes from storage so that he could continue work on the McLennan family portrait. She dropped the clothes she was unpacking and hurried through the access door into the bedroom, looking frantically to find where she had placed her cell phone when she had come upstairs. The ringing persisted and seemed to grow more urgent as the seconds ticked by.

Another woman might let it go and check the message later but I can't seem to learn that skill at this advanced age.

At last she tracked down the vibrating phone under the pillows, on the bed she had made only a few minutes before, and quickly pressed 'talk'.

"*Anna! Thank heaven you're there!*"

"*Fiona! I'm so glad to hear from you. What's up?*"

The young woman laughed with such abandon that Anna began to worry, briefly, about her sanity.

"*Whoa there, girl! That doesn't sound like the serious Fiona I know, and it's too early in the day for you to be drunk, isn't it?*"

"*Sorry, Anna! The truth is I am kind of drunk today but it's happiness rather than alcohol to blame.*"

Anna was immediately intrigued by this comment and asked where Fiona was calling from.

"*I'm at work in Glencoe at the Visitors' Centre giving a talk, but it's my lunch break and I*

just could not wait *to tell you."*

The giggling started again and Anna realized whatever

she was about to hear was something totally unusual in her experience of Fiona Jameson.

"Well then, what are you telling me? I'm sitting down so don't fear I'll fall over with shock."

"Oh, you do know me well, Anna, and that is why I am taking you, and you alone, into my confidence."

There was a pause while Fiona calmed her giggles and became more sensible. Anna could hardly stand the suspense but when Fiona began to talk in a quiet, sober tone, she knew she was hearing a new and important truth.

"I just spent the night in a castle with a Campbell heir who I hardly know. It's completely out of character for me to behave like this but I took a risk and grabbed a chance at happiness and I am so glad I did. So, so glad!"

A host of questions hovered on the end of Anna's tongue but she wisely held most of them back. Fiona had chosen to confide in her and that confidence must be respected. She had felt, before now, that this young woman was like a daughter to her and that feeling must be confirmed in the most subtle and supportive way.

"That's amazing news, Fiona! How did it all happen?"

Fortunately, Fiona did not catch a hint of the inner turmoil leading to Anna's innocuous question. She was too anxious to go on with her story.

"It's incredible, Anna! I had no idea how deeply he felt about me until he took charge and told me his life story. Strangely enough, our lives are a wee bit similar in some ways but, wow, are they different in other ways! You won't believe it! I had to pass a test before he would let me into his bedroom. You should see the size of his dog, Hector! He's part jet-black Labrador and part

Great Dane. He sniffed me once or twice then padded off to guard the door and left us alone there all night. I can't explain what it was like for me, Anna! To fall in love so fast and find

a man so right for me; it's a miracle, I tell you!"

Anna was still trying to digest the suspect information about the dog test. Her one quick comment was all she could summon at this point. *"Wonderful, my dear!"* It almost strangled her to eke that out but, again, Fiona did not seem to notice.

"Oh, what am I thinking? My brain's scrambled this morning. I haven't even told you his name!

It's Gordon Campbell I'm talking about. He's the new estate manager at Glenmorie and I know you will say I haven't known him long enough to be jumping into bed with him and, normally, I would have to agree with you, Anna, yet that's the thing here. None of this is normal at all.

It's all totally magical and it feels so right."

As Fiona drew breath, she noticed a silence on the other end of the line.

"Anna? Are you still there?"

Anna *was* there and about to have a heart attack as she put together the implications of all that Fiona had revealed. This young woman, starting out on a career she had always yearned for, was risking everything on the basis of a very brief acquaintance followed by a night of passion.

What had happened to change her from an eminently practical, level-headed, independent person in charge of all aspects of her life, into this besotted teenager at a rock concert?

None of these questions could be spoken aloud, of course. She would have to tread carefully to keep her contact with Fiona and be there to advise and comfort her if, and when, things went badly wrong.

"I am right here, Fiona. Just wondering where you go from this?"

"Honestly, I can't think beyond today, my head's in such a swirl. I am longing to go back to the castle tonight and see if I have imagined it all but I know he will be there waiting to hold me in his arms and ask me about my day and I'll ask about his day and..........Oh! That sounds like one of those stupid soap operas on the telly but Anna, you suddenly found a true love in Lawren and I knew you, of all people, would know what it feels like."

Anna would not dream of comparing her feelings about Lawren to the crazy stuff she had been listening to on the phone, and yet, there was a kernel of truth in what Fiona had said. Love, whenever it arrives, is a miracle and one not to be questioned too closely. Time would tell whether or not Fiona and her Gordon had found true love. Anna was certain there was not only one path to happiness in love and she was no expert. Each of her romantic relationships had been different and Fiona was living in a more relaxed era than Anna's. So what if Fiona had skipped over months of slow progress in getting to know this Gordon? Anna would not attempt to be the arbiter of appropriate behaviours. After all, some might consider her own romance with Lawren to be far from the standard variety.

She would keep her own counsel about this for now and hope that Fiona would continue to confide in her.

All this passed through Anna's mind in a flash. She composed a suitable response to keep the channels of communication open.

"I am very happy for you, Fiona. He must be a special young man and I hope, in time, to meet him. For now this will remain our secret. Please keep me posted and let's meet soon,"

"Of course, Anna! Thank you for being my listening post. I always value your opinions."

Farewells were made quickly. Anna could hear a voice in the distance calling Fiona's name. The workday beckoned for her.

Anna plopped back onto the pillows and closed her eyes. This business of being a surrogate parent could be exhausting. Hopefully, it would be many years before little Annette might come to her godmother for help and understanding. Anna did a quick calculation and surmised that her goddaughter would be seeking other sources by then, as Anna would be an old, old woman.

There's quite enough to deal with right now without worrying about the distant future. One thing at a time.

Chapter Nineteen

Lawren Drake had made his way through the empty front section of the barn where a car could be parked, and was now in the rear, locked part, where a variety of things from the farmhouse were stored. He quickly found the easel and drawing materials he had left here after the unveiling of the large portrait which now hung above the fireplace in his and Anna's bedroom.

He stopped to take a moment to appreciate how important a role that portrait of Anna and Helen had played in his life. He could never have imagined the results of answering Anna's enquiry about an artist to paint a portrait for her. If he had turned down her very unusual request, his life would have been devoid of the love and companionship he now enjoyed, and so much more than that. Anna had opened up her friendships and connections to him in such a generous way. Every day seemed richer and more full and yet he still had his skills as an artist to concentrate on. Nothing had been taken from his life. So much more had been added.

With renewed enthusiasm, he unwrapped the sketch paper he had encased in plastic against dampness and found the large clips to attach the paper to the frame. The oil paints looked to be in fine shape in their wooden boxes but, for now, he left these aside. Ever since returning to Scotland his mind had been burdened by the overpowering need to get some sketches done. His whole experience in England while searching for his father's family home had impacted his imagination so strongly that the need to get some of his impressions down on paper was becoming overwhelming.

As he moved across the floor, a shaft of light fell upon him and he looked up to see a hole in the rafters above.

Surely Anna would not have allowed a hole in the roof of the barn to remain unrepaired?

He looked again at the dark space just beneath the hole and was amazed to see eyes glittering back at him. A flutter of feathers alerted him to the possibility that there were birds roosting above. Just then a dislodged feather floated down and landed at his feet. Bending to pick it up he recognized the brown and beige barred pattern of a barn owl's feather. The tip was translucent and pointed. He spun it in his fingers and sent a thank you for the gift to the silent birds above. He knew that long ago artists used quills to paint and write. This quill, at this moment, was a sign of approval.

He pulled the easel into position under the shaft of light and clipped the paper in place. Selecting a handful of drawing pencils and setting one behind his ear he began to draw.

Anna had unintentionally fallen asleep upstairs on the comfy bed and she wakened with a jolt when she heard Lawren's voice calling her name. For a moment she could not orient herself in time and space. She had been daydreaming about Fiona and a castle and a knight in armour with a helm that covered his face and obscured his features. *Was he a good or evil knight?*

The dream vanished as Anna struggled to her feet. "I'm up here, Lawren! I'll be right down."

When she reached the kitchen it was to see paper spread

all over the kitchen table and Lawren diving around talking under his breath and shuffling the papers from one position to another.

His excitement was palpable. The air in the room was electric.

"What's all this, my darling?"

"Look over here, Anna! What do you think of this? I tell you the images just poured out of me. It was like a catharsis. I hardly know what I was drawing. Most of them are of Hartfield Hall as I saw it that day in Wiltshire. God! That seems like a year ago!"

"But, Lawren, there's such detail! You were there only the once and not in the best of circumstances, I understand. Where does all that memory come from?"

Anna went around the table looking at each sketch of the house that had once meant so much to Lawren's father. She was astounded at the speed with which Lawren had composed this amount of material. He could not have been at the barn for more than an hour.

"Oh, I don't know, Anna. Years of training, I suppose. Once I look carefully, the images just seem to get burned onto my brain."

"What's this shield bit just under the roof line? I can see something that looks like stars."

"A family crest, I believe. I haven't had the chance to look it up yet."

Anna recognized other monuments like Stonehenge that Lawren had seen on his travels, but again and again her eyes were pulled back to the house drawings. She felt a powerful emotional response to them and could only guess what Lawren's feelings had been to create such sketches.

"You know I love your work, Lawren. I am no expert but these are amazing. You should include them in your show when we get back to London. Would you ever want to give one to your father?"

"I doubt it! I think he is happier with the glory days he remembers. I'd never want to shatter his dreams."

"That's what I was thinking."

She moved over to him and placed her hands on his back. She could feel the excited tension in his shoulders and began automatically to massage them with her warm hands. He had told her how soothing it was to feel that warmth and she was glad to be able to do something to help. She lacked his talents but she could express her appreciation for his skill in this simple way.

In the centre of the table lay a feather. She reached to pick it up and continued to massage Lawren's shoulders with her other hand.

"This is a barn owl's wing feather. Did you see my owls? There are more of them this year since they found the safe place to roost during the day."

"That was a generous thing for you to do, Anna. This feather was a gift from the owls. It inspired me to begin drawing and I felt them watch silently from the rafters as I worked."

Lawren's hands moved the drawings around until he had selected the ones he felt most strongly about. Anna watched the process in fascination. She could see the appeal of some of his favourites. Although oil paints were his usual way of conveying emotion, it was remarkable how even the pencil and charcoal sketches bounced off the page at the viewer.

She focused for a minute on the Avebury stone circle and wondered why it had such a powerful effect on her. It took some time before she spied the tiny figures of children peeking out from between the massive stones sunk into the turf. Immediately she could hear in her head the cries of the children as they played some version of hide and seek with their playmates. No doubt her years in a school playground supplied the sound effects but it had been Lawren's genius to juxtapose the tiny figures with the ancient and formidable stone structures in such a way that the stones lost some of their fearful aspects and became a part of human history.

"Why have you stopped? Are you crying, Anna darling?"

"No, not really! I am just so moved by your artistry, my love. In your hands paper and pencil become something far beyond their everyday purposes. It's a kind of magic, I suppose."

As she spoke, Anna remembered Fiona's use of a similar phrase. She thought it must be love that created this magic. Love for a person, a place or a creature had a transformative quality. Even inanimate objects, when bathed in love, became so much more.

"Don't leave these here, Lawren. Morag may take an interest in sampling them. She likes to exercise her sharp little teeth on the edges of paper occasionally."

"No worries! I'll roll them up carefully. I think they may sell one day."

Anna was sure of it.

"Now, my lady, I want to take you out for a meal tonight. Grant has recommended a restaurant with a spectacular sunset view and he will collect us here in a couple of hours. Go do whatever you need to. I have some business to discuss with George and Jeanette about their family portrait and then I think I'll take a walk up Helen's Hill. I have things to think about and matters to talk over with you later after a fine dinner and a glass or two of wine."

"Yes, my lord!" said Anna, with a quick bob of a curtsey, then she danced up the stairs before he could catch her. Sometimes it was nice to be ordered around.

Back in the cedar-lined closet at the top of the stairs, for the second time in the day, Anna finally unearthed a long-sleeved wool dress in a rich shade of burgundy that Maria had sworn complimented her colouring. She held it against her to check the length and wondered if the belt she had bought in

Glasgow would pull in the waist and add a spark of glamour to what was, in essence, a very plain dress. *Plain perhaps, but classic in style and warm enough for a cool evening.*

She was just emerging from the storage room to begin her search for the belt when the phone rang.

"Not again!" she begged. Another session of surprise revelations with Fiona was not something she needed. She had hardly begun to absorb the last exciting, and worrying, phone conversation.

Thankfully, a familiar voice greeted her.

"Sis, it's me! I am glad to catch you. I want to tell you about our night with Ross and Joyce."

Anna made a quick mental flip back to her brother's departure for Glasgow and the unexpected invitation to meet their father's younger brother at his Kelvinside home.

"Yes, Simon! What did you and Michelle think of them?"

"Well, once I had got over the weird idea that our father actually had a much younger brother none of us knew about, I relaxed and enjoyed them immensely."

"Did you see a resemblance to Dad? I did at first."

"Not at first. Physically, I didn't notice anything, but the more Ross, I suppose he's really Uncle Ross, isn't that strange? The more he spoke, the more I could hear an accent that seemed familiar from my childhood, I guess. What about you?"

"I don't recall that, Simon, but I was with them for only a short time and I think I was in shock for most of it. I am still processing the whole incident. What was it like to spend the night there?"

"Oh, they could not have been more hospitable. Rory came over for supper, and he's just as you described him, Anna. Joyce put on a feast and Michelle was in the kitchen helping out before you could stop her. The two of them were fast friends in minutes. The house is just outstanding. We had a bedroom with an ensuite and Joyce had put in there, flowers and all the bath stuff you could ever want. Donna and Ashley shared a similar room and Michelle said it was superior to most hotels we've ever stayed in."

"I imagine she's right! Joyce struck me as a warm and wonderful woman. I hope to see much more of both of them."

"You'll have to stand in line, Sis! We've invited them to PEI already."

"Surely you haven't moved yet?"

"No, but we will be there before the snow flies out west. Once the idea took hold we couldn't wait to make the change."

"It will be a big change alright. Won't you miss the children and grandkids?"

"We are buying a huge place with room for visitors and we are pretty sure the family will follow us there often, once they see the shoreline, the temperate climate and the gorgeous scenery. It's time for a change and it seems change is in the air. Don't you agree?"

"I can hardly deny it, Simon. My life has changed radically in the last little while and the changes have been good. I will admit I am glad you and Michelle will be closer to Ontario and also to Scotland. I can see a lot more opportunities for our newly-expanded family to get together. It's really amazing how this has all happened. Although Helen Dunlop gave this Oban house to me, I want you to think of it as yours also, Simon. It looked right to me to see Donna and Ashley here."

"That's very good of you, Anna. Donna says you'll have a hard time keeping Ashley away. She really responded to the old place and she is talking of spending holidays with you."

"I would love, that! We'll have to keep track of each other's schedules. For now, you can use the Holiday Home Finder site that lists the Oban house. I guess there will be little space left for other travellers with the way things are going!

Do you know, Simon, it's not so long since I felt quite alone in the world and now I am surrounded with family and friends in an ever-widening circle. Life is certainly full of surprises, isn't it?"

"You bet, Annabanana!"

With the sound of his laughter ringing in her ears, Anna put down the phone.

What a strange day! Phone calls bringing surprises and a date with Lawren to look forward to. I wonder what he wants to discuss?

There are several possibilities. Our lives are rushing ahead like a runaway train these days. Fiona in love, Simon and Michelle moving, Ashley interested in writing about Helen, the new Samba members, Lawren's sketches, Alina and Philip ....what could be next?

After a delicious meal of Scotch broth and Scottish salmon, washed down with wine and finishing with brandy and sherry trifle, Anna was scarcely able to summon enough brain power to focus on Lawren's conversation.

They had talked about the view of the sunset that had appeared through the day's clouds and admired the dining room and the food. Anna was quite replete and ready to go back to Oban and snuggle up in a warm bed.

Lawren, however, seemed to have other ideas.

"Now don't go to sleep yet, my lovely Anna," he begged. "I told you I had something to ask you about and now is the time. I've plied you with food and drink so you will be in a receptive frame of mind so please listen."

Hearing that she had been unwittingly prepared for acquiescence, brought some adrenalin into her body and she looked searchingly at Lawren's golden eyes. She noticed they had the characteristic darkened colour that usually meant he was concentrating on something important. She sat up in her chair and pushed her back into the frame to stiffen her resolve to stay awake.

"I know this is unexpected, my love, but I have a sense of urgency about what I am about to say to you. So much has happened, and so quickly, that it seems the tide in the affairs of men that Shakespeare spoke of is carrying us along with it and I suppose I want to go with the flow."

Lawren had her full attention now. Every last vapour of alcohol had vanished from her brain and trepidation was beginning to take its place. What was coming? She did not dare to speak.

"I'll get right to the point, Anna. I think we should get married."

Her eyebrows shot upward and her eyes opened wide at these words.

What? Where? When?

Lawren continued without a break.

"You always said I should ignore the difference in our finances and you know I care nothing about the minor difference in our ages, so I feel we should waste no time making ours a formal arrangement. That doesn't mean a fancy affair. I will be happy with whatever pleases you. I just want it to be sooner rather than later. I want you to be mine in a way that is acknowledged by the whole world."

Finally, he looked at her and waited anxiously.

"Please, Anna. Say something! I am dying here!"

Lawren's voice ran out of air and energy at the same instant and Anna knew she had to answer swiftly or he would think he had failed to make his case.

Fiona flashed through her mind. *Who's the impulsive one now?*

Alina's face appeared before her but she was smiling approval.

She saw Susan and Maria and Bev and Jeanette nodding their heads and lifting glasses in celebration.

She thought of all the reasons why this was too soon.

And she rejected all of them.

This would not be an easy union, but then, how many of those were around?

This would be a rare second chance and she would be a fool to miss it.

"Oh, Lawren! Yes! Yes! Yes! Of course I'll marry you!"

He came alive again and jumped to his feet, lifting her off the chair and right into his arms. They danced around the dining room to the applause of the few diners who remained at this late hour and who could recognize a seminal moment in the lives of two people in love.

When they settled down enough to catch their respective breaths and stop their insane smiling, it was inevitable that realities and problems began to emerge. They gazed at each other with delight but with an awareness that there were many decisions to make.

Lawren took charge as soon as he saw the shadow of a question on Anna's face.

"Not one word from you tonight, my lady. Let's bask in this glow for now. Whatever we have to do, or decide, will wait until tomorrow and we don't need to tell anyone anything until we are quite ready.

Let's go home."

Chapter Twenty

Anna woke early on the morning following the wedding proposal, and carefully untangled herself from Lawren's arms and legs. She was fully awake and needed a chance to absorb the events of recent days without the distraction of worrying about Lawren's input.

She crept downstairs and found a track suit she kept for gardening hung up under her warm overcoat.

With this layer over her night clothes, and a scarf, and the hood of her coat pulled up and tied, she felt she could face any autumn weather Scotland could throw at her.

Leaving a note beside the kettle and slipping her cell phone into a pocket, she opened the back door and stepped out into the morning. It was a cold, crisp day with a clear blue sky and a temperature low enough to turn the tips of the rain-sodden grass to frost.

She suddenly experienced a pang of longing for Canada. A morning like this in Ontario would warm by the afternoon and a barbecue would finish off the day. The thought of home, (where exactly was her home now?), seemed to crystallize her current discomfort. Was it too much, too soon and was she in danger of making decisions too quickly?

She shrugged off the uncomfortable thoughts and set her sights on climbing to the top of Helen's Hill.

If the exercise did not clear her mind the view from the top would, at least, provide some perspective.

The lower reaches of the hill were still in shadow and Anna had to concentrate on watching where her feet were placed. There were some slippery spots to navigate and once or twice she had to bend down to steady herself on nearby rocks or grasp the strong stems of gorse bushes for leverage.

By the time she was half way up she was feeling warmed through and watching her breath steaming on the cold air. The moment when she broke through the dark and into the light of the rising sun seemed like a blessing. She stopped to catch her breath and look back toward the house.

The sun was glinting on the windows and turning the glass to bright mirrors. Wisps of steam from the heating system escaped from the chimneys and rose straight up into the air. The sun turned the tops of the sheltering line of firs to gold and brightened the last leaves on the rowan tree where bunches of orange berries still hung, waiting to feed the winter birds.

The old farmhouse looked much the same from the rear as it would have looked to Helen Dunlop. The additions and alterations Anna had required were invisible from this angle and the house nestled into its garden and its fenced and stone-walled property as if it would last for a thousand years.

But Anna knew she did not have a thousand years in which to enjoy this house and this view. It was imperative that she made good decisions for the limited span which she could see ahead. Not that there were any guarantees of happiness. She thought of Susan caring each day for Jake's disabilities. She projected forward to a time when her dear Alina might be severely restricted by deteriorating eyesight. She wondered if her own fingers that sometimes ached in the cold, and that nagging stiffness in her back in the early morning were the beginning signs of arthritis, and she remembered Philip's concern about the Alzheimer's disease that had blighted his mother's life.

The future was uncertain for all of them.

Was that a reason for denying the happiness of the present? Was it not better to move forward with the knowledge that illness and sorrow could well happen, as it did to all humans, and accept that chance with hope and belief in the powers of the human spirit to overcome all obstacles? The question remained. Was she strong enough to face the uncertainties?

Was her love for Lawren enough to ward off the fear of failure in a second relationship, one to which she had already committed herself in an uncommonly brief amount of time?

For all of her life she had been conservative, circumspect and unadventurous. This new Anna had already dared to venture into unknown territory. Was it a place where she could continue to live in comfort or was it a temporary location in which she might soon grow uncomfortable?

For a brief moment she wondered what people would think of an older woman marrying a younger, artistic man with a non-traditional lifestyle. Would they think he was taking advantage of her?

"Who cares?" she cried. Mourning doves rose into the air in alarm from the bushes where they had been hidden. Anna followed their slow progress upward and called after them. "My friends know me and they will support my decisions. I've been a quiet observer of life, living on the sidelines for far too long. This is my chance for a full life and I am going to grasp it in both hands!"

She stood up and raised her arms to the sky. It was a physical sign of her open acceptance of Lawren and all that life with him promised.

Suddenly she could not wait one more minute to see his face again. It no longer seemed necessary to climb upward to the top of the hill. She had already attained all the affirmation the summit could have provided and she was ready to begin a new life with the marvelous man who had asked to share it with her.

She scrambled down the slope, conscious that she must not slip and break a leg and spoil this moment.

Safely on flat ground again, she ran through the field, threw open the iron gate in the wall and skipped over the hummocks of grass in the garden.

Lawren was waiting for her in the kitchen with a mug of coffee in his hand.

"There you are!" he exclaimed. One glance had assured him that Anna was happy and relieved of all doubts. "You look exhilarated! All flushed and excited! Come and let me warm you up, my darling! Bacon's in the oven and you can sip my coffee while I pour you a cup. We have a lot to plan for, future Mrs. Drake."

The wedding news raced around the Samba friends as soon as Alina had put down the phone after talking to Anna. Alina had insisted she was not at all surprised. "You two are made for each other. Neither one of you would have been happy with some ordinary partner. It took me a while to recognize that, but I am convinced of it now."

Anna had asked if Lawren's suggestion of allowing Alina and Philip to stay in their condo had helped to make up her mind in his favour, and her friend had to agree it was a contributing factor, for certain.

The good news was that Alina had already found a condo unit in the same complex just a few doors away that she felt sure would be ideal for Anna and Lawren.

"I'll be happy to take over the garden for you, if you want, and of course we'll help with the move," she had added.

Anna asked if Philip was intending to stay in London for much longer and was informed that he was glad to take a break from work and investigate the pleasures of his surroundings. Apparently he had taken a liking to Springbank Park and was encouraging Alina to walk there most days.

"I tell you," she had declared, *"I haven't been this healthy and happy for many years!"*

What followed was a heart-to-heart between the old friends about the men in their lives.

Alina volunteered that she would not be marrying Philip any time soon.

"You must remember that you have been married before, Anna, and you can imagine what that would entail. As far as Philip and I are concerned, we are both stepping into unknown territory and we are not the type to rush ahead.

Not that we haven't talked about it. We have talked about everything you can think of. Frankly, I believe the man has been silent too much in his life. It's high time his secrets and worries were released and I am pleased to be the recipient of his confidences.

These weeks here on our own with nobody to interfere have been so good for both of us. I am feeling more relaxed about our friendship and our future. I think the new start here in Ontario is giving him a chance to reinvent himself. He certainly needed to have a focus apart from his endless work demands."

Anna was surprised to hear Alina wax lyrical about Philip in this way. The time on their own had definitely brought their relationship into a closer sphere and having a chance to live in the condo together would have given Philip a look at what life with Alina would be like.

That's all good, then, she thought.

Alina's next question brought Anna back to the present.

"So what's been happening with you two, apart from the big wedding news, of course?"

"Really, Alina, I'm not too sure about the wedding emphasis."

"What? You're not having second thoughts already?"

"No, no! The marriage idea is what I want, more than a fancy wedding ceremony. Lawren said it could be just as I wished and the more I think about it, the more I feel I don't want all the fuss of a formal occasion."

"Well, I hope you don't think you'll be running off somewhere by yourselves to do the deed. I know a Samba group who would track you down and march you up the aisle no matter where you might flee to!"

Anna laughed at this comment but she had a strong feeling that Alina's humour concealed a true fact.

She thought about Bev and Alan's lovely wedding in Oban. It was a beautiful occasion, and by chance and some good organization, almost all the Sambas were in attendance. This brought up the thorny issue of where such an event would take place for Lawren and herself.

London, or Oban, or Glasgow, or somewhere else entirely?

The complexities that could occur were even now beginning to give her a headache.

"Are you there, Anna?"

"I'm right here! Just thinking about things."

"Well, don't think too long. There will be lots to plan before such an event.

Now, enough about that! How is Lawren coping?"

"Lawren is constantly amazing me! For someone who was an only child and who lived and worked alone for most of his life, he is adapting to a more social environment much more easily than I would have guessed. Despite being thrown into my family at the deep end, as it were, he actually made some astute observations about them after only hours together and he went off for a hike with Ashley, Simon's granddaughter, and charmed her greatly as far as I could see. And, he's been able to work here!"

"How would he get time to work, and what's his subject?"

"Oh, he has commissions for family portraits and he is also drawing sights he saw in the south of England. The sketches are quite wonderful, Alina. I can't believe his talent."

"Huh! You are not a creditable judge, my dear. You are obviously smitten with the man."

"I would hope so since I just agreed to be his wife!"

The laughter zinged through the lines and Anna ended

the conversation with thanks and good wishes for her forever friend and her half-brother.

"Hmmmm!," she pondered aloud, "if we could get one of Simon's clan or one of the Sambas or even one of Maria's daughters to move into the complex, we would have an exclusive enclave there in London, Ontario, and the parties would be wild!"

The thought of parties made her remember her doubts about a wedding venue.

Anna was not the only one thinking about this.

"Maria! Have you heard about Anna and Lawren?"

"Of course! Alina has been on the phone already."

"So have you been approached about a dress for Anna?"

"Susan, I don't think the woman has had time to catch her breath never mind plan a wedding dress. There's not much any of us can do until we find out the where and when."

"You are right, of course, but I am so excited for her that I can hardly contain myself. I keep remembering Bev's beautiful and unusual wedding in Oban. Do you think they will choose something similar?"

"I really have no idea, Susan. You should keep in touch with Bev or Jeanette for the latest news on that front and please keep me in the loop. I'll be travelling for the fashion shows in Milan very soon but you know my cell phone number."

"Yes, I'll be in touch as soon as I hear anything. Isn't it wonderful news?"

"Absolutely! Take care, Susan."

Maria glanced around the busy store where her cruise clientele were eagerly inspecting the latest styles for winter and spring 2013. Nova was doing her best to steer the larger ladies to gowns that would suit them best and Theresa was moving in and out the connecting door between Maria's and her own Babywear Accessories emporium. The teenagers who adored Lucy's styles would be coming along after school hours to see what was new and daring in fall fashion but by then the older customers would have retired to their apartments and luxury flats for their afternoon teas.

Maria stole a moment to think about the differences she now saw from just months ago. She and Paul had their home to themselves again and all was serene there. They organized two busy schedules and made the most of the time they were together. It was like a honeymoon weekend once or twice a month and she loved their closeness.

Lucy had been transformed by finding work in Toronto in the fashion and film industry. As she was often seeing the cutting edge of the business she was able to inform Maria's young set of the up-to-the-minute latest styles. The recent Toronto Film Festival had provided a whole new range of colours and patterned clothes, some of which derived from Europe rather than America, and Maria could see the eager response of local teens reflected in her increased sales.

Another benefit was that Lucy had become very close to her Gran. She occasionally spent a weekend with her Toronto Italian relatives, as much to get away from industry gossip in the flat she shared with two other girls, as to quiz her grandmother about her own fashion roots in Italy and the many stories of how she had established herself in Canada.

When the Toronto Fashion Week was in full flow. Maria booked a hotel room in a downtown spot favoured by the rich and famous. Lucy spent as much of the week with her as she could manage and the two women bonded at the Holt Renfrew shows or sitting in the hotel foyer, dressed to the nines, watching the beautiful people come and go and critiquing their hair styles and outfits.

Maria could hardly credit that this knowledgeable, vital, young woman was the daughter whose teenage antics and bad manners had almost driven her to distraction. Now she was a family girl who loved her parents, her sister's children and her grandparents in equal measure. It seemed that taking her away to Italy and then permitting her to leave school and work in her chosen field had encouraged Lucy to appreciate her family rather than separating her from them, as Maria had once feared.

"Mum! Nova is asking for your help over there. I have to nip next door again to see a customer. I'll be back later."

Maria shook her head clear, and concentrated on the present. It was such a comfort to be working alongside her elder daughter. Theresa was a whiz with the store computer accounts and when she needed to take her kids to doctor appointments or parties it was always possible to arrange the time for her. Whenever she could, Maria elected to look after the two little ones; another treat in her new life.

She checked her watch and saw it was time for the teens who ran Lucia's Lines to arrive. They came in most days after school and Maria had taken them on as part-time assistants. The girls were super keen on Lucy's forward-thinking fashion ideas and proudly wore black T shirts declaring, **'We specialize in Lucia's Lines'**.

Their happiest day was Saturday when Lucy's Fashion Picks of the Week arrived by express post and could be exclaimed over and displayed prominently for the teen shoppers. Currently, the girls were running a blog to see which of the Fall Favourite colours, (emerald green or purple), graphic designs or fall florals, would be the most popular this season.

Once again her thoughts returned to Anna's upcoming nuptials. Where would she and Lawren marry? With close friends on both sides of the Atlantic, it was going to be problematic for Anna, whichever venue she chose. Thinking that this was the way of the world at the moment, with families split up and people travelling back and forth between continents, just as she did herself, she decided not to invest any energy on the wedding attire topic until she knew more about the occasion.

Maria's final thought on the subject was how pleased she was that Anna had come into her own. Her mind drifted briefly to Anna's old apartment where the Sambas had gathered to discuss the Scottish inheritance for the first time. What changes Anna had seen since then! From clothing and hairstyle to travel and romance, Anna Mason was a new and happier creature.

With a deep sigh of satisfaction, for both of them, Maria turned back to her work.

"Bev, it's me, Jeanette. I've been very patient but I can't wait to hear if you know any more about Fiona's romance?"

Bev found herself in the midst of a dilemma. She had just put down her phone after talking to Susan in London, Ontario, and she did not know yet who in Scotland knew about Anna and Lawren, or, whether she was free to spread the news or not. She had a strong impulse to tell what little she did know to Jeanette. After all wasn't she now a Samba member?

"Well, Jeanette, how are the children doing?"

"What? You saw them yesterday."

Two seconds later and Jeanette had figured out that she was being deliberately distracted.

"All right! You can't fool another Canuck. What's going on? Do you know something about Fiona or not?"

"I really haven't heard anything more about Fiona and her boyfriend. I've been busy lately."

"OK then! If you know nothing about Fiona, what else is it you are hiding from me?"

Bev realized she could not keep up this subterfuge much longer. Jeanette would guess eventually anyway.

"I have heard something, Jeanette, but it came from Canada and I am not sure if the secret is out yet. I don't want to break a confidence or spoil a surprise."

"Now you've really got me curious! Spill, Bev! You can trust me. My lips are sealed tight if that's what will make you feel more comfortable."

"Oh, I do want to tell you! It's choking me to keep silent. Susan

just called to tell me Lawren proposed to Anna!"

"What!!! When did this happen?"

"Recently, as far as I know. Alina told Susan. But since Anna hasn't told you or I, I think we can presume it's hush hush for now. They probably need time to get used to the idea. Promise me you won't say word one until Anna tells us herself."

"No problem! This is great news! If they were a younger couple I would be thinking there was a pregnancy in the wind but that's not possible."

"Oh Jeanette! What a thing to say! Don't let Anna hear you suggesting such an idea. She would be horribly embarrassed."

"Of course not! I'm only fooling! It's fantastic news though. They are certainly not letting grass grow under their feet. I wonder where they will choose and when? Goodness there's a lot of excitement to come."

"You are right about that! Now remember your promise."

"Don't worry about me. I'm a new member of the Samba group. I don't want to be thrown out this soon. Let me know if you hear anything more."

"I will do. I may have to call Canada if I can't stand the suspense."

"You do that, Bev. I'll be waiting."

Bev practically hugged herself at the thought of Anna and Lawren living nearby as a married couple. They would be even closer than before and she and Alan could do things with Anna and Lawren as couples together. There were places to show Anna that Alan had shared with her that neither Anna nor Lawren had ever had time to see. They could go to Skye and see Kirsty again and explore the island and then there was a tour of the Black Isle that Bev had heard about and Edinburgh was a must……..

She wandered into the kitchen and began to mix up a cake without really knowing what she was doing. Her mind was full of exciting times ahead with her Samba friend and somewhere inside her it seemed appropriate to make a cake to celebrate.

Chapter Twenty-One

Fiona settled quickly into a routine. None of her neighbours in Oban would suspect that she was not living in the cottage. Her hours were often erratic and unless someone looked to see if her Land Rover was parked in the town lot overnight, they would be unlikely to think anything unusual was happening.

That was exactly how Fiona wanted things for the time being.

She continued to concentrate on her work during the day but as the evening drew nearer, she had difficulty keeping her feelings under control. She could not wait to rush back to the castle, track down Gordon, (usually by looking for Hector's noble head sticking up from bracken or heather), and make her way carefully to his side. If he was with the ghillies and their clients fly-fishing in the dusk on the estate's rivers, she would wait until she had caught his attention then tiptoe off back to his office with Hector for a guardian. Gordon came to the office later to join her and they would relax with coffee from the drip coffee maker she had installed there, discussing their respective days and planning the evening.

Fiona discovered there was a daily woman who tidied, changed beds and prepared an evening meal for Gordon. He had refused to let Fiona cook for him, declaring there was more than enough for two and she needed her rest in the evenings. Fiona was delighted to accede to this request and to spend the time getting to know Gordon in more than a physical way. She was increasingly impressed with the depth of the man. He had ambitious plans for the estate and wanted to implement sustainable environmental methods of stocking and hunting the livestock. He was not against the installation of the huge, controversial wind vanes to create electricity but insisted they should be far enough distant from the castle as to be invisible on the skyline and not near any animal trails.

Fiona was an eager participant in their discussions. It seemed that everything she had learned in her courses and everything she saw in her daily work had an application to Gordon's future development plan.

She had spent a day with children from the Eigg Primary School who had won an award for having a Green Tree program at school. The students grew tree seeds and planted the saplings on their island to replace the forests that once flourished in the sheltered vales there.

Gordon had already instigated a similar project at Glenmorie Castle and a line of sturdy oaks and sycamores was progressing up the bare slopes of old hill ranges. He had also, to Fiona's delight, re-homed a family of otters from an animal sanctuary and the frisky fellows were to be seen in one of the more secluded rivers, away from the paying customers. Watching them lie on their backs sleeping in a sunny stream with their paws clasped over their chests like little old men, was one of the joys the couple shared on Sunday rambles on the estate.

Fiona Jameson could not believe how happy she was. To have found such a compatible mate was far beyond her expectations. She had dated local Oban boys once or twice but the occasions were rare because of her taxi driving schedule and the chance that she would have to cancel at the last minute if Grant could not do a night delivery. She was glad to have an excuse. Her life was so different from that of the secondary school kids in her classes. She had worked from the day she got her driving license and done odd jobs for years before that. She did not have the time to focus on her appearance or the money to buy the make-up and clothes the other girls desired. She had always felt older than her classmates and shared few of their interests. In her mind they were characterized as "silly lassies" and she dismissed them and their mindless pursuit of fashion and boyfriends.

Now she was a woman with a lover. It was as if she had skipped over a few stages on the way to a fulfilling adult relationship. Gone were the tentative advances and insecure longings she had known only from romance novels, most of which had been left in the taxi by some traveller who had read assiduously all the way to Fort William or Inverness. She had found the real love of her life and it was wondrous indeed. She trusted Gordon utterly with her heart. She had found no flaw in the man to mar her happiness. He was perfect for her.

On reflection, there was only one fly in the ointment. Fiona was bursting to tell someone how she felt, face to face.

Her thoughts flew to Anna Mason. At the first opportunity she must check to see if Anna and her beau, Lawren, were still in the McCaig Farmhouse. If so, she would arrange to visit there as soon as possible. She could hardly wait. Anna was sure to understand her feelings about Gordon. Anna would share her joy and they could compare notes.

The opportunity arose the very next day. Fiona was working locally. The seas and weather permitting, she was to board a motor boat at the harbour and ride to Cutler's Rock in the Sound of Kerrera, not far off shore, to see the seaweed cultivation farm there. In ancient times farmers relied on seaweed to fertilize their fields and the rich source of nutrients was now coming back into style. When the right kind of seaweed was cultivated and dried it could be exported as an inexpensive way to feed the fields of subsistence farmers who lived in lands far from the sea.

This was an initiative supported by Marine Scotland and Fiona had been selected to write a report on the effects on sea creatures in the area for Wildlife Services.

"It's in your back yard, Miss Jameson, so to speak!" she had been informed by Kenneth MacNeil.

Fiona spent the night in her cottage so as to be ready for the boat ride in the morning. Before she went to sleep in her own wee bed she called Anna's mobile number and was very pleased to hear that familiar voice on the line.

"Anna, it's you! You are still in Oban. I am so glad. Will you be at home this evening? I really need to talk to you. I am just off to work now but I will drive over around six o'clock. Is that all right?"

"Yes, of course, Fiona! I'll be happy to see you then."

Anna was glad about two things related to the unexpected call. Lawren had arranged with Jeanette and George to paint the next stage of their portrait in the early evening before the children were put to bed. Anna and Fiona would have the house to themselves.

Next, she had judged from Fiona's tone of voice, that there had not yet been a calamity in her love life.

Although Anna would have been prepared to support and comfort the girl, she was exceedingly happy that this would not be required of her. There was nothing so depressing as hearing the demise of a love affair when one was in the midst of a happy love story.

As if he had sensed her thoughts, Lawren entered the kitchen at this exact moment.

"Anna, my love, we are now down to cheese and crackers. The larder is bare and all that delicious cuisine Michelle left for us has been consumed. It's time for a shopping expedition or I shall faint from lack of nourishment when I return from painting tonight."

"We can't have that, sirrah! I'll call Grant and we shall

depart forthwith for Oban and the Castle Tesco and load up with supplies."

"A goodly plan, my lady! I shall assemble my painting materials and we can drop in to see Liam and Annette together. If Grant brings you back here, I don't doubt George will provide a ride home for me."

Better and better, thought Anna.

Despite a very raw and chilly wind blowing spume off the sea, Fiona enjoyed the boat ride to Cutlers Rock. She was well protected by a sou'wester on her head and a standard issue Barbour which covered her from neck to knees.

The problem was that this attire made it almost impossible to move around on the shore where the seaweed ponds were located. Her hat blew off when the wind caught the brim and her coat belled out so that she could not see what was at the level of her feet. She soon divested herself of the outer wear and followed the supervisor of the project who had been sent to escort her and answer any questions. All went well at the start, but the rain began to pour after about an hour and Fiona felt miserable. Her hands became too cold to write.

The supervisor was a hardy type who continued to expound on the principles of marine culture and the methods to protect the seaweed beds from seal and seagull predation. Not until a shaking Fiona had dropped her pencil into a pond from her frozen fingers, did he realize her predicament.

"Och, lass, Ah'm so used to the cold I canna even notice whit you're doin' there. Come away by the shed here. Ah've aye got a kettle on the hob."

Fiona followed along gratefully and soon sat by a driftwood fire with an old blanket around her shoulders, sipping a mug of builders' tea. Her Granny always called a strong cup of tea by that name. "If the spoon can stand up in it all by itself," she would say, "it's builders' tea, not the weak lady's version you can see right through!"

In the smoky warmth of the shed she finished the notes on her report and asked the supervisor a few more questions about yields and harvesting times. The motor boat for her return trip to shore arrived shortly after she had completed the notes and she thanked her host, pulled on her waterproof coat and waded out to the boat.

They were heading into the wind now but it did not take long to cross the Sound and deposit Fiona on the harbour side. She climbed the slippery steps with care and was soon congratulating herself on saving hours of her day. She would arrive early at Anna's but no doubt she would get a bowl of hot soup there to warm her thoroughly.

The Land Rover was waiting for her in the parking lot. She threw her heavy coat inside and started the heater as she still felt chilled from the morning's exposure. As she stowed the report's pages in her briefcase for later transcription to the laptop, she began to notice a strange odour inside the car.

Looking all around, she could not see a source for the smell which was now becoming quite sickly.

Rolling down the windows did not seem to help. The aroma grew stronger by the minute until Fiona began to feel ill. She switched off the engine and hopped out of the vehicle so she could inspect under the hood in case some youngster had thrown a dead fish inside, but there was no sign of anything nasty.

The wind was blowing her hair around her face and she reached up to push the loose strands out of her eyes when she realized the awful smell was coming from her uniform jacket.

She remembered her jacket had got a soaking in the rain but that would not account for this horrible stink. She hesitated to analyze the component parts of the stink but got as far as putrid garbage before she retched and dragged the offending garment off immediately. There was a large plastic rubbish bag in the back of the car and the jacket was deposited in there, firmly sealed with a knot. It would require dry cleaning as soon as possible.

Fiona returned to the driver's seat, wound down all the windows and breathed shallow breaths through her mouth until she had banished her nausea.

What on earth had caused the awful smell?

She ran through the events of the morning in her mind and concluded the only solution had to be the blanket that had been wrapped around her shoulders while she sat by the supervisor's fire. Heaven only knew what had resided in that old blanket before Fiona's wet jacket had brought the smell to life.

There was only one thing to do. She could not appear at Anna's in this condition. She would have to go to the castle, have a bath and change her clothes. Only her old summer things remained at the Oban cottage now, and none of those would be suitable for such a cold day.

With the decision made, she drove out of the town and headed for Glenmorie.

No real harm done, she told herself. She would not arrive at Anna's as early as she had thought but Anna was not expecting her until six anyway. A scrub in a warm bath would soon put all to rights and she could set out fresh. Gordon was surveying the farther reaches of the estate and would not return until much later. She would still have time for a cozy session with dear Anna.

Traffic was light at this time of day and she sped along the familiar road at a good speed. The Connel Bridge proved to be no obstacle and soon the gates of the estate came into view. Fallen leaves had blown onto the driveway but there were still tall scots pines to mark the curving road. She knew the pines would lose their dark green colour as the weather grew colder and they would appear as stately black sentinels until the spring returned.

When the tower castle came into view, Fiona was surprised to see a Rolls-Royce car parked in front of the entrance doors. She drove past and parked by the stableyard gates. Gordon had not mentioned visitors but then he did not expect her to be in the area at this time of day. Perhaps they were future clients who wanted to see how the operation was run. Fiona felt obliged to do something. Estate workers would be out on the hills for hours and there was no one else around to deal with any enquiries. She would have to provide some basic information. Gordon depended on rich clients to keep the estate solvent.

She approached the large, elegant vehicle tentatively. She had no intention of getting close enough to allow the strangers a whiff of her rancid smell which still permeated her shirt and trousers.

A man emerged from the elegant car and turned toward her. He was tall and well-built wearing a comfortable tweed suit and a trilby hat. His features were partly obscured by a resplendent beard, mustache and sideburns in which grey, white and black strands competed for precedence but his eyes, peering out at her from eyebrows which could only be described as 'beetling', were dark and piercing.

"Glad you arrived, young lady. I am not expected but I was hoping to see the estate manager, Gordon Campbell. Do you know where he might be found?"

Fiona was suddenly conscious of the fact that she was standing at some distance from this man wearing an outfit, much the worse for wear. Under normal circumstances she might have welcomed him with a smile and a handshake but that was not going to happen today.

She cleared her throat and managed a feeble, "I'm afraid Mr. Campbell is not around today. I can contact him by mobile phone but it would be some time before he could return."

The man pursed his lips and seemed annoyed. "Can you give him a message?"

Fiona nodded, but kept her distance, always conscious of the taint of rotten fish around her.

"Tell him I will be at a hotel in Oban for two more days and I would like to see him before I leave."

Fiona hesitated to ask for a contact number then realized she still had no idea who this stranger was.

He was about to settle back into the luxurious interior of his car when Fiona thought to ask for a business card. This was produced from the dashboard and she nipped forward quickly to secure it, bouncing back immediately as the door was closed.

With a sigh of relief, she walked back to the stableyard gates intending to enter the tower house by the rear door and run up to the bathroom before anyone, man or beast, could get near her. On the way she glanced at the business card. Yes, there was a contact number.

"Oh, God!" she exclaimed. In a second she put all the clues together; his manner of speech, the upright stance, the cravat around his neck and the Oxford-cloth shirt under the worn, but expensive tweeds. The realization was confirmed by the name printed on his card:

Capt. Diarmid Campbell RN (ret'd)

"That was Gordon's father! He saw me looking like a scared chicken. I was borderline rude to the man who is of ultra importance to the man I love. I didn't even invite him inside. What will Gordon say?"

She began to shake uncontrollably and walked up the remaining stairs at a slower pace as the import of the meeting weighed in on her. The shaking could be from shock or cold but she knew she had to get dry and warm as quickly as possible. Nothing else could be done before she had reclaimed her confidence.

After soaking in a steaming bath and dressing in clean, dry clothes, Fiona took stock of her situation.

Primarily, she had the duty of informing Gordon that his father was in the area. This she could accomplish but she would also have to confess that she had met him briefly and also the reason why she was at the castle. Gordon might well enquire about *how* she had described herself. It was likely that he had not told his parents about his association with Fiona. It had been only a short time and doubtless he was waiting for the right moment to tell them.

That was not the right moment out there!

She could always leave the business card in the office and let Gordon draw his own conclusions. If she did not volunteer any information about the meeting, perhaps Gordon would assume she had never met his father.

She looked in the mirror of the bathroom and wondered if the senior Mr. Campbell would recognize her now that she was bathed and decently attired. Was it possible that she could actually pretend they had never met?

"What have I done?" she moaned.

She knew she was not behaving in her normal, self-sufficient way but she felt she could not deal with anything more in this problematic day. She decided to wait until she saw Gordon later in the day and then try to explain what had happened. Face to face she might have a better chance to persuade him to overlook her incompetence and make excuses to his father on her behalf.

Once this solution had entered her mind it was as if a weight had been lifted and she was free once more to pursue her original plan to talk to Anna. Now there were even more reasons to seek Anna's wise counsel and suddenly she could not abide a further delay.

She fled from what was increasingly becoming 'the scene of the crime' in her mind, and gunned the Land Rover all the way to the outskirts of Oban and around by the rough back roads to the McCaig Estate Farmhouse. It felt like coming home again and on this day Fiona needed a safe place to hide for a while.

Anna was waiting at the door with Morag in her arms and Fiona cried out to see them there.

"What's wrong, Fiona? You look shattered. Has something happened to you?"

The warm, sympathetic voice undid Fiona's resolve and she collapsed in tears into Anna's arms, ejecting an alarmed Morag onto the floor.

Anna was immediately concerned for Fiona. In all the time she had known the girl, she had never seen her so upset. She had always met every challenge with resolve and a steady confidence but this different version of Fiona was a quivering wreck.

"Right, my dear, through into the lounge with you. There's a fire on and I will be in with a tray of tea and a whisky for you and I think some fresh scones and cheese are called for. Lucky for you, Lawren and I did some shopping earlier."

Fiona did not protest. She made a beeline for the fireside and sank back against the tapestry cushions with a sigh of relief. Everything would be all right now.

Anna found her there a few minutes later, curled up like a child with her head on a cushion. Fiona's eyes were shut, giving the older woman a chance to look carefully at her features. She was definitely pale and worn looking. Was the new romance, added to the rigours of a new career, taxing her strength? Were things suddenly going wrong between Gordon Campbell and Fiona? She could hardly imagine what would have caused Fiona to react like this. The girl was one of the strongest, most independent females Anna had ever known.

She put the tray down on a table and the small noise woke Fiona up.

"I wasn't really sleeping," she said. "I just felt so glad to be here with you."

"Good!" replied Anna. "Now, start with this whisky. You need a pick-me-up, I think."

Fiona reached for the glass and took a tiny sip of the amber liquor. Instead of swallowing, she snatched up a napkin and spat the liquid into it. "Sorry, Anna! It just turned my stomach. I think I've had a bit too much stress today."

Anna was shocked but she hid her feelings and poured tea for both of them, saying tea had never been known to upset anyone's stomach. "Do you think you are ill, Fiona?"

"I don't know, Anna. But I do know I need to tell you what's been happening today. You can decide for yourself."

Chapter Twenty-Two

By the time Anna had heard Fiona's tale of the day's disasters, she knew two things.

One was that Fiona was desperately in love with Gordon Campbell and the other was that Fiona Jameson was probably pregnant.

She had not ventured to reveal this latter conclusion to the girl because she had no proof, only a deep conviction that this could account for her strange behavior. The chill she had had earlier in the day combined with acute nausea and the feeling of panic during the unfortunate incident with Gordon's father, and, again, the way in which her stomach had rejected the sip of whisky, all added up to something unusual for Fiona. Anna had never known the girl suffer from a simple cold, never mind anything more serious. She had always claimed an ironclad constitution inherited from her seafaring ancestors and Anna had had no reason to doubt this claim.

Also contributing to Anna's suspicion, was the way in which Fiona had described her nights with her lover. This brought a blush to Anna's cheeks. It did not sound as if either of the young people had stopped to think about protection. Certainly, their first night together in the castle had been quite spontaneous and it did not seem as if Gordon had entertained any other woman since he had taken on the manager's role. Buying condoms did not appear to be high on his list of necessities.

Anna had heard of 'first time' pregnancies. This might be the case but, if so, it merely added to the complexities facing Fiona. Even if Gordon welcomed the news of a child so soon in their relationship, he would have to tell his father he had found a girlfriend, and a mother for his children, in a relatively short space of time while he was far from home and supposed to be establishing a new career. Anna thought how this might sound to a proud father and landowner like the captain Fiona had described to her. It meant Fiona's motives would likely be suspect right from the start of their relationship and it did not bode well for her future.

Of course, Fiona was in the same position with regard to a new career. Although many might assume that all of this was none of Anna Mason's business, she was rapidly amassing a strong feeling akin to that of a mother cat defending her lone kitten. This Captain Campbell would have to reckon with Anna Mason if he dared disparage Fiona Jameson in any way.

There had been occasions in Anna's teaching career when she had defended a child's interests against those of parents and administrators. Reluctant to defend herself when challenged, she had nevertheless rushed to protect the innocent. She could feel the old emotions stirring again. Captain Campbell did not know the able opponent he was about to deal with.

None of this internal conversation could be shared with Fiona in her present state. Anna retired to the kitchen and returned with dry toast and scrambled eggs. She spoonfed Fiona all the while reassuring her that she would be fine once she had eaten and rested.

The heat of the fire soon did the trick and the girl fell into a deep sleep. Anna covered her with a tartan throw and tiptoed out, closing the door behind her.

This is the best thing for her for now, but I need to think what to do to prevent further disaster.

It was going to be difficult to determine how far she could go without interfering in Gordon and Fiona's lives. Anna had never even met Gordon Campbell. She could hardly intervene with him. She was a stranger to him.

Who else knew this Gordon? She remembered Jeanette saying something about George giving him some advice about a will.

"Ah, George has some standing in the community. He could speak to Gordon, and Jeanette would be an ally who would be better at spotting a pregnancy than I am. I wonder if I can reach either one of them? Oh, darn! Lawren is over there right now, painting their portrait. That won't work!"

Anna sat down at the kitchen table and thought again. Approaching Gordon was definitely not such a good idea. That whole issue was between him and Fiona. But she was older and possibly could soften the blow by accidentally running into the senior Campbell. This idea appealed at once. What did she know about his whereabouts? *'Staying at a hotel in Oban'.* Which hotel? She thought of Grant but co-opting him would mean revealing Fiona's secrets. Who knew the town, could supply a vehicle and could be trusted to ask nothing other than what Anna wanted to tell?

Alan Matthews. Bev's husband was of the silent Scot variety and he should be safely off the hills by now.

Perfect. She dialed Bev's number at once and young Eric picked up the phone after a few rings.

Anna was tapping her foot in annoyance. This could be complicated.

"Hi, Eric, can I speak to your dad?"

"Oh, hullo Aunt Anna, he's not here. I'll get my mum for you."

Darn again!! Another road block.

"Anna, is that you? I hope everything's all right. It's a bit late for you to be calling."

"Bev, I'll cut to the chase. Can you come and get me and drive me into Oban? I have a mission of mercy to perform tonight and I haven't much time."

"You mean right now?"

"Yes! The sooner, the better."

"Just tell me there's no blood involved."

"Definitely not!"

"Right, meet me at the gate in three minutes."

"Thank God for old friends," breathed Anna. "They don't ask too many questions."

She peeked in and checked that the lounge fire was banked down enough to keep Fiona warm for the next hour or so, then grabbed her coat and purse and wrote a quick noncommittal note for Fiona or Lawren, whoever should get to it first. If she had good luck, and better timing, she might be back at the farmhouse before either one of them knew she had left.

Bev was as good as her word. She kept the engine of the old Ford running and said nothing until Anna was settled in the front seat and the car was heading in the direction of Oban. Anna knew she owed her friend an explanation but her first announcement was to ask Bev where a person with finances would stay in Oban if that person needed a hotel.

"Someone with money, eh? Male or female?"

"Male."

"An outsider, then?"

"Yes, as far as I know he isn't familiar with Oban."

"Canadian, or Scot?"

"Definitely, Scot!"

"Old, or young?"

"Probably, my age."

"Young, then."

At this point both women dissolved in laughter and once the ice was broken and the tension relieved, Anna gladly told

Bev everything she knew and all that she was hoping to achieve."

"I will now require a Solemn Samba Swear of Secrecy," she cautioned her friend.

"Given, without question," was the reply. "I feel like a CIA agent, heading off into the night on some dangerous mission. Some day I may tell my sons about this."

"Oh, hush up and concentrate on the road, Bev. I admire your driving skills but I want to arrive in one piece."

The consensus between the two women was that Captain Campbell would likely choose to spend the night at the Columba Hotel on the pier. As Anna said, "An old salt would always prefer the sight and sound of the sea to a room far up the hill."

Bev drove into the parking lot of the Columba and dimmed the lights while Anna went inside and rang the bell on the front desk. After a few moments, a smart-looking young man arrived from the rear of the hotel and asked if she needed a room.

"No, I live just outside Oban in the McCaig Estate Farmhouse."

"Then you'll be Mrs. Mason? I haven't had the pleasure, but I've heard a lot about you, Mrs. Mason.

My grandmother is one of your knitters."

Excellent! This is a good start!

She glanced quickly at the nametag on the man's navy jacket.

"Pleased to meet you, Finlay. I hope you can help me. I have some important information for a gentleman who should be staying here tonight."

Finlay began to turn the pages of the hotel's visitor book and asked who she wanted to talk to.

Anna crossed her fingers and provided the name.

There was a moment's delay while Finlay checked up and down the current page. Anna bit her lip.

"Would that be a Captain Diarmid Campbell, Mrs. Mason?"

"Er, yes, that's the one!"

"Okay, then. The captain is staying with us, right enough. He's in the bar at the moment. Would you like for me to take you through there?"

"That would be most kind of you, Finlay. I'll be sure to send a note to your grandmother to say how helpful you have been."

"No problem at all, Mrs. Mason. Just follow me."

Now that the first hurdle had been tackled, Anna suddenly realized how risky her behavior might seem to a stranger. She was interfering in something that was patently none of her business. Gordon Campbell's father had no reason to believe one word of her proposed plea. She had never even met his son. His father had surely never heard of her.

Overcome with uncertainty, she stopped to gather her courage and assemble her thoughts.

Finlay noticed her hesitation and enquired if he could take her coat to the cloakroom.

Unfastening her coat and straightening her sweater over the dark wool pants she was wearing, (why hadn't she taken time to change and comb through her hair?) gave her the chance to work out a new strategy.

"Finlay, can I ask you to introduce me to the gentleman? We have never met before and I would hate to take a seat at the bar. He might get the wrong impression."

The young man looked alarmed at this prospect and gladly agreed to make the introductions.

The atmosphere in the hotel bar was warm and welcoming with subdued lighting, a flickering coal fire and a recording playing somewhere in the background. There were only a few visitors present; a middle-aged couple were enjoying a bar meal at a table near the windows and three men were seated at the bar chatting amicably. Anna spotted

Diarmid Campbell right away from Fiona's description. The beard and mustache were unmistakable.

She waited by the door while Finlay advanced. He proved to be as good as his word, politely interrupting the conversation and announcing, "Captain Campbell, there is a lady here who would like to speak to you. Her name is Anna Mason. She's a Canadian but she is very well liked and respected here in Oban. May I show you both to a table by the fire?"

Well done young Finlay! I shall be adding to that letter to your grandmother.

Anna was subjected to an inspection from beneath a pair of overhanging eyebrows. She smiled faintly and stood her ground until she perceived a spark of curiosity in the dark eyes.

Diarmid Campbell graciously pulled out a chair for her and inquired as to her drink preference. She considered it might be churlish to refuse and selected a gin and tonic as a fairly innocuous choice.

The order given to Finlay, who moved off with a wink at Anna, the captain sat down, folded his hands together on the table top and waited. His eyes never wavered from her face.

"Captain Campbell," she began, but he interrupted to insist she call him by his first name. Anna was glad she had paid attention when Finlay had pronounced the name as her version of 'Der-mid' might have insulted its owner and antagonized him from the start.

"*Diarmid*, then, I must thank you for agreeing to talk to me. The circumstances are most unusual, I know, but I am compelled to speak on behalf of a person I care for deeply. If you will indulge me, I would like to tell you a little of my story."

The eyebrows frowned a little at this introduction but his gaze remained steady.

"I first came here to Oban from Canada a few years ago. I was a stranger on a mission to find out about my Scottish parents and family members. I was most fortunate to encounter help and support right from the very first day in this lovely little town and one of the people I met was Fiona Jameson, a delightful girl who drove me around for the next two months and who was to become a cherished friend.

Fiona was orphaned at an early age and lived with her grandmother who encouraged the young girl to be independent in thought and deed. She worked hard from childhood to help support herself and a more honest, caring and talented person you could never hope to meet."

Anna could tell that her companion was wondering what this story had to do with him. She decided to tackle that worry immediately.

"Today you met that young woman, Diarmid, under the most difficult of circumstances and I am here to plead for your understanding."

"Excuse me, may I call you Anna? I do not believe I have met the person of whom you speak. I have been in the area for only a short time today."

"I know. You visited Glenmorie Castle and enquired after Gordon Campbell. The young woman who informed you he was not available was Fiona Jameson."

"But, I only saw one person very briefly. I hardly noticed her. I thought she was a servant of some kind. Why on earth are you telling me all this?"

His body language displayed doubt and tension and his tone was brusque. Anna feared he would get up and leave before she had finished making her case. She hurried on.

"Fiona was totally surprised at meeting you, Diarmid. She is now a Scottish Wildlife officer and through her work she met your son. She had a difficult morning today involving getting soaked to the skin and had returned to the castle, where she has been staying, to change her clothes. That is why she kept her distance and looked somewhat distraught. That is also why you overlooked her."

Anna watched anxiously as this information percolated

through his brain and the pertinent fact was extracted. She sipped her drink to relieve the dryness of her throat.

"Are you saying that my son and this girl are involved in some way?"

This was the crux of the matter and Anna knew she had to be cautious.

"That is for your son to explain. All I ask is that you not dismiss Fiona Jameson because of the less-than-ideal circumstances of your first meeting."

"What, specifically, are you asking me to do?"

"It's simple, but I believe it will be vital to the future of your son and of Fiona and, not to put too fine a point on it, it may affect your own future."

"Forgive me, Ms. Mason, but I think you are in no position to comment on my family affairs."

Ah, how little you know, sir, of these family affairs!

"Please excuse my presumption. If you will consider wiping today's encounter with Fiona from your mind and starting anew, that is all I can ask. I won't take up any more of your time but thank you once again for allowing me this opportunity."

She got up and exited quickly before he could protest. She had done what she could. Please God she had not made matters worse for the young couple.

Her coat was lying across the hotel desk. Obviously Finlay had not had time to stow it away.

She grabbed it and left by the door. Bev had turned the car around and once more the engine was purring.

"More and more like a movie get-away," she chuckled gleefully.

Anna could hardly disagree. She was overcome with delight at escaping with her mission attempted, if not accomplished, and equally exhausted at the effort it had taken.

"Get me home, Bev, and pray Fiona never finds out about this night's work."

. . .

Bev dropped Anna off outside the front gate and waved goodbye. Anna walked softly up the paved pathway, glad once again that she had dispensed with the noisy gravel. She entered through the red door and stopped to listen. Not a sound. Perhaps she would have no need to explain her absence after all. But first she must dispose of the note she had left in the kitchen.

She was just tossing the note into the garbage can when Fiona came up behind her and said, "I thought I heard someone in here. I feel so much better after that sleep, Anna. I woke up and was sick once. I must have had a stomach upset. You would have been upstairs then. I went right back to sleep afterwards until a minute ago."

She peered at the kitchen clock on the wall and jumped. "Gracious me! Look at the time! Gordon will be back by now and wondering where I am."

Fiona rushed out with her car coat over her arm and headed for the driveway at the side of the house where her Land Rover was parked. Over her shoulder she assured Anna that she was ready to tell Gordon everything, or almost everything. There were some embarrassing things she would eliminate.

"I feel much more able to cope now, Anna, thanks to you! We'll talk again soon!"

With that, the big car was gone in a swirl of dust and Anna could relax at last. She was happy that she had not had to lie to Fiona. The girl would not suspect the devious nature of her dear friend's evening activities.

Anna closed the front door, shutting out the world.

So Fiona had been sick to her stomach again? It was still possible there was a baby on the way.

Early days yet.

No one knows of my suspicions. Not even Bev.

Time, as with all things, would tell.

Chapter Twenty-Three

"All right, sleeping beauty! Enough of this lazing around! You were sound asleep when I got back last night and here you are in the broad light of day still snoozing away! Just as well Jeanette insisted on feeding me a meal before I left town or I would have been famished by now."

Anna was just coming to the surface and only caught a portion of Lawren's complaint. She could believe she had slept straight through the night. She could not remember being that tired for years. Bev's notion that spy work was thrilling for the participants, was not Anna's opinion.

Once her eyes were open fully, she saw that Lawren was dressed to go out and carrying a tray with, not only a boiled egg and brown toast, but also juice, a pot of tea and an autumn crocus in a tiny glass vase.

"Oh, my darling! This is a wonderful treat and I don't deserve it after neglecting you so."

"Nonsense, woman! I am the one who deserted you last night although it was a highly productive session with the McLennan family. I am off to the barn now to finish up some painting details so take your time and eat every little crumb."

"Lawren, I would kiss you madly but I suspect my teeth need brushing."

"See if I care about that!"

Anna was only two bites into the toast finger which was now dripping with egg yolk, when the events of the previous evening suddenly flooded into her mind. She stopped chewing and waited while the entire scene in the hotel rushed through her. Had she done anything to jeopardize Fiona's relationship with Gordon? Would Gordon's father think she was some weird woman who had accosted him for no good reason? Would Captain Campbell discuss the incident with his son?

She swallowed convulsively and glanced over at the clock on her bedside table. Ten o'clock already! No wonder Lawren was worried about her. By now Gordon had probably met up with his father at the castle and they were discussing various topics of interest. Anna could only hope that these topics were focused on Gordon's responsibilities at the castle estate and not on Fiona, or a meeting with Fiona's unlikely female champion.

"There's nothing I can do about it now!" she asserted, with rather more confidence than she actually felt. "Fiona will let me know what transpires, eventually."

She hoped that conversation would not be reported anytime soon. She had had enough of the Campbells and their family issues for the time being.

The sun was high in a sky washed clean by the previous day's rain. The impulse to run away filled her. There had been too much happening lately. She needed to escape for a while and talk to Lawren about a wedding and just be with him, without interruption, for a few hours before they headed back home to Canada.

Her appetite returned with a rush and she soon obeyed Lawren's order and cleaned up every crumb and each drop of liquid nourishment. With energy restored, she plucked the flower from the tray and placed it behind her ear before walking across the hall and into the washroom where Lawren had left the heated towel rack on high and the thick towels were comfortingly warm on her body.

She dressed for an outdoor adventure before she had thought what they might do, but by the time she had unearthed Lawren in the barn where he was cleaning brushes, she knew.

"Let's take a day for ourselves my darling man! I have an idea where we can go and I'll explain on the way. I'll call Grant and book him for the day if at all possible, then we can............."

"Wait! If you want a day on our own, we'll hire a car and I'll drive."

"What? You can drive? Why didn't I know this?"

"There wasn't any need for you to know. I cycle everywhere in London but I learned to drive a stick shift years ago on my dad's car and I have a current licence. You never asked me to drive your car so I didn't mention it."

"Well, this is a surprise! We'll get onto Grant right away and see if there's a car for hire in Oban. He'll know, for sure. Oh, I am so looking forward to this!"

By noon it was all settled. Grant picked them up at the farmhouse and drove them to a local garage where the owner kept two cars for use when customers had their own vehicles in for servicing.

It was a neat little two-seater sports model and Lawren's eyes lit up when he saw it.

There are some days in life when the open road beckons irresistibly. Anna remembered such days when she was immersed in teaching and the responsibilities that came with the job. She would occasionally leave the school at lunchtime for a quick bite away from the politics and gossip of the busy staffroom.

Inevitably, on the hurried ride back to the school, she

would get that longing to just keep on driving and bypass the school building, speeding along the roads and out into the country and freedom for a few hours. She had never actually followed that impulse, but today was another time and another place and beside her was the man she might have dreamt of long ago.

They were like two teenagers. They wound down the windows and revved up the engine and turned the radio up to full blast. It was a station with an eclectic mix of music tastes and they sang out loud together whenever an oldie came along. Anna discovered that Lawren was a natural at harmony if he knew the tune. She gazed at him in wonder as their voices blended. What new thing would she find out about him next? He really was a remarkable man. She only hoped she fascinated him half as much as he did her.

The next song on the radio was a new piece the announcer stated to be an early entry in the annual British 'Favourite Christmas Song' contest. As soon as the haunting music began, Anna knew she had heard it somewhere before. Her mind was occupied with trying to remember the place and time and she almost missed the words. In the second verse a solo male voice with a simple piano accompaniment struck right to her heart.

> *"I see your smile and need to tell you*
> *I am here, right now.*
> *All of my love is yours forever*
> *All my life*
> *All that I am*
> *Is here for you*
> *I vow*
> *I vow*
> *I vow"*

There was silence inside the speeding car. Anna had no idea if the plaintive words had also struck a chord in Lawren.

She hesitated to break the spell by looking at him but it was he who moved first. He turned off the radio and the road noise filled the space where the music had faded away.

"What *was* that?" he gasped.

"I think I have heard it in the background once or twice since I've been here, but not like that. The words are so powerful. I think my heart stopped for a moment."

He reached over and grasped her hand bringing it to his chest. "I think mine speeded up incredibly. Those are the words I will promise you, with my whole heart, when we marry."

"Lawren!" She could say no more. She was overcome with emotion.

He pulled the car off the road at the next side road and they sat there, hand in hand, speechless, as the sounds of nature gradually drifted in through the open window.

Finally, Anna had to retrieve her hand so she could wipe the tears from her cheeks. The moment was right to discuss the wedding. The event which, it was now abundantly clear, they both wished for.

"When should we do it, Lawren, and where?"

"I said it would be your choice Anna, and I haven't changed my mind; anywhere and anytime will suit me. Your decision is much more complicated, I realize."

"You are right, of course. There are friends and family who would be hurt if they were not included but those people are on two different sides of the Atlantic. I would hate to exclude Susan and Jake if we had a ceremony here. Fiona and Bev and Jeanette would have to travel to Canada at great expense and inconvenience if we wait until we are back home. I don't know what to do for the best."

Lawren heard the dismay in her voice and turned her face to his.

"Listen, my lovely, I won't have you troubled by this. It's about us; just the two of us. We can have a simple civil ceremony and host two parties afterward with everyone who wants to, coming to Canada or Scotland, or both, to celebrate with us."

"Oh, Lawren, that's a wonderful idea. I really don't want a lot of fuss. I do want it to be special for us and I could cope with parties much better when we are officially a couple. There are marvelous places here in Scotland from mansions and grand hotels to castles and islands where we could book an event and in London we could use the Elsie Perrin Williams estate or Elmhurst or................"

Anna's eager voice tailed off as she caught sight of her partner's expression. She took a breath and calmed down.

"I know. I know. You were right. It's not about all that. I promise to concentrate on what is important. The rest will fall into place when it's time."

"Exactly! Now where did you say you wanted to go *today*, right now?"

"Just drive on! I'll tell you later. Let's enjoy this magical day together."

Lawren obliged and happily turned his attention to the road ahead. They were traveling north on a coastal road with the sea on their left and spectacular views everywhere they looked. They reached a sea loch and soon the town of Fort William came into view. Anna indicated they should carry on and they left the town behind and continued inland until they saw something so remarkable that they agreed to take a break.

Snow was on the tops of the high mountains to their right but in the valley, miles from anywhere, was a most impressive bronze memorial. Three soldiers, in full uniform stood looking out to the mountains. Their courage and determination was evident in every carved line.

Anna and Lawren walked around the base of the monument and read the information. The three men represented thousands of allied British volunteer troops who trained near this spot for warfare during World War II. Those who survived their rigorous training earned the right to wear the green beret and call themselves Commandos. Their motto was United We Conquer.

For the second time that day, Anna was speechless. This reminder of the sacrifices made by soldiers and by extraordinary men and women for the freedoms many take for granted in the 21st century, did not allow for any facile comment. It was a moment to tuck away in the heart.

When they walked back to the car, Lawren asked, "Was that what you wanted to see?"

"Not really. I didn't know about the monument but I am very glad we saw it together.

We need to find the A 87 now and go a bit further. There's a special castle I want to see."

Lawren was happy to oblige. The roads were quiet and although it was turning colder as the afternoon advanced, he was content to be sitting beside Anna and listening as she reminded him about her meeting in Glasgow with her Uncle Ross and the story of how her grandmother had revealed an unknown family history involving Anna's father Angus, when they visited Eilean Donan.

"I have thought about going there ever since then and as it is one of the most romantic places in Scotland I felt we should go together."

"Aren't you just full of the unexpected today!" he murmured.

Anna snuggled into her warm coat and watched the scenery fly by. She was as happy as she had ever felt in her life. The future no longer scared her. The time she and Lawren might have together was not to be measured in decades as an earlier marriage might be, yet it was clear to her that each and every minute would be precious beyond counting. No one could take away what they had shared already. Even if, God forbid, they should decide to part, she would never regret one second of their time.

Lawren shook her awake some time later and gently asked if this might be what she was looking for.

Anna began to apologize for falling asleep and leaving him to navigate on his own but he stopped her with a raised hand and said, "Just look down there."

Anna blinked several times to clear her vision. She could hardly believe what she was seeing. Below the rise where they were parked lay a stronghold linked to the land by a triple-arched bridge built of the same stone. The rugged castle projected out into the sea on a spit of land and the scene was lit by the low sun of the late afternoon. It was breathtaking.

"That's it! That's Eilean Donan! Lawren, thank you! Can we go down the hill and go in?"

"Your wish is my command, my lady!"

They parked and bought tickets in the gift shop where they were cautioned that the castle closed in one hour. Anna looked worried at this news but Lawren pointed out that there were very few cars in the parking lot so the chances were good that they would be able to explore by themselves and get around more quickly.

Hand in hand they crossed the bridge and followed signs to the entrance. Inside there were plaques here and there pointing out interesting facts. The castle was not as old as it looked, having been rebuilt in the 19th century, but there had been a MacRae Clan fortification on the site 800 years ago. Its location at the junction of three lochs gave the castle huge advantage against invaders from the sea.

There were several floors of accommodation reached by spiral stone stairs which had to be negotiated carefully as excess speed caused dizziness. They wandered through banquet halls and four-poster bedrooms and descended below ground level to dungeons. Anna quickly left these areas as she hated the sad, dank, cold atmosphere there.

"Let's go up to the battlements now. I want to look out at the view."

Lawren soon figured out she was searching for something in particular and he let her forge ahead just out of his reach but within calling distance. As he ascended to a higher level he saw a dark figure leaning on a guard railing that spanned an arch of stone. The figure was that of an older woman and immediately he had the feeling of regret, despair and longing emanating from her in waves of pain.

Shaken at the impact on his senses, he turned away, unwilling to impose on this private moment. He slipped quietly down to the next level and waited there until Anna finally appeared. She was saying a man had told her the land she could see out in the water was the Isle of Skye and beyond that there was almost no more land until the shores of Newfoundland.

"Did you see the old woman?"

"What old woman?"

"The one who was looking out from the stone arch on the level above."

"I saw no one there, Lawren, but I heard someone singing the song 'Speed bonnie boat like a bird on the wing, over the sea to Skye'. My mother used to sing it to Simon and me to lull us to sleep when we were small. I had forgotten it until I heard it again just now."

Something about Lawren's posture and the sudden darkness of his golden eyes drew her attention.

"Wait! *What* did you see? I didn't tell you where Ross and his mother stood that day. I missed it on the way up. Did you see her? Did you see my grandmother?"

No answer was needed. Anna could tell Lawren had had a psychic episode. His super-sensitivity to emotional atmosphere had brought something, or someone, into his sphere.

She pulled at his jacket and dragged him up to the stone arch with the guard rail. There was no one there. Lawren knew there would not be any sign of what he had experienced. Such episodes were fleeting but left a strong and lingering impression.

"Tell me. Please tell me everything," she begged.

"I saw an old woman in dark clothes looking out to the

sea. I heard nothing. I felt how sad she was; how much she longed to be with someone beloved who had gone before her. It was only a fleeting moment. I can't recall anything more than that."

Anna ran her gloved hands over the railing as if to capture a sense of human warmth there.

"Ross said it was in this spot that his mother broke down and told him about his older brother, Angus, who had left Scotland as a young man to emigrate to Canada with his wife and avoid a family scandal. The split in the family was never repaired as Ross' father refused to have his older son's name spoken again.

I can't even imagine how painful it would be for a mother to be cut off from her child in that way. No wonder she was devastated. How could a father impose such a pitiless ban?"

"I have no idea, Anna. It makes me think about my own family situation. My English grandfather must have felt the same way when he rejected my father for marrying the wrong woman. Knowing you, Anna, I can't believe any woman today would lie down and accept these kinds of Draconian decisions."

"I think not! Women finally have more power within marriage, even if it's just earning power. Things have changed all right. Sending someone off across the oceans used to be tantamount to bidding them farewell forever. Thank God today we can fly over those oceans in a matter of hours. Families need never be cruelly severed as they once were."

They stood together, each with their own thoughts about the past and the future.

The peaceful moment was interrupted by the strains of the chorus of The Skye Boat Song as two young girls came clattering down the stairs singing loudly. They did not see Anna and Lawren who both thought that the song of Bonnie Prince Charlie's departure from Scotland during the Jacobite Rising was another episode of leaving these shores for a long goodbye.

A bell clanged somewhere in the castle and brought them back to the present day.

"That must be a warning bell. We'd better make tracks for the exit."

"Wait one minute, Lawren. Standing here I have such a longing to get back home to Canada for Thanksgiving. I need to see the trees flaming with colour before all the leaves fall. I want to see orange pumpkins and turkey cut outs in the stores and huge pots of chrysanthemums of every colour. I want to hear the geese practicing for their long flights south. Am I crazy?"

"Not a bit of it! It's time for us to go home but first we need to escape from this castle before they lock us in for the night."

They ran for the parking lot, laughing at their foolishness but cold reality dawned when they saw how dark the sky had become.

"It's almost night, Lawren. Don't let's drive home now. It's too late. I'll ask inside the gift shop and see if there's anywhere near here where we could stay overnight."

She was back in moments with a card, and directions to the village of Dornie and Birchwood, a house a mere seven minutes away.

"They must be used to this kind of request. They had all the information at the ready and they will phone ahead so the proprietress, a Mrs. Donalda MacRae, can get a fire going for us."

"Excellent! I think we've had enough excitement for one day."

Chapter Twenty-Four

There was one more revelation in store before the day was over. Donalda MacRae, a sturdy Highlander with steel grey hair and a pair of eyes so black as to be almost impenetrable, welcomed them into a cottage where she had lit a fire, turned on all the lights, boiled water, left a tray with quiche and fish to be heated in the microwave, and arranged a plate of griddle scones, cake and cheese for their supper.

"I'll be off now," she declared in a lilting Scottish voice. "But I am just a call away should you be after needing a thing at all. Have a good night."

She was almost out the door when she turned back and looked steadily at Lawren. He was transfixed by her gaze and wondered what else there was for her to say. When she spoke again, he could not have been more astounded.

"You'll be one with the second sight, then."

It was not a question, merely a statement, and she did not expect it to be contradicted.

"My man was a seventh son of a seventh son. He had the sight all his life and I can see it in your eyes even now. Never doubt it."

With that, she was gone. Lawren stood, blinking rapidly as if he had dreamed the entire incident.

"Anna?"

"I know! That was the most incredible thing to happen at the end of this incredible day."

All at once the day seemed to have gone on too long and she suspected neither one of them had strength for much more.

"Come over to this lovely fire, my dear. We'll have something to eat and get right to bed. We can talk about it all tomorrow."

They set off early, after eating what remained of the evening's feast and downing hot tea. Lawren left cash on the table for their accommodation and food. He was wary of another encounter with their prescient hostess.

They drove into the sunrise and stopped briefly at the first garage they saw to fill the gas tank and ask for the fastest route back to Oban. This took them away from the sea views but meant they were home well before noon.

Anna felt impelled to pack some clothes and check over everything in the farmhouse to prepare for their departure. She was sorting out washing when she remembered the cell phone in her handbag had been turned off since their departure from Oban. She had not wanted any possible interruptions to mar their special day.

As soon as she powered up the cell phone she saw a list of missed messages. There were two from Bev who had tried to get in touch and then worried when she was unsuccessful. There was one from Grant asking if the hired car had worked out. There was one from Alina wondering when they were coming back to London, and there was an urgent request from Fiona insisting on Anna's arrival at Glenmorie Castle at 7:00pm sharp this evening.

Anna replied to all the other messages but left Fiona's until last.

She found Lawren in the kitchen where he was carefully packing his drawings into a cardboard box and laying out the canvas of the oil painting of George and Jeanette's lovely family.

"Lawren, that's the first time I've seen the portrait. It's quite beautiful. The children are painted with such care. Jeanette will always have an unforgettable record of how their family grew. Are you taking it home?"

"No, this one stays here. Jeanette wants to find a frame for it and she knows a firm who will stretch the canvas and install it for her. I have preliminary sketches of the group if you would like to have them."

"Thank you! That's a wonderful idea. I will love to have my goddaughter, that precious little Annette, with me in our new home.

That reminds me, Lawren. We have a condo to decorate when we get to London. We can have some fun with that. I want you to choose whatever style makes you feel most at home there."

"I don't know much about interior decorating Anna," he laughed, thinking of his chaotic studio, "but we can explore options together. Something else to look forward to, I believe."

"Ah, about that! We have one more castle to see before we leave here."

"What! another road trip so soon?"

"Not exactly. The truth is I really need you to come with me to meet the Campbells at Glenmorie Castle. Fiona has requested my attendance at dinner tonight and I am afraid I may have interfered in her life far beyond the scope of friendship."

"That doesn't sound like you, Anna. What is it you are afraid of?"

There was nothing for it but to confess everything she had done two nights before. She would rather have kept the secret but the need to have Lawren's support at the castle outweighed the desire to keep her impulsive actions to herself.

Lawren listened without comment until Anna had finished. There was a frown between his golden eyes which Anna had not seen before and she felt a sense of guilt that she had caused the frown to appear. She was about to launch into an apology for drawing him into her mess when he stated firmly that he could understand why she needed backup on such an occasion.

"I don't personally know Fiona well, but I know how important she is to you. I do *not* like the sound of this Captain Campbell one little bit and I will be right beside you this evening no matter what happens. We'll stand together, come what may."

Anna exhaled. As long as they were of one mind, nothing could harm her although the thought did occur that it was not a bad thing they were leaving Oban in a day or two.

Bolstered by Lawren's support, she called Fiona immediately.

"Anna? I am so glad you called back. Grant told me you were out of town and I was

afraid you would miss our dinner date.

Can't talk now, I am working. See you at seven o'clock at Glenmorie.

And, Anna, please bring Lawren too!"

Short and sweet, thought Anna. She was no further forward about the guest list or the reason behind this special occasion but Fiona was back to work and seemed in fine fettle. So far; so good!

When about to face the dragon, it was essential to go well armed. In this case the armour would consist of an appropriate outfit for an evening at a castle.

Anna groaned to herself as she mentally contrasted the previous day at Eilean Donan castle with what might happen at Glenmorie. Hopefully, there would be no ghosts there.

Several outfits later, Anna was doubting whether she had anything suitable for a formal event in a Scottish castle. Every article of clothing she had packed for her trip was spread out on her bed and most of it had been rejected. The full black skirt and white sweater she had worn in Glasgow was the best bet by far but the sparkly belt would have to go, and the red leather shoes would not look right either.

She picked over her jewellery to see what would add a more classic look and found pearl earrings, always a safe choice. She had black court shoes with a small heel that might be acceptable but still the outfit lacked something. In desperation she went back to the cedar closet in the tower where she stored winter clothing to save packing heavy items for her trips. She flipped through the hangers aimlessly, with no idea what she was looking for, when something colourful dropped to the floor at her feet.

It was a square woollen shawl, long enough to be folded into a triangle and wrapped around the shoulders or fastened with a celtic-styled pin. She did not know the tartan but it was a rich mixture of colours. The plaid was mainly red and had green and blue stripes. A distinct, white line outlined the panels. The shawl would add needed warmth to the black and white theme of her proposed outfit.

"Perfect!" she declared. "But why have I never seen this before? Perhaps Alina or Fiona left it behind on one of their visits. No one else has the key to this closet."

Grateful to have her problem solved, Anna locked the door and quickly folded away the rest of her clothes. Lawren would not suspect the mess she could create when making such decisions.

He had nothing to worry about. Whatever he wore he always looked exactly right. It was all a matter of inner confidence, she decided. A quick bath and a different hair style might help her achieve that high standard. It couldn't hurt, and she felt she would need all the help she could get when confronting a certain Captain Diarmid Campbell and his son Gordon.

Warmed through, perfumed, and with her best features accented carefully, Anna donned her outfit and carefully descended the stairs. Lawren looked up from the cell phone he was studying and almost dropped it when he saw the transformation.

"Anna Mason, soon to be Drake, I had temporarily forgotten what a stunning woman you are. Whatever magic you performed in the last two hours, it was worth every minute. I will be immensely proud to escort you to the castle. Together we will be invincible!"

Lawren had arranged to keep the hired car for another day and he had also obtained directions to the castle. They set off in the last rays of the sunset for Glenmorie. Anna sat back with a famous Scottish motto running through her head.

'Wha daur meddle wi' me?'
Bring on the Campbells! They were prepared for them.

It was dark when they drove up the winding driveway. Flood lights on the high, distinctive roofline illuminated the tower-house features and lanterns were lit over doorways and windows on the lower levels. Lawren was impressed and Anna was stunned. *So this magnificent structure was where Fiona had been staying? What a long way from her tiny little cottage on the seafront.*

They left the car on the gravel circle where a large black limousine took up a considerable amount of space. Anna pulled her outfit into place and clutched the tartan shawl around her shoulders. It was not the cold that caused her to do this. It was the unnerving effect of the castle looming above them.

Lawren just smiled and took her hand. As usual, he was not intimidated by anything. His leather jacket and black cords with a white shirt looked like a highlander's garb from a century ago, minus the kilt of course. Anna had a second to wonder what Lawren would look like in a formal kilted outfit but she concluded he would not look any better than he did right now.

Fiona opened the massive oak doors before they could pull the bell's iron handle. She reached forward and enfolded Anna in a warm embrace, whispering in her ear that everything was fine and Gordon's father had not recognized her from the day they had met so briefly.

Anna was immediately reassured and she stepped back to allow Fiona to hug Lawren and welcome him into the castle. Anna saw that Fiona was wearing a long, full-skirted dress with a round neckline and a gathered sleeve. The dress was in a deep crimson shade and gave glowing colour to the girl's cheeks which Anna knew were innocent of artifice.

They followed her up the stone staircase. Anna admired the view of the sweeping train of Fiona's dress and figured out that the girl must be holding up the front.

Gordon Campbell was waiting at the top. He stepped down to take Fiona's hand and in that gesture revealed how respectful of her he was. Anna began to breathe again. One more person to meet and she could relax.

Gordon made flattering comments about Anna's good influence on his girlfriend's life. He shook Lawren's hand firmly as he complimented him on his artistic talent and asked him to assess the castle's paintings. The guests were ushered into the grand banquet room where the imposing figure of Captain Diarmid Campbell waited in front of the fireplace wearing full highland dress including dark velvet jacket, frilled white shirt, sporran and *sgian dhu* tucked into his long wool stockings. Anna thought he could have dispensed with the dramatic attire as his facial decoration was quite imposing enough. She took a quick sidelong glance at Lawren to see how he was taking this display of male fashion and noticed his eyebrows were raised up considerably and there was a gleam of humour in his golden eyes.

The senior Campbell was presented with due formality by his son. Some desultory conversation about the weather and the estate's size ensued, during which Anna received a discreet nod of the head from Diarmid, which she deemed to be a silent signal of approval. Sherry was circulated in an antique glass container and Anna had a chance to look around the huge room.

The first thing she noticed was the preponderance of a dark green tartan fabric similar to that in the attire of the Campbell men. She was almost sure it was the Black Watch plaid as she had once had a waistcoat and tam of that same pattern. The wall decorations of armour and deer antlers were similar to those they had seen the night before at Eilean Donan so they required no further examination. The highly-polished wood table in the middle of the room was another matter. It was adorned with a central line of silver sconces of more than two feet in height. Some held candles and others had a display of fruits and trailing plants.

Only the top section of this table was set out with gleaming silver flatware and an assortment of crystal glasses. Anna was glad the couples would be sitting close to each other rather than have to shout down the length of the table. She also surmised the Laird himself would be taking the carved chair at the head of the table and this was proved to be an accurate assumption when a female figure in white apron, over a dark dress announced that dinner was served.

Anna had been wondering if Fiona was responsible for all this splendour but as she was chatting comfortably with father and son and not knee deep in kitchen preparations, the appearance of a housekeeper made a lot of sense.

Lawren had to be pried away from examining the huge,

dark, oil paintings of highland forbears that dominated the walls, but Gordon assured him there would be time to continue his inspection after the meal.

Anna was seated beside Gordon and facing Lawren and Fiona. As they started the meal with broiled scallops and an edible seaweed vegetable, it became clear that Diarmid was in charge of the conversation. In a manner accustomed to obedience, he sent inquiries down the table and waited imperiously until a satisfactory answer had been offered.

His first question was for Lawren. "I hear you are an artist. What have you been working on lately?"

Lawren responded by praising the McLennan family and outlining his method of capturing each child with one parent only, then combining the two halves into one cohesive portrait."

"That must be timesaving," commented the laird. To which Lawren replied, "Saving time is not the objective. Small children are easily distracted and a formal pose with both parents would be taxing on everyone."

"Indeed! Perhaps you could visit us in the Borders at some point. Gordon's older sisters have produced a brood of children who have not yet been committed to canvas."

Lawren just nodded and continued to eat his scallops.

The next course was rabbit stew with a rich, red wine sauce accompanied by savoury wild mushrooms and a tangle of cress and bean sprouts. Diarmid's focus was now on Anna. "I am reliably informed by Fiona that you are the person who encouraged her to pursue her career aspirations."

"I can assure you, Captain Campbell, Fiona needed little encouragement. She is more than capable of steering her own course and always has been."

Anna bent her head and resumed eating. She was not to be drawn into a discussion about Fiona in case she might reveal something the laird could use against the girl.

When the roast haunch of venison was placed on a platter in front of Diarmid Campbell, he proceeded to carve it with practiced skill while his guests were busy passing plates around. Conversation lapsed for a few minutes and Anna was not the only one to be relieved.

"This is excellent meat, Gordon. Was it hung for the required amount of time?"

"You taught me well, father. I am not likely to forget your teaching on estate matters."

The senior Campbell mumbled into his beard then changed tactics. "So, Gordon, what's this I hear about the endangered Scottish wildcats?"

Gordon took his chance to show off Fiona's knowledge on this topic. "Father, Fiona is in the best position to advise you about this. She came to Glenmorie for the first time to provide information to our keepers about identifying the difference between feral cats and the wildcat species. That is how we met."

The dark eyes now turned their full gaze on Fiona. Anna was proud of the way the girl answered his gaze unflinchingly. This was a topic on which both she and Fiona had intimate knowledge. No one would, or could, challenge her expertise.

"The number of pure-bred wildcats has been falling to a serious level, Captain Campbell. Disease and inter-breeding with domestic and feral cats are believed to be among the main threats to their survival. This a matter of great concern to all wildlife groups and a meeting was held last month to discuss if widespread live trapping, in the few remaining areas where the cats survive, could be the species last hope."

There was no doubting Fiona's knowledge or her enthusiasm for the subject. Gordon's face lit up as he listened to her and even the reserved Diarmid Campbell was impressed.

"Interesting! What is your own opinion, young lady? Would this method be effective?"

"Politicians would insist there is no benefit to society in spending public money on this. Tourists would not ever be likely to catch a glimpse of wildcats, even if they were in the right area at the right time.

I am on the side of the conservationists. A species unique to Scotland deserves to survive. We have lost enough of our national pride in our land and its inhabitants, both human and animal. I am not sure that trapping would be the most effective way to do it. I have experience of what happens when wildcats are exposed to human contact." Fiona exchanged a quick look with Anna at this juncture, then resumed her impassioned plea. "The whole issue deserves more money for research and implementation. I hope to be among those who pioneer this endeavour."

The party at the table erupted in spontaneous applause at the conclusion of Fiona's heartfelt plea.

She blushed like a rose but the tension was gone and the rest of the dinner was much more relaxed and convivial. Gordon gave his girlfriend a hug, a kiss on the cheek, and a warm smile. His father could not misinterpret the significance of this public display of affection. He raised his glass in a toast to Scotland, its wildlife and its people. Anna and Lawren gladly drank to that.

While Gordon acquainted Lawren with the Campbell ancestral portraits, and Diarmid sat back with port and cigars, Fiona motioned to Anna and they slipped away to the restroom together. A few minutes to talk freely was welcomed by both of them.

"Fiona! That is the most beautiful dress. It's silk isn't it?"

"It's the loveliest thing I have ever worn, Anna. Gordon uncovered it weeks ago in an old wooden chest in an attic. He hung it up because he thought it was too delicate to languish there, not knowing he would have someone to wear it before too long."

"And it fits you like a glove! You look so happy Fiona. I am thrilled for you."

"Isn't Gordon wonderful! His father isn't so scary once you get past his appearance. The best part is he'll be leaving tomorrow!"

They laughed and chatted together like schoolgirls in the huge echoing bathroom secure in the fact that the massive door would blanket any sounds of hilarity.

Later, Anna and Diarmid had a moment to talk. He seemed to be mellowed by the plentiful food and drink and the congenial company. Anna could imagine his favourable account of the evening to his wife and daughters when he returned home to the Borders.

Noting the elder Campbell's pride whenever he mentioned his son's plans for Glenmorie, Anna had a feeling that it would not be long before Captain Campbell attempted to restore the castle to Campbell ownership again. The absentee landlord rarely appeared to enjoy his Scottish property, it seemed. If she was right, Gordon and Fiona would have exciting times ahead of them and this castle could become a landmark of environmental and ecological innovation.

"I have been admiring your tartan shawl, Anna," resumed the laird. "Fiona told me your parents were Scottish. Is this your clan tartan?"

"I don't believe so. My family name is McLeod and that plaid is a more subdued colour akin to your own Black Watch, as far as I remember."

"You are correct about that, but perhaps your family had a link to the Fraser clan also?"

Anna registered his use of the Fraser name but replied she was unaware of any such connection.

Hours after this, when she was thinking back over the evening's events, she had a sudden flash of memory. Helen Dunlop was Helen Fraser when she was a married woman. Could the scarf have belonged to her?

Why had it suddenly appeared when it was most needed?

It seemed to Anna a sign that Helen's spirit had finally

accepted her past with all its faults. The Fraser connection, although much feared during her life in Oban, was a part of what had made Helen the remarkable person she became.

Anna decided she would take the scarf back to Canada with her and wear it with pride.

Chapter Twenty-Five

The final day went swiftly, as all days of departure do. The major part of Anna's packing was done, which was fortunate, as friends kept coming to the door all day to wish them well on their journey.

The final house cleaning was going to be a rushed affair until Bev arrived. She insisted she would take care of that, and make sure Morag got home to the farm, once the travellers had left. Consequently, Anna was grateful to have a few minutes to sit and chat with Bev while Lawren re-checked the art packages.

She explained their tentative wedding plans and was relieved to find that Bev approved.

"As long as we can count on seeing you both again, it won't matter if you arrive as a married couple or not. We do love you both, Anna."

"The feeling is mutual, Bev. I hope I can make as much a success of my second marriage as you have done. Be prepared to offer advice, if need be."

"I am sure you won't be needing it! Lawren is truly an exceptional man."

The next group to arrive at the red door was the McLennan family, complete with toys for Liam and a carry-chair for baby Annette. George took Anna aside for a moment while Jeanette was settling Liam at the kitchen table with paper and crayons.

"I admit I have been concerned about Fiona and this Gordon fellow. I don't know how much she has told you but I think I put my foot right in it when I saw Gordon at my office. "

"You can stop worrying, George. Lawren and I had dinner at the castle recently and the two young people could not have been happier. Fiona has even been introduced to Gordon's father, a most imposing ex-naval type. He seemed accepting of their relationship so you need not be concerned."

"Thank you, Anna! That's a relief! I'll continue to watch out for Fiona, nevertheless."

"Good, George! I know you and Jeanette care for her."

"Right! I'm glad that's settled. Now, where is Lawren? I want to tell him how interested in drawing our Liam has become since watching an artist at work."

Anna pointed George in the right direction and then sat with Jeanette who promptly handed over a cooing Annette. The child had her eye fixed on Morag who was firmly defending her usual place on the window seat against all comers. It was as if the cat knew her days there were over for the time being.

"The only thing that makes me sad to leave," sighed Anna, "is knowing that this darling little girl will have grown so much by the time I see her again."

"Oh, I'm sure she'll be skyping with you before too long, Anna, but you're right. They change so fast. That's why I was so keen to get Lawren to do our portrait and I have to tell you, I think it is truly amazing. Everyone who has seen it is astonished and it's not just about the likenesses. It's as if he had the skill to look inside us. It almost embarrasses me to look at my own face. He has brought to the surface my private feelings about George and our children. I understand now how you feel about the picture hanging in your bedroom upstairs."

"He is incredibly talented, Jeanette. I think his career is about to take off in a big way."

The two friends were in the midst of talking about domestic matters including if the farmhouse needed any redecorating during the winter, when Grant arrived to tell them he was ready, but there was no rush to load the luggage.

Anna invited him in for a coffee and encouraged him to take home anything in the food line that remained in the larder.

"Och, that's kind of you Mrs. Mason! The wife will be pleased. If you have a minute I have a message for you from Fiona. She called me this morning. She was feared you might have gone already."

Anna immediately excused herself and led Grant into the lounge.

"Now, what did she say, Grant?"

"I take it you think this is a private message?"

"I don't know yet, Grant. Perhaps you'd better just tell me."

"Well, I'll repeat it as best I can so you can make the choice yourself."

By this time Anna was getting fidgety. She wondered if Grant was on a fishing expedition, trying to get information out of her.

"She said," he began, in a pompous tone as if delivering a royal decree, "tell Anna everything is good at the castle and there will be exciting news soon.'"

Anna made a huge effort to hide her reaction to the news as Grant was watching her very curiously.

She managed to dampen down her feelings and calmly thank him for being the messenger, but inside she was shouting Yes! Yes! The 'exciting news' could only be one of two things. Either Fiona and Gordon were engaged to be married, or Fiona was indeed pregnant. As the thought occurred that *both possibilities* might be true, Anna jumped for joy then had to quickly pretend she had tripped over the carpet. There was no point in alerting Grant. He would find out when Fiona chose to make the news known to all and sundry. Anna tucked the happy thoughts away in her mind for later consideration. No doubt there would be phone calls flying back and forth across the Atlantic very soon.

Another separation, she thought. *This one will not be permanent,* she promised herself.

The final moments arrived at last. Everyone had made their farewells and tears had been shed.

Lawren and Anna took a last look around, closed doors and windows and stowed the McCaig Estate Farmhouse keys safely away in their carry-on luggage. Lawren had only his backpack and several large boxes which he meant to stow in the oversized-item cabin space on the plane. The contents were too precious to be left to the tender mercies of the luggage handlers.

Their return flight was early the next morning so the rest of the day could be taken at a more leisurely pace than usual. Grant would drive them to the train station and they would enjoy the autumn foliage and the swiftly-running rivers and waterfalls on their way to Glasgow. A night at the airport hotel and the flight home awaited them.

"Are you sad to leave, my darling?" asked Lawren.

"Just a little." she replied. "A piece of my heart belongs here and always will, but going home with you is the best compensation I could ever imagine."

Grant caught the whispered exchange and secretly smiled to himself.

Sure now! Did I not tell Fiona these two were meant for each other the first time I set eyes on them?

When it comes to matters of the heart, I am never known to be wrong at all.

Epilogue

She entered the hotel suite like a ship in full sail. A ship well-fitted-out and heading purposely toward a destination. Anna Drake is no stranger to media interviews but, as she tucked strands of her thick white hair neatly behind her ears, the impression is given that she has more interesting places to be.

Question: Mrs. Drake, are you pleased with the critical response to this gallery exhibit? Does it do justice to his talent?

Of course! My husband's work has always garnered a good response from art critics. What mattered most to him, of course, were his own internal criteria.

I am not an art expert but I was privy to his opinions and I feel he is represented well in this retrospective show.

Question: Some from the artistic community have suggested the current exhibit of later work surpasses even the extraordinary pen and ink sketches of the Wiltshire Series. What is your own opinion?

Wiltshire was certainly a departure from his original formal oil portraits but I remember seeing remarkable intuitive paintings in his tiny studio in London.

Question: That studio is something of a place of pilgrimage now. Do aspiring artists arrive at your door also?

It happens occasionally. I have considered moving but I live in a gated community with good friends nearby and I would hate to relinquish my happy memories there.

I am often travelling to my house in Scotland or to visit family in various parts of the world. I do get requests to show people the paintings Lawren did for our home when we first moved there. Only a few of these requests have ever been honoured.

Most people are respectful of private property.

Question: Speaking of privacy; the famous portrait he did for your home near Oban has never been on public view. Why is that?

The painting some have called 'Three Women', is the one that brought Lawren Drake into my life. It is incredibly personal to me. I would not consider moving it from its original position for any reason.

In a way, it encompasses my life with Lawren; a blending of past, present and future. I treasure it beyond any price that could be offered for its purchase or exhibition.

Question: As someone who knew him better than anyone else, to what do you ascribe his incredible success?

Lawren Drake was an empath. He had the ability to see inside a person's soul and transfer that awareness to paint and canvas. His subjects recognized elements of their inner lives no one else knew, even although they had very little conversation with the artist. It is a skill few can command but many can admire when they study his work.

Question: Art historians have been fascinated with the arcane symbols that appear in most of his work. They say this harks back to a much earlier style of art.

Can you explain the shield with the two stars that frequently occurs in his work after your marriage?

It is a tribute to Lawren's distant ancestor, Sir Francis Drake, who navigated between the two poles in his explorations of the world. You might say his own artistic explorations mirrored those of his forefathers, some of whom were also painters.

He used to use a small painting of a duck with a brush in its mouth to signify his name. As he became more famous, the family shield seemed more appropriate.

I still have the sign from his studio with that quaint duck. I rather like it.

Question: I can see you miss him terribly. Do you wish your time together had been longer?

Time is relative, my dear, as you will discover when you are older.

I miss him every day but he would not want me to mourn. I comfort myself by remembering how vital and vibrant our years together were. How could I be sad about that?

Most couples never know the kind of love we shared. The number of years we spent together is irrelevant.

This last question was infringing on personal space. Anna Drake had been known to leave an interview abruptly when questions were too intimate.

I thanked her sincerely for her time and generosity and for all the help she had given me over the years.

I have gained a good reputation as a writer and journalist. Interviews are my specialty yet it was clear to me that I had been given insights that were not available to anyone other than family members. But then, Anna Drake had encouraged my writing ambitions ever since I was a child.

We hugged as she said goodbye. There was a reception to attend in her husband's honour. Nothing else would tempt her to walk into the spotlight again.

As she waved from the doorway, I caught a glimpse of the engraved silver band on the third finger of her left hand. My grandfather had told me its twin was buried with her husband after the aneurism that took his life so unexpectedly.

It seemed a sad conclusion to an epic love story, and yet, no one could deny the success of their married life, however brief.

Lawren Drake often spoke of how Anna's love had awakened a talent in him that had lain dormant for most of his artistic, and his personal life.

No woman could ask for a better tribute.

Excerpted Special to The Telegraph by Ashley Stanton.

The complete text of this interview can be obtained on the newspaper's web site.

The Prime Time Series continues in *Return to Oban: Anna's Next Chapter*, book 7.

Afterword

Prime Time was my first series. I was hoping to find readers in the *prime* of their lives with *time* to read captivating stories, set in real-life locations and featuring women you would like to get to know.

Anna Mason is that woman. She is at a crossroads in her life when she gets a chance to take a new direction and travel to Scotland with the encouragement of her group of faithful friends.

This series is now eight full books and Anna is still going strong with adventures that will transport you to places you might never expect. You will fall in love with Anna, as I have.

Read Ruth's other series, Seafarers, Seven Days, Home Sweet Home, Journey of a Lifetime and Starscopes at retailers everywhere. Also read Borderlines a stand-alone thriller.

www.ruthhay.com

Also by Ruth Hay

Prime Time Series

Auld Acquaintance

Time Out of Mind

Now or Never

Sand in the Wind

With This Ring

The Seas Between Us

Return to Oban: Anna's Next Chapter

Fiona of Glenmorie

Seafarers Series

Sea Changes

Sea Tides

Gwen's Gentleman

Gwen's Choice

Seven Days Series

Seven Days There

Seven Days Back

Seven Days Beyond

Seven Days Away

Seven Days Horizons

Seven Days Destinations

Borderlines (Standalone)

Borderlines

Home Sweet Home Series

Harmony House

Fantasy House

Remedy House

Affinity House

Memory House

Journey of a Lifetime Series

Auralie

Nadine

Mariette

Rosalind

Starscopes Series

Starscopes: Winter

Starscopes: Spring

Starscopes: Summer

Starscopes: Fall

Made in the USA
Columbia, SC
19 October 2020